Stain on the Soul

Michele Drier

Books by Michele Drier

The Amy Hobbes Mysteries
Edited for Death
Labeled for Death
Delta for Death
The Kandesky Vampire Chronicles
SNAP: The World Unfolds
SNAP: New Talent
Plague: A Love Story
Danube: A Tale of Murder
SNAP: Love for Blood
SNAP: Happily Ever After?
SNAP White Nights
SNAP: All That Jazz
SNAP: I, Vampire
SNAP: Red Bear Rising

Ashes of Memories

Stained Glass Murders
Stain on the Soul

Dedication

For my sweetest Bethie… I'll always love and miss you

CHAPTER ONE

Red, blue, red, blue, red, blue…

Colors kaleidoscoped across the grey overcast, reflecting in the puddles left by the morning's rain.

Roz thought she'd heard a faint wail of sirens, but the sound was indistinct, muted by the ocean's constant whispering.

What was this? Sirens and revolving lights belonged to her previous life, not here, not on the Oregon coast, not in her refuge.

She climbed a sand dune behind her house, saw the whirling lights and pinpointed the source, across the street. She'd been walking her dog on the flat sand of the beach.

The flashing colors were a blip, a change, maybe an intrusion in her routine. The routine that included a quarter of an hour getting the greyhound to come back to her.

This morning, until the lights, her routine was usual.

"Tut!" she'd called.

She paused, then "TUT!"

The wind tore the word to fragments, tossing the sounds across the packed sand of the beach and the small rollers coming in from Japan.

"TUT! Come here!"

Her hair whipped across her face, ends stinging and poking her eyes. "I'm going to have to get a whistle," she muttered, these words flung out to sea as well.

A faint line of paw prints ran at the edge of the damp sand, now slowly filling by the incoming tide. Her eyes teared up but something moved way down the beach. She squinted and headed toward the figure, calling his name.

She'd gone about a hundred yards before she could make out it was him, running at her full tilt, keeping to the tide line to increase his speed. "Tut, come here!" She put her hands out to him as the dog skidded up, tongue lolling from his run. "What am I going to do with you?" She snapped on his leash, hugged him, put her face down for a doggie kiss and ran her free hand down his smooth back. "You know it's just you and me, now."

Tut panted and pulled her up the path from the beach that backed up to Hamilton, the small town strung for three miles along the coastal sand. It was one of the Oregon towns with forefathers' names. Jefferson, Lincoln City, Hamilton.

She'd picked Hamilton based on the hit musical. A frivolous way to reinvent herself? It was time to take chances. She'd needed to get as far away from her Los Angeles life as she could, and arrived in the sandy, close-knit town to build a new life at the beginning of the new year.

As she and Tut crested the low dune, she looked toward her house and stopped, Tut almost jerking her off her feet.

Yes, there they were, across the street, the red and blue lights, reflecting off the high fog drifting in. "Wait, Tut, wait a minute." She gathered the leash in, bringing the greyhound to her and slowly walked across her deck, through the French doors.

Standing at her front windows, she watched the emergency vehicles, then noticed two people huddled in jackets, transfixed by the lights. Should she go over? The house they stood in front of, on the other side of the street, was practically wrapped in yellow crime scene tape, warning people to stay back. Surely, she could get close enough to ask questions?

The horror of Winston last year had burned out a lot of Roz' curiosity. After that, she wanted to be alone for a while, left in peace to heal, but this was pulling her. Living for 38 years without drama, in less than a year she'd had cops in her neighborhood, at her house, twice. Was she becoming a lightning rod for disaster?

Stop it, she told herself, this was only a coincidence. She grabbed Tut's leash and they went out her front door, eased over to the people in the street and Roz nodded.

"What's happening?"

One of the bundled-up people, a woman said, "Not sure. The fire engines pulled up a few minutes ago and three guys went into that house with a gurney." The house she pointed out was on a corner, two doors down and catty-corner from Roz' house. As they watched at the edge of the property, a police car, an investigator's van and an ambulance pulled in, light bars flashing and sirens dying.

"Who lives there?"

"An older guy, retired. Doesn't go out much. I never see him at Jules."

At the mention of the town's best-known coffee shop, Roz' stomach growled. She allowed herself only a cup of coffee before she took Tut to the beach for his morning run. Now, after fresh Pacific air and exercise, she craved food. Breakfast. Make it herself or go to Jules for food and gossip? Her mother's words echoed. *Don't be so nosy Roz. People like to have their privacy.*

She couldn't help it, she wanted answers, needed the pieces of her life to fit tightly together. That's what drove her to Hamilton, the quest to find a spot where she could create a space, a situation, that no one could spoil. Where nothing was unknown, all was planned. If the unexpected arose, she had to question it, to dig enough until it emerged, smooth, and slid into place. This, lights and emergency vehicles, was not expected.

Roz pulled Tut close to her again and edged as close to the tape and the investigator's van as she dared. Where the woman already staked a claim.

"Do you live near here?"

The woman nodded. "Around the corner. His yard backs up on mine." Then, "I'm Patsy, Patsy Stoddard. People call me PS, like an afterthought." She grinned, and Roz felt herself warming.

"I'm Roz, well really, Rosalind Duke."

"I haven't seen you around. New here? How do you like it? Where do you live?"

Roz recoiled at Patsy's barrage. How nosy. Well, she thought, it could be small-town friendly, a shortcut to getting to know you. In the L.A. area, Roz hadn't known the neighbors beyond what kind of car they drove as they'd nod to each other while backing out of driveways.

"I am new, well, I've lived here about four months. I really like it so far. My house is there." She gestured across the street to point it out, weathered grey shingles, red front door.

"Oh, you bought the Jamesson house! I've always liked it. Does the noise bother you?"

The noise. Roz zipped through brain cells to find the context for the question and finally gave up. "The noise?"

"You know, the noise of the ocean. That backyard is only a sand dune away from the beach."

"No, no, I don't even hear it now." In her mind, Roz rolled her eyes at Patsy. Coming from L.A. where cars' booming bass stereos, lawn mowers, sirens, were noises set against the constant dull roar of the freeways, she hadn't ever thought of the surf sound as noise. Even the barking seals on the rocks lulled her to sleep some nights.

"Look!" Patsy pointed at a man about to get into the evidence van carrying a clear plastic bag. "It's really bloody. That's not good."

Roz gasped. In the bag was one of her knives. At least, it sure looked like one of hers. One that she'd had specially made for cutting the lead cames she used for her stained glass creations. If it was hers, how could it get from her studio to this neighbor's house, covered in blood?

She forced down panic, took a deep breath, closed her eyes, 1 -2 -3 -4, she counted, making herself take slow breaths and fending off hyperventilation. Fainting in the street would be a terrible first impression.

When had she last looked at her knives? Well, every day, but it was automatic. If she needed a particular knife, she reached for it, not thinking about the tool but concentrating on measuring the lead. The measurements, the cutting, had to be precise for the glass to nestle together tightly, and this knife was one she didn't use often.

If this was her knife. Roz had only a brief glimpse at the bag, maybe she imagined it. She pushed the panic and the question of the knife to the back of her mind. She needed to stay in control right now. Thinking about the knife could come later, when she was alone.

"No, it's not a good sign but it looks like the show's over." The other person, a man Roz now noticed, pulled back the hood of his jacket. A nice face with a lived-in look, dark, collar-length hair graying at the temples. She couldn't see his eyes behind sunglasses. Odd, Roz thought. The morning fog hadn't lifted yet. Was he hiding something?

The man nodded at Roz and Patsy. "Well, I have to get back to work." He turned and walked toward the corner.

Patsy was engrossed in the crime scene. "Hmmm, I know his name is Liam and he doesn't live here full-time."

"Who? The man who lives here?" Roz was finding it difficult to follow Patsy's stream- of-consciousness conversation.

"No, the guy who just left. He's kind of a mystery man here in town. Shows up for a week, maybe a month, then disappears again. He bought the old Neff house down the street from me."

Roz' stomach growled again and Tut let out a whine. "I have to get him fed and I need some breakfast, too. See you later?"

A nondescript sound from Patsy, whose attention was focused on the house swathed in crime scene tape. Roz took this as an acknowledgment and tugged Tut toward home.

Inside her kitchen, she poured kibble in Tut's dish and by the time she'd filled his water dish, he was licking the sides of his bowl, making sure he got every bite.

"You were hungry. You had a long run this morning."

Roz wondered if talking to your pet was a problem. Since her move, she hadn't met many people. What happened in L.A, was too new, too raw and not something she could share. It couldn't be part of holding up her end in a "getting to know you" conversation.

Tut was different. It didn't matter what she said to him, as long as he could hear her voice. Until he ran, at least. A rescue greyhound, he hunted by sight not sound or smell and when he took off, he was focused. She'd adopted him a month before her move. That the move was more than a thousand miles away, in a small town where she knew no one, daunted her, though it had to be done.

Winston's killers had never been caught.

CHAPTER TWO

With Tut fed, it was her turn. She tamped down an urge to go look at her studio, see if a knife was missing. If it was, it wouldn't miraculously show up. That could be later, now she needed people, voices around her, bringing a sense of normal.

Roz looked down at her stained jeans. They'd do for an early morning at the beach but going to breakfast at Jules' called for a bit more. She rummaged through her closet, ending up with a pair of cotton drawstring pants, a cotton sweater and a scarf at her neck. Redid her pony tail, stuck her pencil behind her ear, tucked her notebook in her bag. Not dressy, not touristy, comfy, warm enough for now and not too much when the fog burned off.

Jules coffee shop was packed. Roz stood uncertainly at the door, her look sweeping the room. It was a Tuesday morning for heaven's sake, and even on this spring day she didn't think many people were vacationing. These were Hamilton people. Voices rose and fell, and in the babble she caught "crime scene tape" and "body bag."

Patsy must have been busy, calling people to tell them about the morning excitement. This explained the crowd, townsfolk all coming out to hear the latest. Jules was an old-fashioned coffee shop, probably what would be known as a "caffee" in hip Westwood, Roz thought. In Hamilton, it functioned as a diner until after lunch when it transformed itself into a restaurant with a different menu. Day-long, it was the center of news gathering and sharing. With TV and radio coming from Eugene or Portland and only a once-a-week newspaper, Jules was the town's information central.

A movement caught her eye. Someone waving? At her? She focused and saw the man from this morning—was it Liam?—waving at her. There was an empty chair at his table by the window. Normally, she wouldn't share a table with a stranger, but this wasn't normal. Her stomach was letting out growls she thought other people could hear.

She hula-ed her way through the crowd, weaving around kids having melt-downs in the aisles, canes precariously hung on chairs and extra people holding confabs while standing with friends.

"Wow, this is amazing." She was flustered when she reached the table. "Thanks for the wave. If they found out that you and I were at the scene, we may not be able to get a chance to eat!"

Liam gave a smile that reached his eyes, stood up, stuck out his hand and said, "Hi, I'm Liam. We didn't really meet this morning."

Being careful not to give away that she knew his name, Roz took his hand, a large warm hand. "I'm Roz, Rosalind Duke. I understand we're somewhat neighbors."

As they both sat, Liam wrinkled his brow. "Oh? I assumed you'd just been walking your dog. Greyhound?"

"Yes, I rescued him from a breeder and racer when I knew I was moving up here."

"That begs a couple of questions." Liam waved to a young woman with a coffee pot. "Hey, BethAnn, when you get a chance, coffee and a menu for Roz."

"Sure Liam. It's good to see you back." BethAnn rushed off and Liam turned back to Roz. "Just moved here. When? From where? And neighbors?"

Roz took the menu and tasted the coffee now in front of her. "About four months ago. From Los Angeles. I live across the street from, from…I guess the crime scene house. My house backs up on the beach."

"Ah, you bought the old Jamesson house!" The small lines at the corners of his eyes crinkled as he smiled.

"How did you know it was that?"

"This is such a small town that most places are called by the name of their original owner. I live in the 'old Neff' house', even though the Neffs, whoever they were, owned the place at least three families ago. It's no use bothering with an address, except for people from outside. The only person who usually knows your address is the postmaster."

The coffee was hot and Roz sipped carefully. "This is a small town, I knew that. Didn't realize how small. I met another neighbor this morning, Patsy Stoddard."

"I saw her. She's a font of information and shares it willingly. I hear some people call her Radio Free Patsy."

Roz swallowed so she wouldn't spit coffee. "I'd never have described her like that. It's perfect."

"So, what did you think of our little diversion this morning?"

"Given all the talk, it's not something that happens often here, I suspect."

The waitress came by, took Roz' order for a mushroom omelet, poured more coffee for Liam and took her coffee pot to another table.

"You're right." Liam's eyes slid to look out the window and now Roz noticed the color, a brilliant deep blue. "I think there was one body found on the beach—maybe ten years ago. He was a drifter, wandering up and down the coast, working at the marinas or on fishing boats long enough to get money for drugs. Police figured it was a drug deal gone bad. They never found the murderer."

Roz' stomach quivered despite the omelet she was putting in it. Too much coincidence? Of course. Her rational mind knew about 40 percent of murders were never solved. The L.A. police figured Winston's murder had a drug connection, too. Because of this, she'd spent the better part of three days bring grilled over and over about his habits, his friends, her friends, his money, problems in their marriage, his insurance. By the time they gave up on her as a person of interest, let alone a suspect, she felt dirty, violated. They'd probed some of her innermost secrets, turned her, and their life, inside out.

She shuddered. Knew there were still a few things she held close.

"I wouldn't worry about it." Liam's voice dragged her back.

"Worry? About what?"

"The murder, or whatever it was this morning. This place is beyond safe."

"Why do you assume it was murder? Did you know him?"

He threw a sidelong glance at the rest of the diners and lowered his voice. "Well, the crime scene tape for starters. And Patsy has spread word that the investigation team showed up."

"That makes sense." Roz nodded. "But you said you know him?"

"Yes and no." Liam fiddled with the spoon used for his coffee, spewing small drops of light brown liquid across a napkin.

"Well, yes or no?" Roz surprised herself at her questions. Was she badgering this stranger? One more way she'd changed since Winston.

He jerked his head up and narrowed his eyes. "I'd met him a few times. Exchanged gardening tips. Said hello when we met. More correct to say I think I knew *of* him."

"What does that mean?" Was Liam being cagey? If the knife in the bag was hers, and was the actual murder weapon, Roz needed to get more information. And before any of the cops traced it back to her. Who the dead guy was may help her discover what tied her knife to him.

"I was looking into his background. He never said much about his past, just that he was retired and lived in places around the world. Italy, Australia, Germany, Ireland. His voice had a lilt, a little accent, couldn't tell from where."

"Are you a cop?" Roz leaned back in her chair. Whatever good feelings she'd held about law enforcement had been burned away during her treatment by the L.A. police. They weren't her friends any more.

"No, no. I'm a journalist. Well, a writer. Well, I write stuff."

Roz stared at him. What kind of an answer was that, he wrote stuff?

He didn't seem to notice her confusion. "What do you do? Assuming you do something besides walk your dog on the beach."

"I do work. I'm a stained glass artist."

"Really? Like the things they sell at the By the Sea shop? Pictures of waves and shells you can take home and hang in your window as a souvenir?"

Roz stifled the urge to slug him. Those tacky things were to her creations as a used Yugo was to a Ferrari. "Not exactly. I mostly do commissions, big pieces, windows, for individual homes. Even some churches." She didn't notice Liam pale slightly and look away at the mention of churches. "When I moved up here, I started a do-it-yourself stained glass business. I have an online catalogue, you can order a kit and I ship it with all the glass, cames, solder and instructions. Those are smaller pieces, obviously."

"Ah, maybe that explains it. You sketch things."

"Explains what?" Roz was stumped.

"The pencil behind your ear. Do you always wear it? Most women I've met have earrings."

Roz colored, reached up and pulled the pencil out. "I do wear it, most of the time. I got in the habit when I'd see something I might want to draw, use in a design. My hus…, Win…, friends gave up reminding me and just didn't notice it any more."

He was listening, then twisted his wrist around to look at his watch, put enough money down to cover both breakfasts and abruptly stood. "I just realized the time. I'm sorry to run but I have an important call to make. I hope we see each other again, soon."

He made it to the door before Roz managed to gather her purse and get up.

Was it something I said, she wondered?

CHAPTER THREE

At home, Roz went to her studio and pulled up email. Good thing, she thought. Five new orders for kits were there, which meant for the rest of the day she would be gathering pieces of glass, cutting them to size and shape, cutting the cames and packaging it very carefully. She always taped the edges of the glass for shipment, wrapped them in bubble wrap, taped the cames—the H-shaped pieces of lead gullies that held the glass together—put in a spool of solder and added the packet of instructions.

It was time-consuming, almost rote work and it left her mind free to wander. Who was Liam? Attractive certainly, probably a few years older than she, maybe early 40s. He seemed well-spoken, had nice laugh lines at the corners of his eyes…and his eyes. A brilliant blue, striking with his dark hair. Liam, an Irish name. Was he black Irish, descended from the few Spaniards who survived the destruction of the Armada and washed up on the shores of Ireland?

Picturing Liam, she saw the crime scene this morning. Liam said he knew who the man was. And was investigating him. Turning the information bits over, she didn't pay close enough attention to her job and nicked her index finger with the wickedly sharp knife she used for the cames.

"Yikes! Oh crap." She looked at the cut, a slice into her finger. Not enough for stitches, but it needed a bandage. As she headed to her bathroom for the peroxide and bandage, Tut paced beside her, concerned that her yelp meant either a disaster or some new kind of play.

"It's OK, baby." Once she got the cut cleaned and the finger taped tight, she sat on the toilet lid and pulled him close to her. At this level his head rested on her shoulder and a little ripple of pleasure ran down his skin.

There were times when missing Winston was almost palpable. Not the grief—that was tamped down and the magical thinking of him walking in the door was gone. But the small, everyday things. The way he'd kiss a place she'd cut herself. The way he'd come into her studio when she was wrapped up in a design and put a cup of coffee and a cookie next to her. The way he'd frame a close-up of one of her pieces, a picture she didn't know he'd taken.

Well, Tut was it now and she got crazier and crazier about him as the months went by. She knew she spoiled him, but too bad.

This brought her back to the muttered promise to get a whistle for him, then up popped the memory of emergency vehicles on her street. The man who lived there must be dead, or else why the investigative team? And why the crime scene tape? If he was dead from natural causes, would they use it? And, who called 911 or the police to report something going on? And oddest of all, was that one of her knives in the evidence bag?

Her thoughts came to a halt and she went into her studio. Her knives were out of sequence. She closed her eyes and the scene of the bloody knife in the evidence bag tattooed itself on the inside of her eyelids.

Could she trust her memory? Could that have been her knife because it matched some of her others? She went over them carefully. There were the diamond wheels to score, the steel wheel cutters, the X-acto knives, box cutters, the knives for cutting cames. The knife she'd cut herself with was thrown down but the next slot was empty. This held the longer bladed knife that she'd had specially made. She closed her eyes. My god, she *didn't* imagine the knife in the evidence bag. It must have been hers. But how?

In case she'd read the scene wrong, lost trust in her memory, she scoured the two light tables, the area where she kept the boxes and wrapping for shipping, checked the top of the shelves above the vertical slots that stored uncut glass, even checked her kitchen drawers, thinking she might have picked it up to slice vegetables. Not a thing she ever did, but after Win's murder she found a few strange things happened.

It wasn't anywhere. She cast her mind back to the last time she used it and couldn't remember any time in the last month, maybe more. A mystery. And a cold thread of dread slithered down her spine. She convinced herself she knew where it was.

She walked back into her studio, originally the double car garage, where she'd had two walls taken out and floor to ceiling windows installed. The resulting space, facing west, gave glorious light all afternoon and a perfect space to prop up pieces she was working on. When the light came through, the pieces came alive, whether abstracts or representations, secular or religious. And when the sun dipped low, almost touching the Pacific, the studio exploded with color so rich she could touch it, feel it in her bones. The clear blues and yellows, the deep blood reds, the calm greens.

Overwhelmed with the colors as the day edged into night, the problem with the knife slid out of her mind. She couldn't tell anyone, she had no way of recovering it, she had to let it go. It would eat at her, but she needed to put it in that unanswerable place like Winston's murder. One day, she'd figure it out, one day it would make sense. But not today, not tonight.

Toward sunset, the sky was spectacular when the clouds and fog lifted. Tonight's was one of those. She went out to her back deck and watched for the green flash. When she moved here people told her that occasionally, if the light, the ocean, the clouds were just right, there was a flash of green light just as the sun sank below the horizon. Days when she thought the conditions were just right, she watched and waited but hadn't seen one yet.

This night, no green, but Tut pacing the deck wanting to go for another run. She refused to let him off the leash as it got dark—he'd run and she might never see him again—but went with him through the beach grass to his favorite spot. Roz thought this was a meeting place, maybe a collective potty place, for the neighborhood dogs and they visited it almost every night. She watched the sky darken to a mauvy-purple shade as Tut took roll of who had come to visit.

His business done, he let her lead him back to the house, to the kitchen, where she fed him a snack as she took a container of frozen chili out for herself. She flipped on the television to eat while watching the news and was surprised when a story on the man across the street came up.

They didn't have his name, the reporter said they hadn't found next-of-kin to notify yet. He'd been stabbed, multiple times. The medical examiner hadn't finished an autopsy but estimated the time of death sometime after midnight and before 6 a.m. The body was discovered when an anonymous man called 911 and said the cops needed to do a check on the house.

A sketchy report. Roz watched as the video showed the neighborhood, but the crew got there after he'd been wheeled out because neither she nor Patsy nor Liam showed up on the clip. It was just the empty street, the emergency vehicles and sober-looking law enforcement, doing their jobs.

After finishing her chili and dumping the bowl in the sink—she'd wash it later, a habit picked up from living alone—she grabbed her phone and dialed 411 for Patsy's number. She didn't hear any mention of the knife. Had she imagined that brief look at the evidence bag?

When she moved to Hamilton, she'd gotten a phone book for the entire county. It was so slim she'd used it as a shim under a table in her studio. Now things were precariously balanced and she didn't dare pull it back out.

Patsy's phone was busy. On Roz' second try, Patsy answered with a breathless "Hello?"

"Hi Patsy, it's Roz. We met this morning at the…"

"Oh yes! Wasn't that something? I stayed and tried to talk to the investigation guys. They wouldn't talk to me. Did you see the story on the news? Everybody is talking about it."

The torrent of words slowed enough for Roz to say, "Had you ever met him? Do you know what his name was?"

A moment of silence, then, "Hmmm, I don't think I heard it. He kept to himself mostly. A few times I'd see a young man knock at the door…"

"I thought you were a neighbor in back?"

"I am, I was, but young men would come to his back door, the kitchen, probably. I did think it was odd, like maybe they didn't want to be seen."

"Did you know who the young men were?"

"Nooo…" A moment of quiet. "Come to think of it, I didn't recognize any of them. I guess I assumed they were visiting from out of town."

How much of Patsy's guesses were accurate and worthwhile? They weren't enough beyond gossip to spread around, then Patsy said, "As I've been talking to people, everybody thought he was an odd duck."

"Oh?" Roz wondered who Patsy talked to, the whole town? "Did you talk to the police?"

"Not them. The owner of Jules, and Sally, who does my hair. I had to get to the grocery store today, wow, it was crowded, and I talked to Marge and Betty." Patsy voice droned on and by Roz' count she'd talked to maybe 20 people. Multiply that by how many each of those friends told their friends and it wouldn't be long before the whole town knew. Not necessarily accurate information, but some speculation.

"Sally heard from Janie who talked to Mirabell who heard he was a felon."

"A felon? You mean he was wanted by the police?"

Patsy's snort of laughter made Roz pull the phone away from her ear. "No, silly, he lived here for a bit, more than five years, and if he was wanted, Chief Giffen would have arrested him. I mean he spent time in prison."

Interesting, Roz thought. Liam told her this was a quiet little town, but it looked like it had harbored a criminal, a parolee? "What was he in prison for?"

"I don't know," Patsy conceded. "Not even Mirabell knew. I wonder about Liam…"

Liam. Now dissembling, Roz asked, "Liam? That man we saw this morning?"

"Yeah. I saw him and the dead guy, the victim, chatting a couple of times." A sly note crept into Patsy's voice. "Are you interested? A few locals have been interested. He's never been seen with a woman. Or a man, for that matter."

"I'm just trying to figure out why a quiet, retired man would end up dead, probably murdered in this little town. One of my across-the-street neighbors. Even in L.A…" Roz trailed off. Don't tell a busybody your past, her interior voice told her. "Even in L.A. I didn't know anybody involved in a crime." A lie, but her own secret.

"If you want to talk to him, his name's Liam Karshner and his phone is 503-555-5055."

"O.K. Boy, you had that handy."

A low laugh from Patsy. "Don't get too excited. We have a neighborhood watch group here and have a list of each other's phones. While we're talking, I should add yours."

A sensible reason. Roz mentally shook herself for her suspicions, gave Patsy her number, said good night.

Was it? For the first time since moving to Hamilton, Roz dragged Tut's bed into her bedroom and grabbed a baseball bat she kept in her studio.

CHAPTER FOUR

The weight on her bed the next morning resolved itself from a scary man into Tut, whimpering and pushing on her arm.

"What? What? You think it's time for a walk?" Roz rolled over and checked her bedside clock, 7:40. A gurgle from the kitchen and the smell of fresh coffee was enough to get her out of bed. A quick trip to the bathroom, an armful of jeans, sweatshirt and socks, coffee poured in a small insulated cup and she and Tut were out the back door. He danced around at the end of his leash that was just long enough to reach the sand for a quick pee, while she pulled on her shoes, then they were off.

She thought about keeping him on the leash, but he ran faster than she did, and roamed further. Getting a whistle went on her mental to-do list again as she unsnapped the leash and he tore off, headed for a flock of sandpipers hunting breakfast. Roz followed, slower and taking time to breathe in the cool, salty air. No stranger to a beach, she and Winston went several times a year in Southern California. This was different. There, they shared space on the sand with thousands of people, the air smelled of bodies slathered in sun block and the shrieks of kids dodging waves carried above the cry of gulls.

Here, the morning fog gave off a fine mist, coating the driftwood in a shimmering blanket, the sibilant sound of the waves was a counterpoint to the noise of birds and she could taste the salt, knowing it would stay on her skin until she showered it off. She tucked her coffee mug in the huge roots of a driftwood tree, slipped on sunglasses, jogged down to the tide line and started off at a fast walk, following Tut's prints.

About forty minutes up and down the beach and she stopped to rest, leaned against the tree and sipped her coffee. Her mind shifted to making her list. Finish packing up the orders from yesterday and take them in for shipping. Do an inventory. Yesterday, she thought she was running low on cobalt glass and she needed to look at her came supply.

And, it was time for her weekly call to the LAPD, to check on the hunt for Winston's killers. When she called, she could hear the exasperation in the homicide investigator's voice, but she didn't care. They owed her this and more after her treatment.

Satisfied this was enough for a full day she started on the ritual of calling Tut. She cupped her hands around her mouth and yelled, "Tut!" hoping it would only take one or two calls. Miracles, she saw him far down the beach, running towards her. "Here's my good boy," a sequence of cooing statements reeled him into her and she leashed him. Turning to the path across the dune, a figure waved.

Roz scooted her sunglasses up and saw it was Liam. Oh, good lord, not now. She'd barely had coffee, no chance to clean up. She waved back and led the panting Tut up to the top of the dune.

"He goes far, doesn't he?" By his question, she knew Liam had been watching for a while. This made her shiver and a feeling of unease started up.

"He does. Sometimes I have to call and call. One of my chores today is to find a dog whistle for him."

"I could help with that. The guy who runs the feed store is a friend of mine. We could go after breakfast."

"Breakfast?" This guy Liam was moving pretty fast and making a lot of assumptions about her and her time.

"I had to hurry off yesterday and didn't even say good-bye. My mother raised me better than that. I'm hoping to get another first chance at meeting you."

Despite her internal warning signals, Roz smiled. "Normally, I wouldn't accept such an offer, but I am hungry.

I have to feed Tut, take a shower and clean up. How about half an hour?"

"That's good. See you then." Liam gave a mock salute and headed for the street.

Roz put her getting ready ritual in fast forward, not wanting Liam waiting at Jules for her. As she flipped the hair dryer off, she heard Tut growl and then a knock at the front door.

"Coming," she said, hushed Tut and pulled the door open, holding her hair out of her eyes. "Good lord!"

Liam grinned at the sight of her. "Am I a little early?"

"Ah, ummm, well I thought we'd meet at Jules. I'm not quite ready."

"I'll wait, although I like your hair down."

She opened the door wider. "Come on in. I have a habit of cramming just one more thing into the schedule and sometimes I run late. I have a friend who calls me El Al."

"El Al? Like the airline? Are you Israeli?"

"No. At first I thought it was a pun on my middle name, Eleanor, then she told me she meant the airline. Israelis call it Every Landing, Always Late."

Liam laughed, a genuine full-throated laugh and Roz felt comforted. Somehow, a guy who laughed like that at a bad pun couldn't be scary.

She went to finish her hair, swipe on some mascara and lipstick and came out to find Liam gone. "Well, Tut, I guess we frightened him off," she said then heard a noise in her studio.

Tiptoeing into the room, she saw Liam holding one of her large church window designs against the light, tracing the spaces for the colors with a finger.

"What are you doing?"

He spun around. "I didn't mean to disturb anything. This is an interesting design and I can see how it'll fit together when it's finished. I'm also wondering how you didn't slug me yesterday when I asked about the touristy crap at By the

Sea. You're an artist. A designer. An architect of color using glass as your medium. That's the medieval interpretation of stained glass."

Roz blushed. That was how she thought of herself. Although not religious, her designs were created to reach the soul, to bring the wonder of the universe to the viewer, to stretch the mind through the cosmos. The medieval glass artists strove for teaching and closeness to God, she reached for the limits of the stars and nebula the space explorers were uncovering.

"It's beautiful." Liam's voice was quiet. "Is it a commission?"

Roz nodded.

"For a house? It would have to be big to show this correctly."

"It's for a church, actually a new cathedral." Roz picked up the drawing and absently ran her fingers along the design. She didn't hear Liam's swallowed gasp.

"Should we go?" She grabbed her purse and headed for the front door.

CHAPTER FIVE

In the street, Roz slowed. "Want to walk or drive?"

"I guess it depends where you want to go."

"I guess I was thinking Jules again. Have things calmed down?"

Liam pulled his sunglasses off his head and covered his eyes again. Sorry he did that because Roz was starting to like the bright blue. When she gave him a curious look he said, "I've found out my eyes are as old as the rest of me. The doctor told me to wear sunglasses whenever I went out. They're not a statement of coolness any more."

He grinned. It was infectious, and Roz did too. "I'm probably getting close to that, too. I never know whether to wear them before the fog and haze burns off or wait 'til the sun comes out."

"It can get kind of glary, even with the fog. The moisture in the air makes light do funny things."

"Glary, is that a writerly word?" Roz was out of the habit of making flirty talk. Would he take that as a biting comment? She glanced up and his mouth quirked, at least the beginning of a smile.

"A 'writerly' word? No idea. Aren't most words?"

"I suppose so. Jules?"

Liam raised his hand in a French *comme ci, comme ca* gesture. "You said you wanted to buy a dog whistle. If we go to the feed store down the highway we can eat at an old fisherman's place. Not many tourists. Ever had a salmon omelet for breakfast?"

"No, but I adore bagels and lox or smoked salmon."

"Not sure we can get that, but whatever we get will be good and fresh. Like going to an Asian restaurant where everybody is Asian, this is a fisherman's diner. My car or yours?" He started across the street toward his house.

"I guess yours, since you know where we're going." She shook her head. Is this a *date?* The last person she rode in a car with—except for the cops—was Winston. This is a new place, a new life her brain reminded her.

She followed Liam around the corner and up to a cottage that could have been transplanted from the coast of Ireland. The only thing missing was a thatched roof. Two deep-set windows overlooked a wild front garden, though at a closer look the yard was carefully tended to give the appearance of wildness. The whitewashed exterior glowed in the rising wisps of fog.

"This is wonderful, Liam." Roz was in love with her own house, a grander one with the red trim setting off the weathered gray shingles. A deck wrapped around three sides of it. A neighbor on one side, the wilderness of the Oregon costal forest on the other and in the back, nothing but the vast ocean.

Liam was backing a pickup out of the shed that acted as a garage. He popped open the passenger door. "Hop in. It's not fancy, but it's right for here."

"For here? Where's 'not here'?" She pulled the door to and jumped when a long arm reached across and slammed it.

"It sticks sometimes in the damp." Liam straightened up, twisted his head to make sure he was steering clear of the bushes bordering the street. "Not here is Portland."

Ah ha, that's where he "vanished" to, as Patsy so eloquently put it. "Do you do writerly stuff there, too?"

At the highway, Liam didn't speak as he whipped his head back and forth, checking for a gap in the traffic on U.S. 101. The north-south artery ran from the border of Mexico to the tip of the Olympic peninsula, the Straits of San Juan de Fuca and Canadian waters, and stitched together all the coastal towns. It wasn't L.A. freeway traffic, but a constant flow of cars and trucks along the two-lane road.

"I do." Liam eased back as he pulled into the stream. "That's one of the benefits of being a writerly person."

"Care to tell me what's writerly?" Roz had forgotten how fun easy banter could be. Most of her conversations over the past few months had been business. First the shock and awful arrangements about Win. Then the cops. Then the business of selling the house in L.A., wrapping up Win's estate, finding this house in Hamilton. All serious stuff, helping her work through grief.

"Since you showed me yours last night, I guess I should show you mine." Roz twisted around. Liam was smiling at his bad use of the elementary school jibe. He glanced at her. "Your work, of course."

"Of course." She breathed a silent thanks to the gods that he wasn't serious.

"I was a journalist, a writer for the Portland Oregonian. I covered a lot of local and state politics and wrote features. Outdoorsy things, some travel pieces, stories that let me get outside of the city. When the crunch hit newspapers, the print media, I watched as my friends and colleagues across the country were laid off or forced into early retirement. Here we are."

Liam wrestled the pickup into a gravel parking lot between two buildings. One said The Fisherman's Friend, the other simply Feed. Roz thought it was a toss-up which one was the diner.

Her question was answered when he said, "Let's eat first," and headed for the Fisherman's Friend. A wave of fish-tainted hot grease oozed out the door as they entered, not an enticing smell. She sensed Liam's look of concern, so she pointed out an empty table.

"How's that one? Not too noisy?" The table was close to the door, giving Roz the idea it may get fresh air.

"That's fine. I'll go let Jurgen know we're here."

Jurgen? Did Liam know everybody up and down the coast?

She sat while Liam went toward the kitchen. A large, very large, Nordic-looking man stopped him with an arm thrown out and Roz inhaled a little "erp." Was this dangerous? The Nordic man broke out into a huge grin and Roz relaxed. This had to be Jurgen.

A brotherly hug and a few backslaps and Liam brought the man over. "Roz, I'd like you to meet Jurgen, the best fisherman and second-best fish cook on the Oregon coast."

Roz looked up, and up when she realized she was focused on his belt buckle. Tipped her head back. Holy crow, this man had to be more than six-and-a-half feet tall. "Nice to meet you, Jurgen."

She opened her mouth to ask if he was still a fisherman but Liam already had the floor. "Jurgen and I met when I was doing a freelance piece on the collapse of the Columbia River salmon runs. We went up and down the coast a few times while he talked about fish, fishing, nets, line caught, being out for four days in a storm, lashing himself to the rail to stay aboard and now, diversifying and crabbing."

Roz' head spun. Fish came from fish markets, or the counter at the grocery store. Fish involved a lot of ice and guys in long aprons, maybe guys dropping lines off the piers that dotted the coast. She'd seen fishing boats, they chugged in and out of marinas and ports and she'd been to wharves like Monterey and San Francisco and watched boats unload their catch. Even men mending fishing nets seemed quaint, a way of getting food that dated from the beginning of time. What she hadn't thought about was being at sea for four days with no sleep or tying yourself to something so the ocean didn't take you. Liam must have a lot of curiosity.

"Don't let him tell you tales." Jurgen nodded at Liam. "He asks a lot of questions. Strings words together pretty good. But he's just a landlubber. Wore a life vest the whole time we were out. What can I get you?"

CHAPTER SIX

The Fisherman's Friend did have bagels, as well as salmon and whitefish that Jurgen smoked in a shed behind the building. Liam toyed with the idea of fish and chips—the hot grease—and ended up with an omelet of smoked salmon, onions, green peppers and mushrooms.

Roz kept her questions about being at sea on a small fishing boat without a life vest to herself.

Stuffed with breakfast, across the parking lot the smells of Feed overwhelmed her. Hay, chicken feed, horse tonics, grain, earthy odors that reminded her of an early trip to stables in Griffith Park. Win was going to surprise her with a riding lesson, but one look at the size of the horses did her in. She was too much a city person. In Feed, though, Liam was at home. He chatted with the salesclerk, a young woman in jeans and Western shirt with a pair of leather gloves tucked in a back pocket.

"We just ate at Jurgen's and Roz here needs a dog whistle. She has a greyhound who forgets he's supposed to come back if he's on a chase."

Did Liam just take over her life or was he only being friendly? This was his home, one of his homes, so he knew his way around better than she did. She bit back a snarky comment. "Yes, his name is Tut and he was trained to race. He thinks he's still supposed to do it. Usually the way I get him back is to wait him out. When he's run himself ragged, he comes back but I don't always want to be out that long."

The young woman showed them to the dog aisle and Roz chose a whistle that woke the napping terrier at the back. Good enough. She also grabbed a package of dog treats the young woman said were great for training.

"What do you have planned for the rest of the day?" In the pickup, Liam's head swiveled again, looking for a gap in the traffic.

"I have to take the kits that I packaged up yesterday to be shipped and I need to get an order together for glass and leading." Roz stopped.

Liam glanced at her and saw she was somewhere else. Her eyes glazed over, her brow wrinkled. "Is something wrong?"

Roz gave a shiver and snapped back. "No. No, I sometimes have designs turn over and over in my head. I can see the piece, know where it would have to be installed for maximum effect. I alternate between the emotional reaction and the mundane of shopping lists." And, she reminded herself, to check her supply of knives. She'd left it in the back of her mind because there was no way one of her precious knives could have ended up in the murdered man's house.

"Hope I didn't interrupt your thoughts. Are you going to work on the commission today?"

Odd, why would he care? She wasn't going to tell him that the trip to Feed stirred up memories of Winston she'd buried. She needed some time alone, even an unscheduled call to the LAPD. "I might. Do you have a lot to do?"

Liam twisted his head around. "A few things. I have some research to finish for my book."

"A book? You're writing a book? What's it about?"

He didn't often tell people about his book project. They asked what it was about, how he came up with the idea, told him about their second cousin once removed who'd written a book that was a best-seller, confessed that they knew they had a book in them because their lives were so interesting/difficult/easy/brutal. He was surprised that he'd mentioned it to Roz.

"It's a creative non-fiction story of a crime, well a brutal event, that affected a lot of people. How, even after years, the victims were still living with the trauma."

"It sounds interesting. Are you almost finished?"

Was she asking to be polite? "No. I don't know, really. I've interviewed a lot of people who were involved. I'm still trying to see the patterns, how to weave the story together."

Roz let that sink in. What they did, their interests and jobs, were eerily similar. Taking the large question of "Why", putting it into a concrete object, building up piece by piece until the whole became clear. He used words, she used glass. They both created things that told stories.

They were quiet on the short drive home. At her house, he came around and opened the car door for her, a gesture she didn't expect any more and kind, a throwback to earlier times. "Thank you for breakfast, again, and the trip to Feed. I may go back and browse, they have an amazing assortment."

Liam took her hand to help her down. "They do. I love finding places so eclectic. There are more of them in small towns. A store that specializes in one or two things has a harder time making it here."

She winced as he hit her bandaged finger. "What happened? I didn't notice it before."

"It's a hazard of the job. Or maybe I'm just clumsy. I wasn't paying attention yesterday while cutting cames and the knife slipped. It's nothing, didn't even need stitches."

"Are you a doctor now?"

Roz grinned. Banter with this man was fun and easy. "No, I've done it enough to know when I need to get out the sewing kit."

Liam's turn to smile. "You do it yourself? Do your glass kits come with a needle and thread?"

"No. Only 'BE CAREFUL, GLASS IS SHARP' warnings in big red letters. My insurer insisted on it." She shook her head. "Doubt you have to warn people about your writing."

"Hmmm… sometimes editors' notes that this is my opinion or a 'Don't try this at home'."

"Like on the story that Jurgen goes out for days and doesn't wear a life vest?"

They reached her front door and Liam looked more closely at the stained-glass inset window. "Yeah, kinda like that. Ah, I really like this. Is it Van Gogh's *Starry Night*?"

"Some of it. It was hard to figure out the pieces and colors so I did this small part of the sky. The Van Gogh Museum gave me permission to replicate *Iris* and *Sunflowers*. Those are big sellers in the kit world."

"I may have to go to your website." Liam touched her shoulder. "I'm going to the 'not here' place this afternoon. Can I see you when I get back?"

Roz nodded. "I'd like that. Breakfast seems to be our meal."

She closed the door and was pinned by 70 pounds of dog. "Did you miss me? I wasn't gone that long and I got you something. I guess it's more for me, really." She dropped her purse on the hall table and pulled out the whistle and treats. "Let's go test this, OK?"

On the back desk, Tut looked up expectedly. She always put him on the leash went they went anywhere, even down to the beach where he was allowed to run. "Not now. Stay." She walked down the three steps to the grass and blew the whistle.

Tut's ears pricked up and he tipped his head. Well, at least he heard it, she thought. She blew it again then called him. He was down the steps in a bound. She gave him a treat, said, "Stay," again and walked a few yards to the edge of her property. Beyond were the wild berry bushes that signaled the beginning of the forest. She didn't think he'd try to get through those. Another whistle, another bound of dog. He stopped before he hit the bushes, she called that good, gave him another treat.

Enough for now. He heard the whistle, seemed to respond to it. She'd try it again tonight at the doggy potty place to see if he'd even react.

In her studio, she double checked the addresses on the packages. Carried them out to the car, put them in the trunk and Tut in the backseat. Drove to the all-in-one store that handled post office duties plus all the shipping services, a gift section and a selection of cards and gift wrap. Liam was right. She smiled as his comment about all-in-one shops came back to her.

Outside, at her car, she watched Tut's head hanging out a back window. She left it down enough for air but not enough for escape. Now he stared at a small terrier mix three spaces over that was barking at nothing.

"Good boy!" Tut had a lot of good qualities and not barking incessantly was one of the best. With the exception of ranging so far while on a run, he was a quiet, obedient guy who followed her around the house, or lolled beside her in the studio, not pestering her or demanding attention. She was learning to live alone and found she cherished her solitude.

CHAPTER SEVEN

Roz took a run by the grocery store as long as they were out. Liam fed her breakfast the last two days and she hadn't shopped, now she was out of eggs, the milk was turning and the vegetables couldn't stand up by themselves.

She was in the produce section, deciding on tomatoes, when a voice said, "Roz?" Patsy pushed her cart up. "I thought that was you. I don't often see you here. Thought maybe you went all the way to Salem to shop."

"No, I usually get in here earlier, right after Tut has a run. I'm a little later today. Had breakfast with Liam then had to pack up some things to send off."

This was too much for Patsy, her mouth worked in and out as she mulled over which piece of information needed to be asked first. Finally, Liam won. "You had breakfast with Liam? I thought that was yesterday?"

"Well, yesterday it was convenience. I went to Jules by myself and it was so crowded the only spot was at a table with Liam. Today, he actually asked. We went to The Fisherman's Friend."

"That's nice." If Patsy had been Southern, Roz thought "Bless your heart" would have come out. That Southern saying could cover anything from congratulations to sarcasm. "I don't think he's ever been seen with someone else. Well, sometimes he's with somebody asking questions, has a notepad and everything, but mostly he's alone. Brings like a laptop with him."

How much to say? She and Liam seemed to both relish their privacy. "He told me he's a freelance writer. I don't know what he writes about or where it's published." Little white lies, maybe, probably a sin of omission, but in a good cause. If Liam wanted anyone to know what he did, it was up to him to tell them.

Sensing the subject of Liam was a dry well, Patsy took topic number two. "Sending off souvenirs to friends?"

What's the harm? Roz had been careful not to broadcast her business around for fear of insulting the couple who owned By the Sea. Her clientele was different and out of the area. "I design stained glass windows, big one for churches and some private commissions. And I do produce a few do-it-yourself kits."

"Like the ones that By the Sea sells? Maybe you could put some of yours in there on…"

Better stop this now. "No, my designs are too different. Mostly abstract. I don't think their customers would want mine." Take the lead in this conversation. "What have you heard about the guy who died yesterday? Murdered?"

Ah, Patsy took the treat Roz threw her. "Murdered, yep. Stabbed. A lot. Some of that was on the TV last night. Today I heard," Patsy glanced around for big ears, "that there was blood all over the kitchen where they found him and," her voice sank to a whisper, "there was a big cross drawn in blood on the dining room wall!"

Whoa, this was probably more that Roz wanted to know. "A cross? How awful. Do they have a name yet?"

"I called a friend of mine who works in the County Recorder's office. The name on the deed is William Smith. William Smith? Can you believe that?"

"There are probably a lot of William Smiths in the world. Why does it bother you? Do you think it's a fake name?"

The other woman tapped a finger on her lips. Mum's the word? "Maybe, but there's not a William Smith in the phone book in Hamilton. Not even one in Lincoln City."

"I guess this will be a mystery until they identify him. Sorry, I have to run, I left Tut in the car."

"Tut? Oh, your dog. You had him with you yesterday morning. What kind is he?"

"I did have him with me yesterday." Roz smiled. He wouldn't be any help in identifying the murdered man, he was only interested in things that were moving. "He's a greyhound." She put two organic tomatoes in her basket. "Nice seeing you. Let me know if there's a neighborhood meeting, I'd like to get to know other people, too."

Checking out with both Liam's and her privacy as far under wraps as possible, she put her single bag of groceries on the front seat and drove home. William Smith, huh?

With a glass of iced tea in one hand and her phone in the other, Roz went out to her back deck. The morning fog had lifted, replaced by a hazy mist. Fishing boats a mile or so out in the ocean moved, not close enough to tell if they were coming or going. Coming in, she guessed, they'd head out before sunrise.

Alva Robeson's number was on speed dial. Even if it weren't, she could punch the numbers in eyes closed.

"Robeson." The voice was gravelly, too many late nights, maybe too many cigarettes back in the bad old days. Roz always took solace that the landline phones at his office were so old they didn't have number recognition. Otherwise, she knew that Det. Lt. Alva Robeson of the Los Angeles Police Department would never answer her calls.

"Lt. Robeson, this is…"

His sigh was so deep she imagined her phone vibrating. "Yes Ms. Duke. What can I help you with?" His tone of exquisite boredom lightened. "Wait a minute, this isn't your usual day to call. Has something happened?"

"I don't know for sure. You know I'm not in L.A. anymore?"

"Yes, you're in Hamilton, Oregon, on the coast. Despite you thinking we don't have the ability to find our 'ass in the dark' was how you described it, we do have ways of finding people."

Hmmm, that may not have been one of Roz' best days. Surely she could come up with a better metaphor. "Whatever, I do have a question for you."

"No, we have no suspects. No, we have no evidence, No, we have no witnesses."

"This isn't about Winston's murder."

Robeson's chair squeaked as though he was leaning forward, listening. "What then?"

Roz tamped down the irritation she felt when she talked to this condescending man. "Yesterday, a man, a neighbor here in Hamilton, was murdered."

"That happens sometimes. Your point is?"

"It's more of a question. No one knows the man's name. He was stabbed, apparently a lot of times. I'm worried that it was random, like Winston's shooting."

"Ms. Duke, I can assure you that there's no similarity. Your husband was shot accidently as a bystander in a drive-by in front of a mall. What possible connection could this have to a man stabbed in his house more than a thousand miles away?"

"Me." Roz let out the breath she'd been holding. If the murder weapon was one of her knives, she didn't want to broadcast it.

"You? Why would you think that?"

"Well, after you dragged me in and verbally abused me thinking I had something to do with Winston's death, I began to wonder if I had some link. Some weird thing, a chance accident I didn't remember."

She could hear him tapping on computer keys. What was he searching for?

"Is there something you haven't shared with us?" His voice took on an edge.

"I haven't come up with anything, but having a neighbor murdered brought back not very good memories."

Robeson sighed again this time quieter, kindly. "I can imagine, Ms. Duke. Believe me when I say I'm, we're, all sorry for your loss and we're doing everything we can to find your husband's killer."

"There's one more thing." Roz stared out at the Pacific, wishing for some peace from it. "Someone drew a big cross on the wall of my neighbor's dining room. In blood."

"That's distinctive, but why would this involve you?"

"Don't you remember? I'm a stained glass artist. I do commissions. And a lot of those are for churches. But some aren't. I did a big abstract piece for the mall where Winston was shot."

"Tenuous. And how do you know about the cross? Have the police up there released that to the media?"

Roz mentally kicked herself. He wasn't supposed to ask that. "No, not really, I found it out from another neighbor."

"Ms. Duke. Please. Just stick to your regular weekly calls and we'll let you know if we find anything."

Roz' phone screen said "call ended".

Now that questions were started—damn Lt. Robeson for picking up so fast on the gossip angle—she was going to keep asking about the dead man. She pulled up Patsy's number.

CHAPTER EIGHT

"Patsy? It's Roz, from the grocery store?"

"Hi, I know. Do you want to know if we're having a neighborhood meeting?"

Perfect opportunity! "Well, yes. It seems like there's so much speculation and maybe even worry about the murder. What is the Neighborhood Watch doing? What are the cops doing? Shouldn't we get together and talk about it?"

"I knew we were going to be friends!" Patsy's voice held excitement. "I was just starting to jot down some things to put on an agenda. Are you busy tomorrow night? I can get the phone tree going and see how many people can make it."

"Why don't you just send out an email blast?"

Patsy chuckled. "You city people. A lot of folks here don't have email. A lot don't even have computers. I always do an email, but we also have our phone tree committee, you know, you call five people and they call five people…"

"I do know. Would tomorrow night be enough time to get in touch with everyone?"

"Probably, and better than email. It's harder to ignore a phone call than a message sitting in your inbox."

"What can I do to help with it?"

A pause, then, "Could we have it at your house?"

Oh crap, she'd put her foot in it again, two times in a day getting hooked when she thought she was being the angler. "I guess. What does that mean. Do you have food or drinks?" A cursory inventory of her pantry and Roz groaned. Another trip to the store, maybe even a trip to Salem, loomed for tomorrow.

"We do, but snacks. And we have a committee who provides them. Chips and sodas, that sort of thing. If anyone wants something special, they bring it themselves. If we meet at your house, a lot more people will come. The Jamesson's didn't entertain much. Everybody will want to see the inside of your house, and what you did to the garage."

Had Roz thought she'd keep her privacy? People she didn't know were talking about her, apparently before she even moved in. She'd contracted the garage renovation while still in L.A. and trusted a builder from Salem to oversee the work, sending her pictures and updates on the project. She put a light tone in her voice. "Sure, I can do that. How many people show up?"

"Anywhere from five to 15. It's not the whole town, just our neighborhood, that's why it's called…"

"Right, Neighborhood Watch," Roz finished the sentence. "I can pull out the dining room and kitchen chairs if we need to. What time?"

"We usually start at 7 p.m., give people time to get home and have dinner. It might be good to start tomorrow at 6:30 so everybody has a chance to see your house before we begin." Patsy's voice drifted away from the phone, as though she was hunting for a pen to make lists.

Acckkk, Roz needed to nip this home tour in the bud. "I have no problem with having people over, and if it's a nice night I can show them the deck. One of the reasons I bought the house. But I'm afraid my studio is off limits. Folks can peek in the door but that's it. My insurer insists that I keep visitors limited because of all the sharp glass and cutting tools around." She racked up another sin of omission. True, her insurance broker warned her about too many people wandering around her studio, but how she handled that was her discretion.

"Oh, OK." A tinge of disappointment in Patsy's voice. "I'll start the phone tree and write an email. And I'll make sure Chief Giffen can make it."

"Chief Giffen?"

"The police chief. He assigns someone usually, but if we're going to be discussing the murder, I think it's best if he's here."

What Roz envisioned as a small group of neighbors getting together to swap gossip and share ideas was taking on a life of its own as a formal police presentation. If she worked with the cops here, though, it might give her better standing with Lt. Robeson.

She put her hostess hat on. "I guess I need to know how many are coming." A run to the post office/gift store tomorrow morning and she'd load up on nice cocktail napkins. She wasn't going to get crazy about hostess duties, this was information gathering. "Thanks, Patsy, if I need to do anything else, just let me know. I'll see everybody about 6:30 tomorrow."

So much for her solitude. Damn William Smith, or whoever he was, for getting himself killed and inconveniencing her. She poured a glass of water and took it to her studio. There was time before sunset to get some work done.

There, the whiff of hot lead and solder calmed her. Designing, cutting glass, assembling the pieces carefully and methodically took her away from present problems. The designs and finished work were a far cry from art like the Chartes Rose Window or the birdcage glass of Ste. Chappelle, but she used much the same tools and ways developed in the Middle Ages.

As she laid out a section of the design on a light table, readying to cut some glass, her mother's voice said, *Make this a window into the soul.* Roz started and looked around. The voice was so clear she swore her mother came back to give one more lesson. A rabid Medievalist, her mother chose Roz' names, Rosalind Eleanor, for one of the greatest love stories in English history. Legend said Rosalind, the mistress of Henry II, was poisoned by Queen Eleanor, his wife and the most well-known woman of the age.

Her mind free-wheeled as she laid a small piece of deep yellow glass over the paper design. This would become the tail of a comet.

Roz worked steadily until a shaft of light blinded her at such a low angle she knew the sun dipped into the ocean. Her back creaked as she stood. She'd been bending over for better than two hours, her fingers ached, her eyes blurred and her stomach growled, letting her know it was hours since lunch.

Tut. Where was he? He hadn't made a sound. Roz found him asleep on the couch, stretched out to his full six-foot length. And he snored, softly. She leaned over and ruffled an ear and he looked up, blinking. "Do you need to go out? Let's get some air out back."

She grabbed his leash from the peg by the French doors. Outside, it was the wrap up of a spring day, warming the air and teasing her pots of flowers and herbs bordering the deck with the hint of summer. The leash spooled out to its end, enough for Tut to reach the edges of lawn, while she decided on dinner.

Tuna salad stuffed into one of the heirloom tomatoes she bought this morning. And a toasted piece of French bread. And she'd allow herself a glass of the Pinot Blanc in the fridge. One glass was fine, but more than that when she was alone brought back memories, good times she had with Win, meals, restaurants, trips to France and Italy.

Roz traveled on business several times a year, meeting other artists, touring museums, churches, homes for techniques and ideas. And Win was a professor of European History at UCLA so summers were their times to enjoy—and write the travel off as legitimate expenses. On the cusp of this summer, she didn't plan on travel. Not alone, not without Winston.

The piece she worked on, this commission for a new cathedral in Colorado, would require one trip by the fall, bringing pictures of what was completed for the Bishop and the building committee. They planned the completion and installation for early next spring so Roz had penciled in a two-week window when she'd be gone.

There was enough warmth in the air, and such a stunning palette of sky, she took her dinner out to the back deck. Gulls slued and squawked overhead, sharp eyes watching for any bit she might drop. At the end, two crusts of bread got thrown into the air and snatched. Tut watched, his head swiveling, following the gulls' swooping flight, but he didn't move. On the leash, he wouldn't run.

Too tired, a book and a senseless tv show on for background noise, Roz made it until 10:30 when she dozed off. She hated doing that, it was nasty having to wake up, turn off lights, check the locks, brush her teeth, wash her face, put on a t-shirt for sleep and climb into bed. Then she'd be wide awake and had to read for another hour.

Tonight the surf was white noise, lulling her. She dreamed of galaxies and star nurseries, clouds of pink, purple, orange, red, swirling dust far, far away.

Remember this, she told herself.

CHAPTER NINE

Roz stood in the small section of the garage she'd kept for storage, pulling out the folding chairs. Once a year she and Win hosted a history department party. They'd agreed it wasn't worth buying a whole new set of furniture for, so wooden folding chairs got hauled out every September and arranged on the patio.

The dozen chairs she moved from L.A. made a tight fit in her living room but the people weren't coming for a mixer or a dance. They'd sit, they'd listen, they'd discuss. They may get up and wander to the table for chips or a drink. Then they'd go home. All before 9, she hoped.

Patsy called twice, checking on things and telling Roz who'd responded.

"I was right, Chief Giffen is coming. He said this is too important a case. He doesn't want any gossip going around, just the information he gives out."

"Does he know you tracked down the guy's name?" Roz spent too long in L.A. being questioned by the cops. They were all taken with receiving information, not too keen of giving it back out and she was pretty sure if Giffen knew Patsy was gathering behind his back, he'd shut down instantly. They'd never hear another peep.

"No, silly, I'm playing like a reporter, never give up your sources. My friend just gave me public information, but she's married to one of Giffen's wife's cousins. Doesn't want word getting back to him that someone was nosing around the man's house. I got RSVPs from 19 people, which probably means we'll have 20. Two who said yes won't show and three who didn't respond will come anyway. Do you need anything?"

Patience, Roz thought. "No, I'm fine. It's just folding chairs, couple of bowls for chips."

"I'll see you, then." Before her call ended, Roz heard Patsy say, "Good, he's coming, too." Wondered who she was talking to.

With the chairs set up, Roz went into her studio. She didn't want to leave anything out that might be a slap in the face to the By the Sea couple if they showed up, nor did she want any neighbors helpfully telling her she could sell her work at crafts' fairs in Salem or Eugene. She made a good living, very good truthfully, with her commissions bringing in sometimes $500,000. Granted, the project from initial discussion and design to installation took close to two years, while her online kit sales netted about $75,000 annually.

She didn't gloat, but her designs were proprietary and she wrangled agreements with artist's estates and museums for use of their art in her designs. They required royalty payments on her sales.

Her commissions were big cash infusions but the kits were bread and butter. Tonight, the neighbors could peek in and see the drawing of the piece she was working on, the inventory of glass and lead, the light tables, the arranged knives and X-actos, the pliers and grinding wheels and cloths she used to smooth the edges of the cut glass.

Like packing orders and taking inventory, Roz checked over what was out in the open with part of her mind, another part working on the design and the next section she'd cut.

The mystery of the missing knife niggled at the edge of her consciousness making her tummy queasy, a mystery that wouldn't be solved tonight. Roz threw drop cloths over the storage shelves and table with knives, left the segment of the cathedral window she'd cut yesterday on the light table and went to take a shower. Her guests were about to show up.

It was early, 6:15, when the doorbell rang and Tut pricked up his ears. "Good boy," she patted his head, reached to open the door and her "Hi..." died before she got to "Come on in."

Liam was standing on her mat, wearing a grin and carrying a bottle of wine.

"I heard you're entertaining tonight and thought I'd stop by."

She shut her mouth. "Hmmm…I'm not sure entertaining is exact, but the Neighborhood Watch is coming over. Some of them, I don't know who. Patsy put out the call."

"I know. I got the email. And a phone call from some guy named Clark. Sounded as though she wants everybody to show up."

"I imagine the murder is quite a draw. And she's got Chief Giffen to show."

Liam smiled and held the bottle up. "Can I come in or is this a non-alcohol party?"

A tinge of pink rose up Roz' cheeks. "Yes, come on in. I didn't expect to see you. You were in Portland?"

"I was. It's not that far away you know. I'm a neighbor. I find Neighborhood Watch a way to keep tabs on people, events. You never can tell when a story might pop up."

He was in now, going toward the kitchen to put the bottle of Willamette Valley Chardonney in the fridge. "It looks like you're expecting a crowd."

"Patsy thinks 20. She said the attraction of seeing inside the house would bring people."

"Probably." Liam leaned a hip against the kitchen's island. "When I moved into my house, a steady stream of people showed up with cookies, casseroles, pies. None of them turned down an invitation to come in and look. This town doesn't need a formal home tour, it happens regularly, ad hoc."

The doorbell and this time it *was* Patsy, loaded down with two grocery bags and a big tote.

"Why so much?" Roz took a bag of what turned out to be chips and cookies.

"I got worried. There may be more people and they might want to stay longer to look at your house." Patsy deposited the other bag, six-packs of soda, on the table then spun around as she caught sight of Liam.

"What did I tell you." She looked from him to Roz. "Here's someone who didn't RSVP, but he made it anyway."

"Hi, Patsy. I haven't seen you since the murder morning. It seems you've been busy." Liam waved a hand in her direction. "Even got Chief Giffen to come tonight."

Patsy stood up straighter. My god, she's almost preening, Roz thought and glanced at Liam. Well, he was dishy, in a sort of nerdy, writerly way. She looked from him to Patsy. He was friendly, nothing more. Patsy seemed to be a step-and-a-half beyond friendly, on the verge of interested.

"Yes. People have been talking. A lot of neighbors are afraid. We've never had a murder here. This could be a serial killer, or a killer going after Christians…" Her voice trailed off like rain hitting a desert. She almost mentioned the cross, a fact she wasn't supposed to know.

"Christians?" Liam's voice held interest. "Why Christians?"

"Well, we're all good Christians here. Most of us go to the Church on the Sea although some are Baptists. And there are a few Catholics." Flustered, Patsy jumped as the doorbell rang again.

"If you'll put the chips in the bowls, and here's a plate for the cookies. I'll get the door." Roz was curious about Patsy's rundown of her neighbors' religious makeup and Liam's reaction to it.

A definite undercurrent flowed back and forth between them.

CHAPTER TEN

Chief Giffen turned out to be a roly poly guy, no more than 5' 8". Roz could look him in the eye, and when she did, she saw his intelligence belied his downhome appearance.

"It's nice to meet you, Chief." Roz led him into the living room, now filling with knots of people. "Do you know everyone?"

"I believe I do." Giffen had a slight trace of an accent, not a drawl but a slowing of speech and a drawing out of syllables. "How's everyone tonight? Karshner, good to see you, I wasn't sure you were in town."

"Came back for this, Chief. He was my neighbor, after all." Liam was easy, familiar.

Patsy clapped her hands, pulling the crowd's attention. "First, I want to introduce our hostess and newcomer, Rosalind Duke. She goes by Roz. Probably you're like me and would love a quick tour of the Jamesson house. She's said we can even take a peek into the converted garage. She makes stained glass windows for churches and stuff so we can't mess anything up but we can look."

Roz found 20 sets of eyes on her, took a breath and led off. "Down this way are three bedrooms and two baths, standard arrangements. Back here," she motioned to the French doors, "is the back deck that goes out to the beach. In this section, there's a half bath, living room, dining room, kitchen. I remodeled and put in an island. On the other side of the kitchen is the door to my studio. That used to be the garage. As Patsy says, feel free to look but please don't go in. There are lots of sharp tools and glass and my insurance company doesn't want visitors."

People milled around, ohhing at the kitchen and taking turns peering through the door into the studio. One man,

Roz later heard it was Clark from the phone tree, asked, "What's that big piece of paper on the light table?"

"That's the commission I'm working on right now. It's for a new cathedral in Colorado."

Liam, who'd had a personal tour earlier, hung at the back of the group. Roz caught his eye and thought he looked uneasy. Didn't like people? Uncomfortable in a crowd?

Patsy gave them 20 minutes to wander then herded them into the living room and handed out agendas, sheets of paper with several questions. "You may have questions of your own, but I wanted Chief Giffen to start with these. We'd like to know who the victim was, how he died, if you have any leads on the killer, are there any clues, do you have any witnesses, who made the 911 call. And the big one, should we be worried? I know I am, locking my doors even during the day."

Most of the women nodded, the men silently rolled their eyes.

Giffen started out. "I'm sure you've all seen the newscasts. We don't have much to go on. The man's name was William Smith. We haven't found any next-of-kin nor any history on him, which is odd. He moved to Hamilton six years ago, bought the house for cash through an LLC registered in Boston. He was stabbed to death, the medical examiner counted multiple wounds…"

A hand raised. "How many is multiple?"

"We aren't letting that information out. Let's just say he even had wounds on his arms and legs, not just his torso. As you can imagine, there was a lot of blood. So far, we have no fingerprints which makes us think the murderer was prepared, although it looks like there was intense anger. We've spoken to some of you and we'll be coming around to all the neighborhood asking if any of you saw or heard anything. Anything out of the ordinary, a stranger in the area."

Another hand, this time Clark. "Are you saying it was a stranger?"

"No." Giffen shook his head. "We have no information that would lead us to that conclusion. Every path is open."

Roz had stood, but at this she sat down, hard, on a chair by the fireplace. Waves of memories washed over. Did all the cops go to the same cop speak school? She heard these words so many times from the LAPD, both answering her questions and spilling out in press conferences to the media after Winston's death. She stood, went through the kitchen to her studio needing to be out of hearing range. It had nothing to do with Giffen but she couldn't listen any more.

A woman's voice drifted out. Roz recognized Patsy and walked back to hear the last of her question. "Are we safe?"

"I'd say yes." Giffen took the question seriously. "There's nothing to indicate this is a serial killer, but a lot of things seem to say that Smith knew his killer. It's a murder of passion, anger, and directed toward the victim. This isn't to say don't take precautions. Lock your doors. Know your neighbors. Watch out for any strangers."

At this he turned to the By the Sea couple. "I'm not talking about our visitors who help make our businesses thrive." A tide of low laughter circled the room. "Watch for strangers who seem to be outside of the normal tourist spots. Someone walking down a residential street. A car cruising by your house several times. Don't panic, don't jump to any conclusions, but if something looks suspicious, call us."

The gathering was breaking up into small groups, all talking about where they were, what they were doing when they heard the news. It was an anomaly. Roz understood why people remembered what they were doing when they heard Kennedy was shot, but this was so small. Then she realized this town owned it. They had their own mystery and it knitted them together as few things did.

Liam stayed to help Roz tidy up, gathering napkins, empty soda cans, hauling trash bags out to the bins in the driveway.

"You don't have to do that..." she began when he gave her an odd look and slight frown. She stopped and watched Patsy pick up her tote and the leftovers.

"I can take these to the church youth group tomorrow night. Thanks so much for hosting us, I think it went very well. Chief Giffen was helpful. Has he interviewed you yet? He's coming to talk to me tomorrow morning, as I was the one who watched longest."

"It was good." Roz led Patsy to the door. "Thank you, I enjoyed meeting all the neighbors. Now I have people to talk to when I'm out and about." Oops, another sin of omission, a little white lie. She didn't chat with people. Roz idly wondered if there was a certain number, a weight, of little white lies that tipped over and made a real lie. Despite doing commissions for churches, she wasn't Catholic. She had a hazy spirituality and loved the natural world, astounded at its depth and beauty and amazed at how it was tethered together.

Closing the front door on Patsy's back, she went down the hall and let Tut out of her bedroom. "Hi baby, you were such a good buy. You wouldn't have had any fun, they were boring people. Let's go out and you can see what friends came to visit." At the French doors she reached for his leash and jumped a foot when a male voice said, "Can I come with you?"

"Oh my lord, Liam I thought you'd left, too. You scared years off me."

"Sorry. A man's voice you weren't expecting is nervy-making after that meeting."

"Yes."

"Yes, what? Yes to making you nervous, yes to allowing me to come with you to walk Tut?"

Roz smiled to herself. The banter was back. Liam was quick, a trait she appreciated in a man. Winston was like that, full of puns and wry, almost British, wit. He could make her laugh at his understated speaking and always made her stretch her mind to keep up with him and the conversation. He sparkled and kept her alive and interested.

God, she missed that man.

CHAPTER ELEVEN

There was a chill in the breeze off the ocean. It was spring, but early spring came on in a different way here. In L.A. it would be the first warm days, even hot days before the May and June doom, when the marine layer of cold and fog was sucked in by the deserts heating up. Here, the coastal fog and mist stayed more constant year-round so that the days warmed easier and more gradually.

Roz grabbed a sweater from a hook by the door, wrapping it around her as she stepped out to the deck. "It's brisk, but it feels good. So far, I'm not tiring of this view and sound and smell."

"I agree." Liam watched Tut stretch the length of his leash to reach to communal potty spot. "I love a lot of things about Portland, particularly now it's getting lively. Bars, brew pubs, music, bookstores. There's a kind of critical mass of people, and young people, a place reaches before the culture changes. It's a place I go to check in, to find freelance gigs, to come up with feature ideas, to hang out with writerly friends."

"That all sounds wonderful. Why did you buy your house here?" She could see his gaze, the moon lighting his face.

"Here is where I can recharge. I'm trying to stretch myself as a writer." He turned to her. "A writerly person. I told you a bit of a falsehood the other day. I'm not working on my first book. I have four books out."

"Wow, I had no idea. What are they about?"

"They're genre fiction. Fantasy."

Roz was quiet. Then: "I don't read much fantasy. You mean like the Game of Thrones guy? George Martin?"

"George R.R. Martin. Well, I wish like him. I write under the name of Gregg Garthsom and I haven't sold anything to TV or movies. The one I'm working on now is totally different. I'm writing it under my own name. It's a creative non-fiction account of a horrific crime, or set of crimes. I'm thinking it will sell well, the crimes were headlines all over the country."

"I didn't know I was watching Tut and the moon with a famous author."

Liam let out a breath he'd held when he told her his secret. "Not famous. Not even well-known. Publishing is a hard game to get into these days. I'm what's considered a mid-level author. I sell enough books to keep a contract with my publisher but not enough to make a complete living from it."

"We have a few things in common. You have two businesses that pay you and a big creative project." She stared at the ocean, the tips of lapping waves glimmering in the moonlight. "I have a secret, too."

She'd spoken so softly Liam wasn't sure he heard. "A secret?"

Roz walked to the rail of the deck, keeping her back to Liam. She couldn't look him in the eye. "The reason I moved up here is that my husband was murdered."

Silence. She turned to see if he was still there. He was, just watching her. Had she made a mistake?

"I'm so sorry Roz. I don't know how a person gets through that. Do you want to talk about it?"

She felt the wetness coming and closed her eyes. "There's not much to tell."

"When? How? Have they caught the guy who did it?" He stopped, realizing he was using his journalist's brain.

"It was last summer. He'd gone to a big mall, not someplace we usually shopped. I never knew why he was there. He was walking to the entrance when a car full of guys sped by, shooting. The cops think they were shooting at a rival, another guy who was hit in the arm as he ducked. My husband didn't duck. He was shot three times in the chest.

The cops and the medical examiner told me he didn't even know what hit him. He died instantly."

Early in his career as a journalist, Liam covered a few shifts on the cops beat. It was a story he was familiar with, random killings, injuries from idiots with guns, too much testosterone and no sense. They didn't know and didn't care about the wreckage they left behind. Too many stories and pictures of grieving relatives, friends, neighbors, asking "Why?" There was no answer.

"I'm so sorry."

Roz stiffened and turned to face him. "The hardest part is they've never found the shooters. I call the LAPD homicide detective assigned to the case once a week. Same answer. No leads, no witnesses."

"That happens too often, more so in urban areas."

"I hope it doesn't wind up that way here. With our neighbor. I got the feeling from Giffen that it may not be random. He said the attack, the murder, was angry, passionate. It's not often that strangers get passionate about killing someone."

She sensed Liam nod his head. "It's even more so with a knife. You have to be on top of someone, touching them, to use a knife. That's an intimate killing."

"You said you knew him." Roz began curling up Tut's leash. The chill of the breeze made her shiver, or was it the possibility that one of her knives was a murder weapon?

"Sort of. I ran across who I think he was in my research. When we saw each other here, we talked social chitchat mostly, 'How're your tulips doing, going to plant beans or tomatoes this year?' That kind of thing."

It seemed natural Liam followed her inside. "Patsy doesn't think William Smith was his name. Giffen doesn't either, I get the feeling."

"That's possible. I've been in touch with people in Boston."

"Liam! Are you going to tell Giffen?"

"There's nothing to tell." He brushed the back of Roz' hand, started toward the front door. "Good night. I'm heading back to Portland in the morning, may be gone for a few days. Is it OK if I call or email?"

Startled by the frisson from his hand touching her, Roz smiled. "Sure. Hope we can get together when you come back. Good night." She closed the door and silently watched him walk across the deck and down the driveway through one of Van Gogh's stars.

"Well, Tut, this ended up an interesting evening." He cocked his head, his tailing slowly swishing as though he agreed but waited for more talk. Roz didn't disappoint.

"I guess the town is bringing me into its clique. We're not strangers any more. And it only took a dead man across the street."

She was tired. Enough strings of thoughts slinging around in her head she knew she wouldn't sleep right away. Put on Bach's Toccata and Fugue in D Minor, music that crammed so many notes in it forced your mind to focus. Went into the studio, pulled drop cloths off, folded and put them away. Began a list for tomorrow. Take pictures of all that she'd done on the cathedral job and email them to the diocese. Finish inventorying and place orders with her suppliers. Talk to Patsy and try to worm the name of whoever told her about the bloody cross.

And the knife. Who should she, could she, tell? No one. She'd been a person of interest once. Wasn't going to go through that again. If they managed to track the knife back to her, she'd deal with their questions. For now, she'd continue on her own, feeding off of Liam's research and pumping Patsy.

Telling Robeson that she might be a link between Winston's murder and her neighbor's slaughter wasn't smart. Her brain wasn't letting the pieces fit together. Was she tired or were they parts from different puzzles?

Enough. As she reached to turn the lights off, she saw a flash of movement outside. She went over to the floor-to ceiling glass, cupped her hands around her eyes, leaned against the window. Tut was up, ears alert, head swinging. He'd seen or sensed something too.

"It's probably just an animal. Maybe a deer. Good for you to chase, not for me to worry. Come on, sweetie, we're going to bed."

Outside her studio there was a muffled curse. "Don't make any noise," a voice whispered.

"It's alright. Her bedroom's on the other side of the house. And keep off the sand. We don't want any footprints."

Inside, Roz slipped into a dream. In a European cathedral with Winston. Bach's notes echoed from the organ loft and marched around the interior lit by stained glass. Color and music wove together and she slept.

CHAPTER TWELVE

"Next!"

The line in the coffee shop moved like a sea slug, oozing, while people decided on orders or looked at the pastries.

Northwest Coffee Roasters was Liam's go-to spot in Portland, walking distance from his loft and not corporate, but the casual attitude meant slow. The servers and the clientele pretty much knew each other and held conversations at the cash register.

"I went biking this weekend. Rode 35 miles!" "Tomorrow we're going to Hood to catch the last snow." "Did you hear? Jeb got an email from a venture capitalist."

Liam was an unembarrassed eavesdropper. He picked up feature ideas from the young, hip customers and used the conversations to help build his character's dialogue. These twenty- and thirty-somethings didn't talk about distant worlds or a dystopian future, their casual everydayness gave him tone and structure.

Nothing today struck him. He picked up his latte, took it to a small table and opened his laptop. He didn't work much here, didn't write, but an open laptop gave him camouflage for listening and observing. Plus, he usually got to keep a table by himself. He pulled up the notes for his current project, skimming them. Just as he remembered, he'd asked friends in the business in Boston to check out some names.

Liam sat back in his chair and let his gaze unfocus. What had Giffen said that night at the Neighborhood Watch meeting at Roz' house? The deed to Smith's was held by an LLC in Boston? Many times, that indicated money that somebody didn't want traced. He'd heard stories about dirty money, mobbed-up money, being used that way to launder it. Boston mob money laundered in a single-family house in

Hamilton, Oregon was a stretch. When he got back to Hamilton, he'd try to weasel the name of the LLC out of Giffen.

For now, he'd send a few more emails, see what trees he could shake. He opened Google and typed in Rosalind Duke.

Besides all the royal dukes in the world, there were better than 1,000 hits for Roz. Most of them were her business, the kits she sold and her commissions. Good lord, she was near the top of the profession in creating stained glass windows. She'd gotten commissions from around the world. A window for a $75 million house at Lake Tahoe, a towering piece for the lobby of a luxury hotel and spa in Switzerland, and a window for the nave of a church in Sao Paulo, Brazil.

Interesting. Now he narrowed the search for Duke and LAPD. Half-a-dozen things came up, all of them stories from the L.A. Times and smaller papers around the basin. They told the same facts he heard last night from Roz, Winston Duke was a professor of European History at UCLA. While on a shopping trip to a mall, he was caught in a drive-by feud between two rival gangs, was shot three times and died at the scene.

Police had no suspects, although they'd talked to his wife, the well-known stained-glass artist, Rosalind Duke. The case was open, but LAPD wasn't holding out much hope for an arrest soon. One small paper had unearthed an odd correlation, the mall developers had commissioned a window from Rosalind Duke to install over their entrance.

There were pictures of the scene in the parking lot, a mug shot of Winston from the university, a shot of Roz talking to police outside her house, a file picture of the window she designed for a house in the hills above Malibu. She looked younger but distressed. Liam thought it had been taken when they brought her home after talking to her.

His cell rang with a number he didn't recognize so he let it go to voice mail. When he listened to the message, he closed his laptop, took the remains of his latte and walked quickly outside. Slinging his computer bag over his chest, he hit the number.

"Sam? It's Liam."

"I know." The man's voice was quiet. "Glad you called right back. I can't talk much, I called on my personal cell. Hang on."

Liam could hear someone walking, a door whooshed shut. "Ok, I'm back in the photo lab. That LLC you wanted me to trace? The craziest thing came up. I still don't know who or what it is, but one of the entities that came up in the search string was…" The call ended.

Liam stared at the screen willing it to light up with an incoming call. Nothing. What happened? Sam wasn't usually mysterious, but he was careful to keep anything he did as a favor to friends away from his job with a Boston television station. In today's culture, everybody was wary of leaks.

There must be something about the LLC. If Sam was a dead end for information, he'd try Giffen, and now sooner than he'd planned to.

He trotted back to his loft, looked around. He'd come back to Portland three days ago, anticipating he'd be here up to two weeks this trip. He needed to get some free-lance gigs lined up, his books sales were slumping and he hadn't even sent off a proposal to his agent for the one he was working on.

There were key pieces missing. Biggest was the identity of William Smith. If he was who Liam thought, the answers to the puzzle were in Hamilton and he could winkle them out there, not here.

He threw a few things into a backpack, hoisted it and the laptop case and headed for the car. He never hauled much between the houses. It nudged his conscience to buy two of everything; soap, toothpaste, deodorant, but this way he could leave a house quickly and stay for as long as he needed to.

As he drove south on I-5, toward Salem and catching the state highway that would take him west to the coast, a call came in from Sam. "Sorry about the interruption, someone came in. I'm out of the building now."

"Things happen, I know. I figured you'd call back when you could. What did you run across?"

"This LLC came up in a thread when I was tracing money. It was somewhere in the middle, not the beginning or the end, but odd. It was registered to a diocese."

"A what? A church group?"

"Yep. There were some holding companies, some non-descript names like SkyWays and Black Opals. One sounded vaguely Italian, Sciotto Investments. Then up pops the Diocese of Eastern Kansas. Not a place I'd put together with money laundering."

Liam signaled for the off ramp to the coast. "I have to agree. Didn't even know Eastern Kansas had a diocese. I'm headed to Hamilton now. Email me what you have, I'll talk to the police chief tomorrow. He didn't give out the name of the LLC so if I hit him with that, I should get a good reaction."

Sam's voice was gleeful. "More likely you'll get a 'stay out of my investigation,' or 'you're getting close to a person of interest, let's chat'. Do you have someone to bail you out?"

"Funny. It's not going to get to that point. Thanks for the info, I owe you one."

"Just write me a letter of introduction to your agent." Sam's call ended.

When Liam started writing fiction and snagged an agent, all his previous colleagues got in touch to let him know they'd written, were writing, a book and could he help?

After he recommended ten or so of these, he got a call from his agent. "Stop sending me these. You know what I handle. Have you even read any of them?"

Liam admitted he hadn't, the agent said, "Don't send me any others unless you've read them first and you know they're well-written, polished and fit my genres." Chastened, he was careful about recommendations now and his friends knew it.

As he hit the end of this highway and turned south, along the coast, the setting sun paved a golden path across the water. Too late to fix some food for himself, he pulled into the lot beside Jules. It was in the middle of their dinner rush, filled with both tourists and regulars. Patsy spotted him and frantically waved him over.

"Boy am I glad you're here. Something's happened!"

CHAPTER THIRTEEN

Liam was tired, hungry and butt-weary after his drive and the last thing he wanted was Patsy yakking. Then he slapped himself up along-side the head, mentally. She was wired into this town and related by blood or marriage to half the population. If he was going fishing here, he needed her as a lure.

"What's up?" He slid into the booth across from her and nodded as the waitress held up a coffee pot.

"We think Roz had a visitor a couple of nights ago."

The waitress poured coffee, handed him a menu, Liam ordered a bowl of clam chowder and a small salad, she scribbled and walked away.

"OK, since when is Roz having a visitor any of your, or mine, or anyone's, business?"

Patsy twisted the napkin she was holding. Any tighter and somebody might die from strangulation. "It wasn't the kind of visitor who knocks on the front door, if you know what I mean."

Liam closed his eyes and heard Patsy squirm. "Sorry, just tired from driving. I'm not sure, what do you mean?'

She leaned across the table, lowered her voice. "The visitors were in her side yard. Clarence, her neighbor on that side, thought he heard something. Figured it was deer or neighborhood dogs, went out with his flashlight and shotgun. Saw the backs of two people running down the street."

"What happened then? Did he call the police?"

"No, he's such a nimrod. Didn't tell anybody until he got in here the next morning then was bragging to his fishing cronies about how he scared off burglars last night. The young cop, the one they call Smiley, heard them, dragged

Clarence down to the station to tell his story to Chief Giffen."

"That was this morning?"

"No, two days ago. They all trooped up to Roz' house, got her out of bed. She didn't see or hear anything, her bedroom's on the other side of the house. She did say Tut, that dog of hers, looked out the window of her studio but she thought he was watching another animal. If you ask me, that dog's less than useful. Who wants a dog that doesn't bark, particularly at strangers?"

No comment that Liam thought of would be appropriate or helpful. "Well, she wanted to adopt a guy who'd had a bad puppyhood and a dangerous life. So, did they find anything?"

"No. Whoever it was, and Clarence thinks they were teenagers looking for drugs, was careful. Walked on the grass so they didn't leave prints in the sand. Some of the gravel at the foot of her driveway was messed up, like someone had run through and pieces of gravel got pushed around."

"Wait a minute, was that the night of the Neighborhood Watch meeting?"

Patsy looked up at the ceiling and Liam watched her calculating. "Yes, it was. That same night. I'm surprised you didn't hear the search."

"I left a little after 6 that next morning. Was probably half-way to Salem. So, it's just hanging? Nobody found lurkers, nothing more?" Liam scooped up soup, stopped long enough to butter a piece of fresh French bread.

"You're pretty picky." Patsy pouted. She'd brought Liam good gossip and he poo-pooed it. "That's the most excitement we've had for a while. First a murder then a possible burglary, all in a week and both in the area where a stranger moved it."

Put like that, it did sound too coincidental. Liam couldn't see the link but thought there might be one. Someone who knew about Roz' past, Winston's murder, her being grilled. She said she hadn't told anyone besides him about her past.

The night of the Neighborhood Watch meeting, there were 20 strangers in her house, and they all peered into her studio. He knew how easy it was to find her background, he'd just done it.

"I'm going to be here for a while this time." No reason to let Patsy in on any reasons. "I wanted to get together with Chief Giffen and I'll ask about this, too."

"Too?" Patsy leaned forward again. Was she going to get information about Liam's business?

"I wanted to follow up on the meeting. It was distressing that they had no leads on who killed Smith. Has anything happened with that investigation?"

"No, not even the cross..." Patsy's eyes got big and she slapped a hand across her mouth. "Oops."

"Oops? What's that about?" Maybe because of the coffee and the food. Liam felt a new wind take hold.

"Nothing, nothing. Just something I overheard at a family dinner last night, but I don't think it means anything. I need to run. Glad to see you back, hope we run into each other again." She stood up, left money for her pie and coffee and bolted.

Odd.

Liam had split his time between Hamilton and Portland for about five years. He'd met people in each place, felt comfortable, was accepted as a member of the community. He called men like Jurgen friends, chatted about their jobs, businesses, interests, even hobbies. This helped his bread and butter income, the free-lance pieces on human nature, slices of interesting life, like why fisherman went out to sea without life vests.

What he didn't write about was crime. Sure, there was the project he was working on, and sure, that was a crime, but he was more interested in the breadth of it, the reasons behind it, the cover-ups that made it so invisible and possibly even continuing. But, day to day stuff, not so much.

Because of this, he didn't have established relationships with local law enforcement. With his background, he could talk the talk and walk the walk but there wasn't the intimacy that grew with those reporters who covered the police beat on a regular basis.

Tomorrow, he'd call Chief Giffen. Tonight, should he call Roz?

No. She'd said they seemed to do breakfast, so breakfast it would be.

Paid for his dinner, drove home, but couldn't resist a swing by Roz' home. There were lights on in the studio and the kitchen so he knew she was up, no doubt working.

At his cottage, he opened windows to let in the sea air. His main source of heat was a fireplace and the house always had a slightly smoky smell. Poured himself a beer to take the edge off the coffee, set up his laptop in the space he'd turned into an office. Here was the email from Sam, an attached file. Opened, it was five pages of notes, with footnotes and comments on some of the information.

The total amount of money that ran through the channels was just over $1 million, certainly way more than Smith's house around the corner cost. What else were they laundering money for? Or if not laundering, where did the money come from and where did it go? Liam was too young to remember the ins and outs of Watergate, but every reporter from that time to this lived for the day they'd uncover corruption and cover-up like Woodward and Bernstein did. And they made a mantra of the famous Deep Throat line, "Follow the money."

Here was the money, now what to do with the information? Liam jotted notes to himself. Smith: Who? The LLC: Where? Eastern Diocese of Kansas: WHAT? Peepers/burglars in Roz' yard: Who/why?

And the Neighborhood Watch. A group of 20 strangers to Roz?

CHAPTER FOURTEEN

"Tut!"

She knew it was next to useless to call him, so she wrapped her hair into a loose bun, held by her pencil, to keep it out of her eyes. Took the whistle from her pocket and blew. She had no idea if it worked, she couldn't hear it. She hoped he did.

Roz turned to walk toward the beach path when she saw a figure at the top of a dune. She squinted. Liam? It couldn't be him, he went to Portland. Said he'd be gone for a few weeks. She heard sand shifting behind her and Tut was at her side, winded but grinning. Maybe the whistle worked?

"Hey Tut, look who's here. He said he wouldn't be back for a while. I wonder if something's wrong?" After the town responded to her having nighttime, uninvited visitors, she admitted to herself that some of the residual fear from Winston's murder resurfaced. Between that and Smith's killing, the placid surface of the small town might hide things she didn't want to know.

She topped the dune, smiled at Liam. "Hi. I didn't except to see you so soon?"

"Some things came up and I needed to get back. It turns out this may be the spot where my book is centered. I heard you had some unexpected guests the other night?"

"I wouldn't say guests. I never saw or heard anything but it gave Clarence a chance to be a hero for about eight hours. Until he got taken down to the police department and questioned. That gave him first-hand knowledge about police procedures though, and he's been happy to share with anyone who'll listen. Or at least stand still." She smiled again. Even though she relished her quiet, her space, she was comforted that the town was taking her in as one of theirs.

"You said a few days ago that we seemed to do breakfast well. Want to try again?"

"You always hit me up at my most vulnerable, when I'm starving after Tut's run. Sure, can you wait for 20 minutes or so?"

Liam reached out to give Tut an ear rub and a head pat. "Yes, of course. Jules, Fisherman's Friend?"

"I think Jules this morning. I don't want people to get the idea that I'm frightened, I want them to see me out. Let me feed Tut and take a quick shower."

Inside, Liam walked into the studio while she fixed Tut's breakfast then headed off to her bedroom. A clean pair of jeans, sweater, fast shower, hair back in a scrunchy and she was out again.

"Not much has changed since what you saw the other day."

Liam was hunched over a light table. "I just noticed your knives and blades. Those look nasty and sharp."

"They are. Lead is a soft metal but the cleaner the cut, the less you have to reshape to give the glass a tight seat. You want the cames as smooth as possible. It's kind of like dough. It needs to be worked a little, but too much, or you lose the elasticity."

Mention the missing knife to him? No, he was in the business of asking questions. Let him ask away to other people, then bring the information back to her and she could decide how much to let him in on the secret.

As they went out, Liam asked, "You want to walk?" The morning sun had burnt off the early fog. She lifted her face. "Spring is definitely on the way. Sure, I can look at neighbor's gardens. Maybe get some ideas."

"I like yours. The rhododendrons are about to bloom. Do you know what color they are?"

"No idea. I found this place in the late fall and moved in winter. This is going to be a surprise. Are all the bushes rhododendrons?"

"I'm not an expert, but I think you have some azaleas as well. What's in the pots?"

Roz grinned. "I'm not sure they'll come up, but I planted some bulbs. Daffodils and tulips. I'm from the place where jade plants and ficus trees are outdoor plants. This is a learning experience."

"It's different here, all right. Lots of moisture, less sun, way less heat. Bulbs should do well. There are even places where daffodils grow wild and California, just below the border, has acres of lily fields. Grown commercially."

She slid her eyes to him. "You said you and Smith talked about gardening. It's a hobby?"

"No, just conversational grease. I'm not comfortable with chatting, but I had to learn to do some as a reporter and writerly person. People will tell you amazing things when you talk to them. Last night…" Wait, Patsy slapped a hand over her mouth at the mention of a cross. What did Roz know?

"Last night? Last night was quiet, no visitors, no guests. I worked until almost midnight. Did you drive down last night?"

"I did. I was too tired to shop for food so I went to Jules. Saw Patsy. She told me about your 'visitors' the night of the meeting. That must have freaked you."

Roz absently leaned over to pick a bud off a tree beginning to flower. "Yes and no. I didn't hear a thing. When I designed my studio, I had the contractor remove two walls. I knew it might be like working in a fishbowl, but the trade-off for the light was worth it. I'm thinking about installing motion sensor floodlights. At first, I didn't want to because of the animals roving around. Thought it would disturb Clarence. Turns out, he gets disturbed anyway. Maybe he wouldn't come running with his shotgun." She was quiet, then, "Although he might like that."

"His shotgun?"

"No, telling the tale, being the center of attention." Roz laughed. "Even with the murder, this town doesn't have much excitement."

"That's what Patsy said last night."

Roz' eyes rounded. "You talked to her?"

OK, Liam thought. Do this carefully and don't spook her. "She told me about your visitors. Then she said the strangest thing. She was talking about the excitement and mentioned a cross."

"A cross?" Roz squinched her brows. "She told you about that?"

Aha, pay dirt. "I guess. That's all she said. Do you know what she was talking about?"

Liam could see that Roz was torn. She knew something yet wasn't sure about passing it along. He was silent, letting it play out.

She went through her mind, weighing. If Patsy knew, it could be all over town instantly, but Patsy didn't tell Liam. Where was Roz' loyalty? Should she keep a secret? On the other hand, she'd already told Robeson.

"Patsy told me that one of her contacts told her that the house was bloody. Particularly the dining room. And someone had drawn a big cross on the wall, in blood."

"A bloody cross? That could be significant. The cops must be keeping quiet about that." If this was true, Liam had a hole card for his conversation with Giffen. He'd have to play it carefully or he might get shut out completely. "Why do you think it was there?"

"I don't know, but it makes me nervous." She took a breath and Liam wondered if he'd pushed too far.

"It's pretty weird, but why would it make you nervous?"

"Because." Roz hesitated. "Because I have commissions from churches. I'm working on that big one for a cathedral right now. And now everybody in town knows it. They saw some of the drawing when they looked in my studio during the meeting."

CHAPTER FIFTEEN

Liam stopped. "You can't think like that. Why would you put together your designing window for churches with the guy across the street getting murdered and then the killer drawing a cross? That's a web that wouldn't hold a fly."

"This is probably the downside of trying to live like a recluse. I start with these ideas, then pile on other facts, then draw conclusions." Roz gave a low laugh. "It's hard living in my head. It started when the cops questioned me about Winston. Their questions began making me think that something I did or said, even subconsciously, caused his murder."

They were at Jules. Before they went in, Liam said, "I'd like to keep this between us. I don't know if Patsy told anyone else about the cross, but I'm leery of having information the cops haven't made public." He looked at Roz. "Or have they?"

She shook her head, "Not that I know of, but Chief Giffen doesn't confide in me. I heard it from Patsy before the Neighborhood Watch meeting, but she hasn't mentioned it since. Mum's the word."

The early morning crowd had thinned. Four tables held vacationing couples, dressed in long pants, shirts, sun hats and walking shoes. Too early in the year for families with kids, this time of the spring the coast attracted retired people who came to walk the beach and look at the first rhododendrons.

Five guys took up a big table at the back and Liam waved, said quietly to Roz, "Are you up for some gossip?"

She angled her eyes, saw him smiling at the group. "Sure. Who are they?"

"They're retired fishermen. Spent 40 or 50 years taking their boats out in all kinds of weather. Bought houses, cars, educated their kids, paid taxes. The economy rested on their money. Fishing is harder now. Areas are overfished, salmon runs are decimated. Each of the little towns up and down the coast from Southern California to Washington had a fleet of boats. Now, every town has a place like Jules where they come, drink coffee, talk about the good old days."

They were at the table now. Roz saw the men ranged from their late 60s to maybe 80, all with weather-burned skin, rheumy-eyed from watching the water, looking after their trawl lines and nets.

"Hi guys. This is Roz." Liam stepped back so she was front and center. "She's the one who bought the Jamesson house. Clarence's neighbor."

What a suitable introduction, Roz thought. She'd been placed in the neighborhood and vetted because of Clarence, so these men could fit her into the right slot.

"Any more midnight visitors?" one of the guys asked.

"Now Yonson," the man to his left said. "We haven't even said hello and you start with the questions. I'm Schneider and this rude old man is Yonson."

"Yonson? That's a different name." Roz kept her voice light.

"Really, it's Johnson," Schneider said. "When he showed up here he had such a Svenski accent, couldn't pronounce the J, so it stayed Yonson." They all laughed and Johnson/Yonson turned a deep red.

"Don't listen to them," he said. "They're all rude. They come down here every day because their wives kick 'em out of the house."

These were old, polished jokes and slams, gentle ribbing between men who'd worked together, been friends for years.

"We came in for breakfast. Roz here walks her dog every morning before she eats." At a raised eyebrow from

Schneider, Liam added, "Crazy, huh? She's a city girl, L.A. You know those folks are different."

They found a booth across the room and Roz said, "Should I be pleased that you dissed me in front of those guys?"

"Dissed you? How?"

"That crack about how I don't eat until after I run Tut, then saying you know those 'city girls' are crazy."

"I'm sorry you thought that was dissing. What I just did was give you gravitas with the guys who carry a lot of gossip here. If you're part of their in-group, and you should be, now, they'll go to bat for you against anyone they consider an outsider. And that may include Chief Giffen."

Roz narrowed her eyes. "Well, then, I guess thanks. And you used that writerly word, gravitas, too. I had no idea they were the trend-setters."

"Naw, they're just a bunch of old guys who used to fish for a living. The coastal version of good ol' boys. Clarence is one of them, a little bit dotty, kind of over-eager but with a good heart. It doesn't hurt to have some of them in your corner."

Roz had to agree. Clarence didn't do any harm the other night and may have chased off two people planning to break into her house.

BethAnn came by with her coffee pot, they both said yes, Roz ordered French toast and Liam had corned beef hash with eggs on top. Roz silently giggled, she hadn't seen that on a menu for years. Avocado toast was the current rage in L.A.

"You said you were back here for a while. Did you find something else in your research? Or is this part of your book?"

Liam laughed. "Everything's part of a book, if not the crime one, then it gets used in the fantasy ones. But yes, I ran across a lead for the crime one."

"Care to tell me?"

He looked at her. Saw a woman in her late 30s, probably. Good looking, blond-streaked hair pulled back in a ponytail, dark brown eyes with laugh lines at the corners, small wrinkles beginning to form. And that ever-present pencil tucked behind her ear. He'd never seen her take it down and use it, though. A face with character. And a haunting sadness deep in her eyes. How much could he trust her? As far as he knew, she'd been open with him. Having one's spouse murdered had to be hard. It wasn't a thing you talked easily about to strangers.

And she was modest about her success. After Googling her and discovering who she was in her professional life, he was deeply embarrassed about the crack he'd made, likening her work to the tacky souvenirs at By the Sea. She didn't get angry, just quietly showed him her work and let him discover his goof by himself.

He could open up a crack. "I don't have a lot to tell. Remember when Giffen said Smith's house was owned by an LLC? That seemed like a bizarre thing. Would anyone be using that way to launder money in Hamilton, Oregon? Crazy-making. A friend of mine in Boston traced the LLC. The money, about $1 million, went through several holding companies and one strange thing. A diocese in eastern Kansas."

"A church? The Catholic church owns that house?"

"We haven't tracked it down to that, yet. The diocese is just one of the companies the money ran through."

"I never thought of the church as a company." Roz mopped a piece of French toast through syrup.

"Sure. You've heard about the Vatican bank, the church owns a lot of stuff. Property where facilities are. Churches, abbeys, rectories, schools. Even the cars the priests drive are registered to whatever order the priest belongs."

Liam pulled out money for breakfast, but Roz put her hand out. "You've paid for breakfast the last two times. It's my turn."

Outside, he said, "What are your plans for today?"

"I'm working on the cathedral commission. There's a section that's kind of a comet coming down from the edge of a star cluster. I'm basing it on the comet in the Bayeaux Tapestry that appeared over Westminster Abbey, but I'm not sure it's fits."

He stared at her.

"What? It is for a church, after all."

CHAPTER SIXTEEN

Liam had his own agenda.

First, a call to set up a meeting with Chief Giffen. He needed to cover the LLC and the midnight visitors to Roz' house. He toyed with the idea of asking about the cross on the wall, but no, he knew better than to give away information while fishing for it.

Then another email or call to Sam. Had he been able to trace the William Smith name through the diocese? And most important, get started on the book proposal and send it off to his agent. He talked to her about it, it wasn't a genre she usually repped, but she knew him and trusted his judgement.

Taking a chance that crime was light this morning, he walked to the police department and asked the volunteer staffing the desk if the chief was in. He was and Liam was ushered in.

Giffen's office was the only one besides an interrogation room that had a door. "Do you mind if I close it?" Liam asked.

"Go ahead, I guess. I didn't know this was going to be formal." Giffen had the usual pictures and plaques on the wall; him being sworn by a judge, him with a mayor, him at the state house in Salem. Pride of place was him graduating from the FBI Academy.

He leaned forward, picked up his coffee cup. "What can I do for you?"

Liam cleared his throat. "There are a couple things. First, I was wondering what progress there is on the Smith murder and second, have you gotten any leads on the incident the other night at Roz Duke's house?"

"Have you appointed yourself her bloodhound? Why are you asking and why should I tell you?"

"Sorry, I let my enthusiasm get away from me. I'm working up a free-lance piece, hoping to sell it to someplace like The Atlantic or New Yorker. How crime and policing in a small town is changing." Not quite a lie, he just hadn't told his agent yet. And if he did find enough in digging around, it might make a good piece.

"Well, I don't know what to tell you. No, all we know so far is that William Smith is a ghost. No trace of him in any of the state or national databases, no fingerprints, no next-of-kin. As I said the other night, his house was owned by an LLC, but we haven't had time to track that down. That kind of stuff usually goes through a financial crimes or RICO team and we don't have that. The state guys aren't even interested. It's just a murder of a possible John Doe."

"How about the autopsy? Or the crime scene? Anything different or interesting?"

Giffen seemed to be deciding how much to tell. "The manner of death was homicide, the cause was exsanguination, he bled out from stab wounds."

"How many wounds?"

"The ME found 27 total. Most on his torso, several deep ones on his thighs, more shallow ones on his hands and arms. Probably defensive ones." The chief was silent. Liam watched him and his reporter's instincts told him there was more.

"And?"

Giffen sighed. "This is absolutely off the record."

Liam nodded. "Yes."

"He had wounds to his privates."

"You mean…" Liam gestured to his own lap.

The chief nodded. "Yep. His penis was almost completely severed."

"Wow, that's unusual. You said it was probably someone he knew, and a crime of passion and anger. You'd have to be pretty angry to cut off some guy's…" He was looking for information about the cross of blood but this was good, also. "There must have been a lot of blood at the scene."

"The first responders, my guys as well as the EMTs, said it was a like a slaughterhouse in there. Even with booties and care, they couldn't help tracking blood everywhere. The investigators finally gave up, there was just too much to collect prints or anything."

Once Giffen began, more information came out. "No trace stuff, no hairs or fabric threads. The killer wore gloves, but he had to have been covered in blood. We've checked laundromats, dumpsters. There are boot prints, like Wellingtons, up to the back door—who around here doesn't have at least one or two pair of those. And you never worry if they fit right, you just add another pair of wool socks, so the size doesn't matter."

Liam had written enough cops and crime scene stories to know how frustrated Giffen must be. This was what a lot of cops he knew called a "stone case," stone cold with little chance of solving. Should he tell the chief about Sam's information? About the angle he was looking at? What his assumptions were about the man called William Smith?

Instead, he asked about the murder weapon. "You said there were more than 20 wounds, and that his penis was almost severed. It must have been a sharp, heavy knife to do that."

"It was. At least we think it was. We found a knife that's probably the weapon."

"One from Smith's kitchen?" This didn't fit well with the other information Giffen gave him.

"No. If a murderer wears untraceable boots and gloves, he, or she, usually shows up at the scene with a weapon already. The impulse stabbings are the ones where the guy grabs a butcher knife. This was an unusual one. Handmade, with a long blade, sharp on one side. The handle was wood, shaped maybe by a lathe. Round and smooth. It could have been used at any angle."

Liam jotted a note and something jogged in his memory. Had he seen a knife like that recently? It may come to him later. "How about any leads on Roz Duke's nighttime visitors?"

Giffen snorted. "You mean the ones Clarence thinks are druggies?"

"I take it you don't?"

"Naw, I'm leaning toward kids. Pepping toms, curiosity about the single woman new to town. A lot of people met Ms. Duke and saw the inside of her house earlier that evening. Probably went home and talked about her. The kids overheard, called some friends went to see for themselves."

The police chief picked up his coffee cup, eyeing Liam over the edge of it. "Do you have more information on Ms. Duke? You two seem to have gotten awfully pally."

"It's not my place to say anything. Did you take a look at her studio?"

"A quick peek. Nothing jumped out. Her work seems different from stuff that people around here would be interested in."

Liam stood, stuffed his notebook into his pocket. "That's true. Have you researched her? You might try Google."

He was almost to the front door of the station before he heard Giffen's "Well, well, will you look at that."

Liam smiled and went out to the bright day.

CHAPTER SEVENTEEN

Roz flipped to a new page in her sketch book, took her pencil from over her ear. What about this? Her mind was watching the soft dunes being sculpted by the wind, thin streams of individual particles lifting into the air. The beach grass leaning over, as though to capture the sand. Could she translate this movement into the world of spinning galaxies, streaming star clusters?

It would tie the natural movement here on earth to the cosmic movement in the universe, but she despaired that she'd be able to transcribe it glass.

Instead, she turned to the view of the Oregon forest, south of her deck. This she could do. The thickets of wild blackberries, salmon berries and Marionberries, the cypress and pines bent inland from the constant wind. If she got it right, she could add it to her online kit catalogue, something that visitors could recreate.

A vision of By the Sea popped up. If she began a design like this, would she be in competition? She was successful, they held on by their fingernails, dependent on the spring and summer months when Highway 101 was almost bumper-to-bumper traffic. Tourists and sightseers from both north and south drove the road and businesses like By the Sea did whatever they could to have travelers stop, visit, shop, take home a souvenir.

By the Sea owners Bob and Betty Snook came to the Neighborhood Watch meeting. They'd checked out Roz' studio. Maybe it was time for her to visit them. If they had stained glass pieces, maybe they had the tools to make one. Glass? Knives?

She went in, ran a brush through her hair, wrapped it into a loose knot on the top of her head skewered by her pencil.

Lipstick and mascara, flip-flops on her feet, now decisions. Should she walk or drive? Should she take Tut?

She decided on her car in case she bought anything and had to schlepp it home, and against Tut. He'd either have to stay in the car or get tethered in front of a store.

"Bye, sweetie, be good. I won't be gone long." She looked at herself in the rearview mirror as she pulled into the street. Had living alone gotten to the point that she told her dog how long she'd be away? She was pretty sure he had no concept of passing time.

The short strip of downtown Hamilton was crowded, all the parking meters full. The town set aside a paved section on the edge of the beach as a municipal park for picnicking and parking and Roz pulled into a spot. Families flew kites, kids rushed to the incoming waves and screamed as the cold water hit their toes.

By the Sea was in a building from the 1920s, when the economy thrived with fishing and logging. Originally the Fishermen's Hall, it saw meetings, dances, classes and was a central gathering place for the town. Even women and children came there for vigils when a storm blew up on the Pacific and their men weren't home yet.

The years rode lightly on the building, now renovated into a sales room up front and a gallery in the back which featured local artists as well as painters specializing in seascapes. Roz shopped through the space, looking at shells, cards, jars of Marionberry preserves. Sweatshirts and tees with the By the Sea logo, a weathered log on a shoreline with the Pacific in the distance, hung from hooks on the walls.

One shelf held the stained glass pieces, a dolphin jumping out of blue, blue water; an avocet strutting along the tideline; weathered wood half-buried in sand.

A voice said, "Ms. Duke?" Roz turned. "I'm Bob Snook. I was at your house the other night?"

"Of course, Mr. Snook. I was hoping I'd see you."

"Please, call me Bob. There aren't enough of us in Hamilton to use last names. Thank you for hosting the Neighborhood Watch meeting. Your house is well-known here, but not many have been inside. I know I enjoyed the look."

Roz smiled. "I'm Roz, and you're welcome. Patsy suggested it. I'm glad she did. I got to meet most of my new neighbors at one time."

"Not everybody had a chance to talk to you. Betty and I had to get back to our dogs. We don't like to leave them alone too long, they get into mischief." He twisted his hands together. "One time they got into our entire laundry basket. Clothes all over the house. Of course, we had to wash them all again."

How to stop this train before it got stuck on a siding? She had to ask this guy whether he had glass or make-it-yourself kits or knives in stock. When he slowed to take a breath, she said, "I understand. I don't think you missed anything, the meeting was breaking up."

"That's good to hear." Bob waved Roz into the back gallery. "Let's go in here, we can chat easier without interruption. One of the things I most enjoyed about your house was your studio."

And here it comes, Roz thought, he wants some of my things to sell in his store. "Thank you. I'm sorry people couldn't see more, but my insurer insists on very few visitors and usually one or two at a time."

"That makes sense, your pieces are so large. And almost all commission?"

Was this the time for the little lie? "Most of them, although I do have some online kits for sale. I'm thinking about designing one that could be a souvenir of the Oregon coast."

Bob's faced scrunched and a look of worry flashed across his eyes. "Do you mean like we sell? These are all done by a woman in Portland. We're the exclusive outlet for her on this stretch of the cost."

"No, I'm imagining something very different." Here Roz pulled her sketch pad out. "I'm thinking more of trying to capture the wildness of the coast. Maybe the forest? Possibly the beach, the way the wind sculpts the sand and grass."

Bob's face relaxed a degree though he still held worry in his eyes. "That would be different. Would you make them and sell them?"

"No, I don't sell any direct to customers. I sell kits so people can make them for themselves."

"Ahhh…" Roz could see the shop owner was calculating. Was this an opportunity?

"I've been thinking about classes." Wow, Roz wasn't sure where that came from, but it made Bob's eyes light up.

"Like the adult ed kind of thing?"

"More like private ones. I can't use my studio because of insurance, plus I spread my work out all over the place. I don't want to have to put everything away whenever a class comes." She paused, as though considering. Was it time for the bait? "Do you know of a place…"

Snook leapt at the bait like a hungry salmon. "Maybe you could have them here?"

Roz surveyed the space while her brain chugged through which track to take. "Well, I wouldn't want to take any space away from your gallery. I imagine these artists are depending on you for sales and exposure."

"Not right here, I meant next door." He took out a set of keys and went to a door at the side. "We had to put another door in for an emergency exit to outside so when we redid it, we walled off a space for storage." He unlocked the door and waved Roz over.

She hadn't noticed the width of the store and the gallery earlier, but now saw there was a jog where a false wall narrowed the gallery portion of the space. The room Bob led her into was long and slim and crammed with boxes, easels, shipping containers. One corner had been sheet-rocked off and a toilet and sink installed. And the outside wall had two large windows, boarded up.

"Hmmm…this could work." Roz paced the width. "I could get a light table in here. Install a cabinet to store the glass, cames, knives. Can you take the covering off the windows?"

"Sure. We put the plywood up to stop vandalism, but we can take it off and install bars. We didn't want to bother if we just used this for storage."

A bit more discussion and Roz left By the Sea with a quickly typed contract. She'd hold two classes a week for three hours each to teach people the rudiments of making stained glass. Her fee would cover the materials to make a 6" by 9" piece, she thought probably a Celtic cross. Enough cuts and curves to expose students to basics of measuring and cutting, not so complicated that they'd get discouraged.

Bob Snook would clear out enough room to move in a small light table and half a dozen chairs. Plus, he'd design flyers, put them up in all the other businesses and the Chamber of Commerce and Visitor's Center.

Roz was now tied into the town, had an open and easy way to start watching people.

And a reason to talk to them about knives.

CHAPTER EIGHTEEN

Roz sketched a couple of Celtic crosses, settled on one that only required 20 pieces of glass. Basic colors, red, blue yellow and a light grey. A quick inventory and she saw she had enough glass and cames for the first two weeks of students.

She'd ask each to bring their sharpest knife and Bob could sell X-actos for tourists who'd dabble in the class then head home again. A roll of solder and a cheap iron and she was in business, for at least as long as she could ferret information on who had or who needed a good, sharp knife. And who might have helped himself to hers.

Restless, Roz wandered through her house. When she was engrossed in a commission she let things go. Since the meeting a few nights ago she hadn't straightened, put things away, picked up her clothes. Now she put together a load of wash, swept and mopped floors, dusted tables. The simple physical jobs let her mind wrestle with the idea for the new design.

There was a glass wholesaler in Portland she ordered from much of the time, particularly when she needed odd or different colors. With the floors clean, the house neat, she went into her studio and pulled up their website. One of the tricky parts of the design would be the berries. She found an opalescent orange that was perfect for the salmonberries, some deep red for the Marionberries, several shades of green for the trees and bushes.

How to design, though. If she used it for a kit, she didn't want lots of teeny circles of glass, one for each berry. Maybe a more abstract version, splashes of color in the middle of the greenery. For the next two hours, Roz worked over the design, until Tut nudged her.

"Oh sweetheart, I've ignored you all day, haven't I?" She leaned over, gave him a kiss and hug, ruffled his ears. "Would you like to go out? Not a long run, but we'll walk up the beach, clear these pesky details out of my head."

Picking up a hoodie for her and his leash, she went out the French doors. Tut danced on the deck until she attached his leash then headed for the dog telegraph at the edge of the lawn. She gave him a few minutes to identify all the visitors then tugged him gently across the dune and began a brisk pace. Tut pulled a little, letting her know he'd like to run, but this break was for her as well as him and she didn't want to spend time chasing him down.

She'd done as well as she could, pushing the missing knife to the back of her mind. It didn't go away, sat there covered in blood, mocking her. Twice, she'd sorted through her knife collection, imaging, believing, she'd misplaced it. Hadn't seen it in that evidence bag. Knew, though, her eyes hadn't lied to her.

Was it time to talk to someone about it? Who? Not Patsy, although she could call her and pump for information. Not Chief Giffen. All he'd said publicly was that the man was stabbed. Det. Robeson? No, he'd tell her to talk to the local cops. Liam?

She could send him a text, invite him over for a glass of wine. Resolute that she had a small action, she turned toward her house. As they came over the dune, Tut tensed and stared at the side of the house. Roz was silent. When he went into his hunt mode he was focused. On what?

Roz grabbed his leash, holding it and his collar tight so that nothing jingled and tiptoed across the patch of lawn to the deck. She didn't want to take the three steps up, it might creak, but slid silently along the bottom of it until she could peek around the corner of the house. There was a figure, leaning against the window, looking into the studio.

"What are you doing?" Roz yelled as loud as she could through her fear. "Get away from that window. Get off my property!"

The figure—all Roz saw was a tallish person, probably a male, in a grey hoodie, the hood pulled up, and wearing sunglasses—turned and ran toward the street, not caring if he was leaving tracks in the sand.

She must have yelled pretty loud because Clarence came bursting out his door, shotgun in hand. "What's all the commotion?"

"Oh, Clarence, I'm sorry if I disturbed you. I had another peeping tom. Someone was leaning against the window watching my studio. When I yelled, he took off running."

"Want me to chase him?"

At the image of Clarence, better than 70 years old and half crippled with rheumatism, chasing a young man down the street, Roz burst into a stream of giggles.

He limped across the grass. "What's so funny?

"It's not you, I'm just so nervous, I guess. I never had any peeping toms in L.A. and it seems funny that someone up here would be interested in me, in what I do."

"Do you think I should call Smiley?"

Smiley? Because she was giggling? Oh, *Smiley,* the young cop. "No, I don't think so, what would I tell him? Someone was looking in my studio. He had on a grey hoodie and sunglasses, When I yelled, he took off running."

Clarence didn't look appeased. "Maybe they can come over with their investigative stuff. You know, take fingerprints or shoe prints. Maybe he dropped something. We should at least look."

Not to be mean or ungracious at Clarence's offer, Roz said, "Let me take Tut inside then we can look along the side of the house."

For the next half hour, she and Clarence stooped over and crab walked along the side of the studio, finding some flattened grass and a small, stepped on fuchsia.

"There's just nothing here, Clarence." Roz straightened up, her back now aching in earnest. "I'll call Chief Giffen just to let him know. I think it was a young guy, maybe a teen, curious. He wasn't inside my house, and I don't have anything worth stealing. Well, a tv set and a computer. Everybody has those."

Clarence nodded in agreement. The excitement was over. His back and legs hurt and he wanted to get back to his recliner, his beer and his own tv. "That's sensible, Ms. Roz. Just yell, though, if you see anything else."

"I will, thanks, Clarence." She moved the motion sensing light up to the top of her shopping list. Now it was time to share some of this. She went in to text Liam.

You brought a bottle of wine to the Neighborhood Watch meeting. Would you like to come over tonight and share it?

CHAPTER NINETEEN

When Liam texted back, *Sure. Are we foregoing breakfasts now?* Roz wondered if he thought she meant dinner. In case, she sent, *How about 7:30? We can catch the sunset on the deck.*

After a bowl of soup, she gathered up cocktail napkins, wineglasses and some feta and crackers. Took the wine out of the fridge, but she'd wait until Liam showed up to uncork it. In her bathroom, she ran a brush through her hair, left it down, smiled as she slicked gloss over her lips. This wasn't a date, but the familiar ritual of getting ready for the evening made her happy, with a sadness underneath. Was she forgetting Win? Never.

Liam's knock at the front door roused Tut from the couch and he strolled over for a head pat.

"I think he's getting accustomed to you." Roz grinned.

Liam smiled back. "The feeling's mutual." He handed Roz a bouquet of yellow tulips. "These are early ones. I have some in my backyard."

"Thank you!" She took them into the kitchen, put them in a small vase, centered it on her kitchen table. "Cheery things to have coffee with. Let me open the wine."

"While you do that, do you mind if I look at your studio? You must have a spectacular light during the sunset."

"I do. Go ahead. I'll get things on a tray for the deck."

This was going well, Liam thought. In the shower this evening, he had a flash, thought he remembered where he'd seen a knife like the one Giffen described. He wanted to check out Roz's tools before she came in. He went to the shelf where he'd seen her knives and picked one up. It was a shorter blade, but had a heavy, smooth knob of wood for a handle, a knife that could easily be turned to make a cut at an angle.

This fit with the description Giffen gave him of the murder weapon. Might Roz have been the killer? No, she wasn't anywhere near the theories he had for either the victim's identity or the killer. He heard her step and turned to see her illuminated in the door of the studio, imagined what she'd look like bathed in the deep red of the colored glass.

"With the sun at this angle, I can understand why you had the garage renovated. This must be spectacular with one of your creations against the window."

Roz smiled at him, glad that he understood her vision. "It is, and it's a true test for each piece. Not all the installations will be in west-facing locations, but this way I can see the colors and design are at their optimum."

They were silent for a minute, watching each other bathed in the early evening light. It looked to Liam that she had a halo, an outline of pure light around her, picking out wisps of hair and the fluidity of her arms as she motioned him toward the deck. He followed her outside.

"Do you want some wine to toast the sunset?" She held up a glass.

He took it from her. "I'm seeing all kinds of reasons why you bought here. For me, all this movement and light could be a distraction. Writers tend to be in a cocoon when they're working. But you, your craft is to capture this, to replicate it, to allow people to watch it daily in their homes."

Roz felt the heat rising from her chest. "Honeyed words. I get why you're a writer, now. Thank you." She turned to the ocean. "I'm hoping there's a green flash tonight."

"Do you believe that?" Liam moved over to stand beside her.

"I don't know, I guess so. I've never seen it. Do you think it's a myth?"

He took a sip of wine and shrugged his shoulders. "No idea. I've heard it most of my life, never seen it, never met anyone who's seen it. It's a nice thought."

"Hmmm." Had Liam poked a hole in her belief? Or maybe belief was more of a wish. She liked the idea of having a fitting good-bye, a salute to the end of a day. "Regardless, I keep watching. You never know." She walked back to two chairs she'd arranged with a table between them. "You've already had dinner I imagine, but I have some cheese and crackers."

He came to sit. "I have, but cheese and wine are always welcome. Breakfast with you is good, here's to winding up the day with you." He raised his glass in a toast.

"I feel the same." She raised her glass, sipped. Then: "This is relaxing and peaceful and I hate to interrupt it, but there's something I want to talk to you about."

Internally, he braced himself. Had he read her wrong all along? Did she have a confession?

Roz took a deep breath. "One of my knives that I use for cutting cames is missing."

Smack. There it was. He hadn't imagined it when Giffen described the weapon. "How long has it been missing?"

"That's part of the problem, I don't know. It's not one that I use every day. It could have been gone for a few weeks."

"You've had it since you moved here?"

She gave him a look that could have shriveled grapes into raisins. "*Of course* I've had it here. What? You think I'm dropping knives along my path as I head north?"

He beat a fast retreat, conversation-wise. "No, no, not that. I'm trying to help you figure out where you saw it, used it, last."

"Nice save. I probably used it three weeks or so ago. I was cutting cames in bulk to put together kits. I usually have a few on hand. A lot of times I wait until I have orders, though. Never know what's going to be a big seller."

"If you didn't misplace it, how could it have gotten out of here?" He waved a hand at the studio.

"That's a question I've been wrestling with. I lock my house every night."

"What about during the day?"

Roz gave him a speculative glance. Had he heard something about her peeping toms? "If I'm going out, I lock the front door. I don't lock the French doors when I'm out on the beach with Tut."

"There were your visitors the other night who Clarence scared off."

Time to confess all. "I haven't told anyone—well Clarence knows—that I had a 'visitor' today, this afternoon." She gave Liam an edited version of the search. "We ended up with nothing but sore backs."

"Does everyone know your schedule with Tut?"

Roz snorted. "*Everyone* doesn't know anything about me. Until the murder and the Neighborhood Watch meeting, I hadn't met anyone in town. I knew who people were in general but beyond talking vegetables with the guys at the market and chatting about shipping with the post office lady I hadn't had any conversations."

Liam was silent, staring out at the fingernail sliver of the sun as it slid under the Pacific. How much should he tell her? "I looked at your knives tonight. Did you have them specially made?"

"Some of them, yes. Why?"

He took a breath and dove in, hoping she wouldn't think he'd been prying behind her back. Which he had.

"I talked to Chief Giffen about an idea I have for a story on policing in a small town. We got to talking about the murder. He didn't tell me any specifics, but he did say the knife, the murder weapon, was a long-bladed one with a knob-like wooden handle. Probably custom made."

"Oh, my god." Roz took in a deep breath, feeling the panic begin. "That's what I've been afraid of. I saw the cops, I guess the investigator, come out of the house with a bloody knife in a plastic evidence bag and I knew, in my heart, it was one of mine."

CHAPTER TWENTY

They looked at each other in the rising dark. Skirting around the edge of opening up to each other.

"What have you done about it possibly being your knife? Who have you told?"

"No one, Liam. Except you. Right now. I've been thinking about who the dead guy is. Maybe if I can figure out who he was, it might help me with why *my* knife."

"Good thinking." She's further along in her search than I imagined, he thought. Liam sifted through how much he felt he could tell her. His quest was opposite to hers. He needed to identify the victim so that he could understand the killing. "I know Patsy found the house was owned by William Smith and she couldn't find any William Smiths in the phone books around here. Has she done anything else?"

Roz hesitated. Had Patsy done any more? Without guilt, she said, "I haven't talked to her for a few days." Not a lie of commission, though she did know about the cross. Patsy told her that.

"I saw her when I came back from Portland. I was tired and stopped in at Jules of a bowl of soup. Patsy grabbed me and told me about your nighttime visitors." Liam was quiet for a beat, then the scales tipped in favor of more disclosure. "She started to say something, mentioned 'cross', then slapped a hand over her mouth and bolted."

Roz leaned her head into her hand. Was Liam fishing, or did he know? Either way, it was time to share information. Her new gig at By the Sea may shake loose some knowledge of what knives the locals owned and used. But it would be weeks, if not more, before that would yield any results. "Patsy swore me to secrecy about the cross. She probably does that to everybody."

"Was it a blood oath?" Liam injected some levity, not wanting Roz feeling guilt over sharing with him.

"No, no, nothing like that. She talked to a shirttail relative who was at the scene. One of the investigators, I think. She knew there was blood all over and someone had painted a big, bloody cross on the dining room wall."

"That's one of those facts the cops will keep quiet about. The only person who would know that detail is the killer." Liam stopped. Closed his eyes. "Except for everyone who Patsy told. God, no wonder Giffen is playing this close to his vest. Not much to go on and one major fact being blabbed all over town by a busybody."

Roz took a sip of wine. Now that she and Liam were talking about this, she could tell him her other fears. "I know. And I don't want the cops to find out it was my knife. They'll make me a person of interest, if not a suspect."

"Why would they do that?"

"Well, he was my neighbor. Nobody knows, knew, much about me. He was killed with one of my knives, one made specially for me. And I design stained glass windows for churches."

He had to lean over to hear her, her voice was growing fainter. "Those are all barely circumstantial reasons, Roz. Unless it turns out that you knew him." Was than even possible? Liam doubted it.

"No, I didn't know him. I don't even know what his name was. I'm not sure I ever saw him. Patsy did tell me she used to see some visitors he had. Young men who'd come to his back door." Then: "Could those guys have anything to do with my 'visitors'?"

Could they? This was the first Liam heard about the young men visiting, but if the victim was who he thought it was, that made sense. A leopard didn't change his spots even though he was caged in a zoo.

"Maybe we need to work together. I'm tracking down who might be the legal owner of the house. It's somewhere in the morass of holding companies, LLCs, and the Eastern Diocese of Kansas. I doubt the victim owned the house, but there should be some lease agreement, contract, that allowed him to live there."

Roz licked her finger and picked up crumbs of feta from her napkin. "Are we overlooking something?"

"Probably a lot. What did you have in mind?

"Fingerprints."

Liam shook his head. "Dead end. Giffen told me there weren't any prints. The killer used gloves."

"Not the killer's prints, the victim's prints. Or his DNA. There was plenty of blood."

In the silence, all they could hear was the relentless hiss of the surf. "I didn't ask Giffen about that. I got so wrapped up in the Eastern Diocese of Kansas. Maybe my research and investigative skills have gone to seed. I'll do that tomorrow."

The last wash of light was gone. Liam and Roz were each wrapped in their own thoughts. They'd believed they were on divergent paths. Now these paths seemed to intersect in places. How much reliance could they put on the other person's story?

Liam broke the silence when he put his glass down. "I need to go. I haven't written my compulsory 1,000 words today."

"You write 1,000 words every day?"

"That's a minimum. I need to write that many every day in a book, either the fantasy ones or the crime one I'm writing now, or I'll never get finished. That doesn't include anything I'm writing for a blog or a newspaper or magazine, the bread-and-butter features."

Roz sensed him tensing in the dark. "When do you do your research?"

"I fit that in around the actual writing. Some days I can write a blog and a magazine article, so I'm ahead of the game. Some days I write maybe 2,000 words in a book. It gives me few hours of slack to do other things."

"You must be chained to your computer. How many hours a day do you have to write?"

"Usually four or five. I consider it full-time and don't let anything interfere unless I've already scheduled it. This is my job, just like I used to go into a newspaper office every day."

He felt her nod. "That's how I think of my stained glass, too" Roz stretched. "I probably average about the same hours, concentrated, as you do. There's time spent on researching glass manufacturers, although I know most of them now, doing inventory, packaging kits. And some free-floating idea time. I have a loose folder in my head of new designs I'd like to try."

They went in through the French doors, Roz carrying the cheese plate and Liam the wine and glasses. "What's your day tomorrow?" He set the glasses down on the island.

She smiled. "Tomorrow is actually an interesting day. The archbishop and the building committee members for the cathedral in Colorado are coming to see my progress and talk about the window. This will be the first time since I took the commission that we've met. They're flying into Portland and driving down."

"You've never met them?"

"We've met, it's just been a while. We met once when I flew back to Colorado to give them the bid and the preliminary sketches. Then they came out to L.A, to approve the design and sign the contract." She stopped talking and drew a design on the counter top with her finger. He waited. "Then Winston happened. We agreed on a six-month extension, so I began work on it again two months ago. "

Her smile was wry. "I think they're coming to bolster me, give me pastoral help. And, make sure I'm in a condition to finish. They have $500,000 of the church's money riding on me."

CHAPTER TWENTY-ONE

Her visitors showed up shortly after 10 in the morning. She'd given Tut a run, fed both of them and made a fresh pot of coffee.

"Thank you for making time to meet with us." The Archbishop was a cultured man who'd risen through the ranks of the church to oversee several dioceses. He wouldn't make the Colorado cathedral his headquarters, he'd stay in the Eastern Diocese of Kansas, but he exercised approval of purchases and commissions, like Roz'.

The contingent included the bishop, the architect and the head of the building committee, who said, "We do appreciate it. We flew into Portland last night and drove down this morning. My first time in this part of the country. The coastline is beautiful."

"It is." Roz nodded her agreement. "I wasn't sure in the beginning. It's very different from Southern California. Both in landscape and size. It takes about ten minutes to drive from one end of town to the other."

The men smiled. "I can appreciate the change," the architect said. "Do you find it's affected your designs?"

Roz poured coffee for the group before saying, "I don't know. Yet. I'm working on an idea that's specific to this place, that will capture the wildness. It's preliminary, but if it works out I'll put it in my catalogue." She stood, "Would you like to see my studio?"

The archbishop nodded. She escorted the group across the kitchen and out to her studio, where they gave a collective intake of breath. Not a gasp, a murmur of appreciation.

"This is stunning." The first words from the bishop. "You must have a glorious view of the sunset."

'I do. That's one of the primary reasons for buying here. You're standing in what was the garage before I had it renovated and two walls removed. This gives me shelter from the weather and still allows me to be part of nature. I've seen two storms sweep in, but I'm protected by the beach and the dunes. I get a lot of rain, strong winds, but no erosion so far." She walked to the back wall of glass that overlooked the dunes and the ocean. "I use this when the sun sets as a final test of the colors and composition. Not every piece will face west, I know."

The men nodded, um-hmmmed, glanced at each other. Then the building committee head said, "Do you have some things from our commission that you can show us?"

"I do." She went to a shelf, pulled out a stack of folded drafting paper. "If one of you could hold this?" She unfolded the paper and began taping it against the window. "As we discussed and agreed, the piece will be 27 feet tall and 15 feet wide and be installed in the nave. The proportions are designed to pull the eye up. I'll lay the design out on its side, but you'll be able to understand how it will fit." As she talked, she taped the paper up until she'd covered most of the two walls of window.

She began at the left, what would be the bottom of the piece, directing the men's attention to the rising swirl of clouds and streaks of color punctuated by pin pricks of stars and clusters of nebula. She'd used a photo from the Hubble Space Telescope as the basis for her design.

"This is beautiful." The bishop's voice was quiet. "It's a sweep of majesty and wonder on an epic scale."

"Thank you." Roz was pleased they liked and understood what she was creating. It was a departure from the usual designs in churches and cathedrals, but she believed it captured some of the mystery of the nature of the universe.

They chatted for a time about the building, how the construction was going, whether the time frame she'd roughed out for a visit and the ultimate period she'd spend overseeing the installation would still fit. She and the architect compared notes and ideas about how the installation would be anchored and what braces might be needed against strong winds sweeping down from the Rockies.

After a couple of hours she asked if they were hungry. "I thought I'd show you the beach and then we could go into town. The main restaurant is Jules, closer to a diner, but you'll get a feel for the place. Some of the emotion from here will end up being worked into your window."

They agreed and walked into Jules just before 1 p.m., the last of the lunch rush. Roz hadn't thought about how it might look, coming in for lunch with two men in Roman Catholic collars, and wondered when BethAnn grew flustered and quickly showed them to a table by the window.

"I'm still new here and people are trying to place me," Roz said as she nodded to Patsy, who watched with raised eyebrows, backed into a chair and knocked over a water glass.

The archbishop laughed. "We get that sometimes. People forget we're all humans and do all the human things, eat, drink, travel."

People's attention shifted back to their lunches, their conversations, Patsy made her escape and normalcy returned. Until Liam came in.

BethAnn stopped her rounds so suddenly the coffee in her ever-present pot sloshed on the floor. Roz started and looked around, catching Liam's face, pale and grimacing. What was this about?

She pushed her chair back to go over and invite him, but Liam walked past her, homing in on the archbishop.

"I'm Liam Karshner. And I believe you're Archbishop Malone."

Malone rose and put out a hand. "I am. Do I know you?"

"No, we've never met. But I know of you. You're assigned to the Eastern Kansas Diocese, I understand."

"Yes, now, although I've served in many places, many dioceses before my assignment there. Are you a Catholic?"

Color was returning to Liam's face. "No, I'm not a member of any particular faith. I'm a journalist, a writer. I guess I'm more of a dabbler, interested in many things." He paused. "What brings you to Hamilton, Oregon? I'd think it's a bit out of your normal path."

The archbishop smiled. "It is, but it's church business. This lovely lady," and he gestured at Roz whose mouth was gaping, "is making a stained glass window for our new cathedral in Colorado."

Liam stared at Roz. "Ah, I had no idea this was where your commission was from." He turned back to the table, "Enjoy your lunch gentleman. Will I see you again?"

"No, we have a plane to catch early this evening. We're driving back to Portland after lunch." The bishop finally spoke.

"I hope I'll see you later." Liam's brilliant blue eyes drilled into Roz and she almost flinched.

"Yes, I hope so," she managed to get out as he turned away and went to join the retired fishermen at the table in the back.

What was that all about? She shook her head, clearing the awkward scene. Between Patsy jumping like a frightened rabbit, BethAnn scurrying around and Liam being just an inch away from rude, there were strange undercurrents.

She dragged her attention back to the conversation about travel arrangements, schedules that the men were putting together, how they'd handle the logistics of the installation and the Mass that would celebrate the consecration of the new cathedral. Again, she was reminded that the church was also a business, a big business in the world.

Finishing lunch, the group said their goodbyes to Roz on the street before piling into the car for the trip back to the airport. It was a quick trip, she thought, but they saw what they needed to, checked on her progress, seemed happy with her design and explanations. As she worked on parts, put together sections, she'd take pictures and send them to the architect and building committee chair. Then the last the months would be taken up with the final logistics. Shipping the sections to the site, arranging for other glass workers and construction workers who'd do the final welds, installing the bars that would keep the window stable.

She'd penciled in two weeks for that portion of the work, but she knew it would have to be flexible. The window would tell her what it needed.

Putting the visitors and commission aside, Roz walked down the street to By the Sea. As she came in, Bob stood up from behind the cash register. "I'm glad you're here. I wanted to show you what we've done."

"Good! I'm working on some designs and checked my inventory. If we don't have more than five in a class—which is about the limit—I have enough supplies for a couple of weeks."

He reached under the counter and pulled out a stack of flyers. "These are what I designed. Are they OK?"

He'd sketched a window designed to hang in the light, showing a mass of wild berry bushes under two towering trees with the line, "Take home a bit of wildness." It also included two sentences about Roz, how she was an award-winning local artist, the dates and times, the cost and location.

The invitation was overstated, the students would have to spend a few years getting the expertise in the craft to tackle something that complicated. What she was offering was a taste, a few hours of the basics. Cutting glass, cutting cames, learning to use a soldering iron without burning oneself.

Maybe Bob went overboard in his enthusiasm, but it would bring people into his shop. Tourists would buy, locals would swap information and Roz could ask questions. "Don't forget to order five X-Actos knives, too, plus some of the small rolls of solder. I'm bringing two basic irons for them to get started with. If anyone gets excited, we can sit down with them to order additional supplies."

He showed her how they'd rearranged and cleaned out the storeroom, taken down the plywood from the windows. It was looking like it would work well.

Roz headed home, mentally tired from doing her song and dance for the Archbishop's group. All nice men, easy to work with, but there was always some tension when discussing a commission.

And the odd scene at Jules over lunch. What was wrong with Liam?

CHAPTER TWENTY-TWO

Saturday, Roz loaded up a soldering iron, some glass, cames and a roll of solder after she took Tut for his morning run. She planned to spend an hour or so at By the Sea, randomly cutting some glass and soldering cames together so that people could see what this stained glass stuff was all about.

She unloaded the box and was struggling to open the door to the shop when Betty rushed over. "Wait, let me help you," the shop owner said as she held the door open. "We didn't expect you."

"I probably should have called." Roz acknowledged Betty with a smile. "I woke up this morning and it's such a great spring day I figured there'd be lots of tourists in town. I have an idea." She went into the side room, dumped her box, carefully, on one of the light tables. "What would you think about putting a sign out that there's a stained glass making exhibition this weekend?"

"A sign?" Betty looked doubtful.

"Don't you have one of those a-frame-y easel signs that go out in front? On the sidewalk?"

"You mean the chalkboard ones? We used to have one, but I don't know where Bob put it. We haven't used it for years."

"Is it in the storeroom? There's a bunch of stuff down at one end."

The two women unearthed an a-frame chalkboard after twenty minutes of digging and rearranging, Betty found an old box of sidewalk chalk and they had a sign. It read "TODAY, Stained glass demonstration, famous artist. Come in." As they hauled it to the sidewalk in front of By the Sea, Bob came in and they sent him to the supermarket on the highway for some Mylar balloons. Without much fuss, they'd given the street an air of excitement.

One of their first drop-by's would help spread the word. Roz heard "Hi Patsy" and came out to the main part of the store.

"This is new." She narrowed her eyes at Roz. "I didn't know you were planning this."

Roz thought, well I didn't think I need your permission, but held her tongue. If she were going to poke, pry and gather information, gossip, she should use sweetness.

Betty said, "Roz came in this morning with this great idea! The weather's so nice we should get lots of visitors this weekend."

"It was just a spur of the moment thing." Roz went over to Patsy and touched her arm. "Are you OK? I saw you almost trip over a table yesterday at Jules."

As that, Patsy turned pink. "Uh, yeah, I'm OK. I was just surprised."

"Surprised at what?"

The color on Patsy's face deepened. "Well, uh, I, uh…I thought you were sort of seeing Liam. It surprised me to see you with four other men."

Roz burst out laughing. "Didn't you notice that two of the men had Roman collars on? They're priests."

It was Betty's turn to look at Roz. "You were out with priests?"

"I thought I told everyone. I'm doing a commission for a new cathedral in Colorado. That group of men was the archbishop of the Eastern Diocese of Kansas, the bishop of the cathedral, the chair of the building committee and the architect. They came to meet with me and see how the window is doing."

"That makes sense, I guess." If she couldn't put a personal relationship together with Roz and one of the men, Patsy's interest waned.

Roz watched her, reading her thoughts as Patsy's face shifted toward disinterest. "When I took the commission and first worked with them, I was living in L.A. I think they wanted to see if anything changed when I moved up here. I…" She stopped, seeing Patsy's eyes beginning to glaze over. No sense talking about Winston, Patsy's involvement began and ended with Hamilton.

"Now that you're here, do you want to come back and see how this works?"

"Sure, I guess so." Patsy wasn't enthusiastic but curiosity got the better of her.

Roz led her into the converted storeroom and began unpacking glass, lead, solder. When she got to some of the knives, Patsy's eyes lit up. "Those look like that one…"

The knives caught Patsy's interest, but then they would. She and Roz had both seen the evidence bag coming out of the murder house. By letting Patsy see she owned the same type of knife, Roz hoped she was priming the pump for any locals who might have swiped one of hers, used it in the murder.

"I don't always use those." Roz picked up an X-acto knife. "This is usually the easiest to get and use and does the job well for most small pieces. See." She pulled a short length of caming toward her and cut it in half, demonstrating clean ends. "You need to have a fast, sharp cut so the edges don't get smushed."

Roz held up the came so that Patsy could see how easily the lead bent under light pressure, then straightened the end so that the edges were true. "You have to fit the glass in like this." She slid the edge of a random piece of glass into the came.

"Do you cut the glass like that, too?" Betty and Bob both watched as well and Roz felt this was her first class.

"No. Once you have your pattern drown on paper, you tape it down to the light table." She'd brought a Celtic cross design. "You lay the glass on top and trace the glass cutting wheel along the pattern. You have to be careful here because you only want to score the glass one time."

She demonstrated a single curved score on a piece of yellow glass, then used pliers to gently break off along the score line.

"Are you open?" A woman's voice rang from the front of the store, Bob scooted out of the storeroom. "Yes, we are. What can I help you with?"

"I wanted to look at your driftwood sculptures. We're from Wyoming, driving down the coast, and want to take home something for our grandchildren." The customer was eyeing small pieces of wood carved to resemble a flock of sea birds, a seal, a fish.

"Those are light and small enough to carry home, even if you're flying, although we do pack and ship." Bob handed one to her. As they were talking, Betty and Patsy came out of the storeroom and the woman asked, "What would you buy?"

In the storeroom, Roz idly listened to the flow of conversation, not paying any attention to the words, as she laid out some cames, a few pieces of glass, cutter, knives, soldering iron and a roll of solder. She was hoping people would drift in by twos or threes so she could keep the demonstrations simple. With luck, Patsy would spread the word for locals to get a look at the newbie who used knives in her everyday work.

It was a close call when Patsy almost blurted out about the evidence bag, but she had to take a chance on the busybody telling the right people. What if the wrong people heard. Like the one who stole the knife and murdered the man. Would he or she come after Roz, them?

No, more likely that person would give anonymous tips to the police about the knife's owner. Framing Roz. But why would she have a reason to kill a stranger?

Unless it turned out the man wasn't a stranger.

CHAPTER TWENTY-THREE

She left a message when Liam didn't pick up. "Are you here or not here? I want to talk to you about our murdered man. I need to know who he is."

She hoped she'd set some traps and thrown out some nets. It was all she could do right now until she compared notes with Liam.

Yesterday, three more people wandered into By the Sea for a stained glass demo; she cut glass, cut cames, talked about sharp edges and knives and got nowhere with them recognizing any knives—other than Patsy's blurt. Bob and Betty were pleased, their sales were up by $100 or so and they'd added five people to their mailing list. Roz just left all her stuff in the storeroom and locked the door, planning to come back today, Sunday.

Another glorious warm spring day, Tut ran and ran. Roz had to whistle three times before she saw his streaking form down the beach on a collision course for her mid-section. He slid up to her and she whirled him around for a hug. "Isn't it wonderful this morning? Did you find some things, chase a rabbit? Are you my best boy?"

Tut nodded happily, his tongue lolling and his intelligent dark eyes on her face.

"I bet you're hungry and thirsty. Let's go get breakfast." They walked to the path, over the dunes, up the deck steps and through the French doors. Roz stopped. The doors weren't locked and she'd promised Liam she'd lock them when she took Tut out.

Making as much noise as she could, she carried on a running conversation with Tut. "What are you planning to do today? Have any friends coming over? Do you want something special for dinner?" If she talked as though there was another person. If someone had come in while she was gone, they may have to get out as fast as they could.

A voice said, "I don't have plans…"

Roz squeaked. "Liam, what are you doing? You scared me half to death."

"The front door was locked but not the French doors. If I can just walk in, anyone can."

"I know, I remember. I had that thought. Now that you're in, do you want some coffee?"

"Sure. You wanted to talk to me?"

Roz hurried through feeding Tut, poured coffee, got out cream and sugar. "Black is fine with me." Liam's voice held some contained laughter. "You didn't notice BethAnn and her endless pot?"

It was Roz' turn to smile. "I did, but now I wanted to be a good hostess." She moved the coffee mugs to a small kitchen table. "I wanted to know where you stood with digging out the real name of William Smith. When I had lunch the other day with the archbishop and bishop, it seemed to fluster a lot of people. BethAnn, Patsy…" she stared at Liam, "and you."

Liam absently added some cream to his coffee and Roz gaped. "I thought you said black?"

He raised his eyebrows. "I did. I do. Every so often, I add some cream. It gives me something mindless to do with my hands while I'm thinking." He grinned. "And when I'm with you, I need to keep my mind on track."

Was he flirting with her? Roz shook her head mentally. He might be. She looked at him, saw an attractive man, just old enough to have laugh lines forming at the corner of his blue, blue eyes, one side of his mouth quivering on the edge of a quirky smile. As interesting and flattering as this might be, she was still wrapped up in Winston. Although it was warming to have his interest.

"Thanks, but there's another track I want to talk about. You came over to the archbishop and acted as if you knew him."

"What I said was that I knew *of* him." Liam corrected her. "I've followed his career since he was a parish priest." He stopped. "More accurately, I researched his career."

Roz' gaze went blank as she looked out the window to the dunes. He did say he knew of Archbishop Malone, but where…wait a minute, Malone was the archbishop of the Eastern Diocese of Kansas. The house across the street was owned by the same diocese.

"I'm putting a trail of crumbs together. The house? The diocese? Malone? Is this a path or a conspiracy theory?"

Liam broke out in a smile. "I hope it's not a theory because it's the same path I've been heading down. There are just a few too many coincidences here."

"Well, what do you know?"

"I don't have a name…" Liam was interrupted by a phone call. He began to ask the caller to leave a message then stopped and said, "I understand. Not a problem. Yes, we'll be there."

Roz threw him a questioning look as her own phone rang and Chief Giffen's voice said, "Ms. Duke, I wonder if you could come by the office this morning. There are a few things I want to clear up. "

"Of course, Chief. I can be there about 10 if that's convenient."

"Fine. I'll see you then," and the called ended.

Roz looked at her phone. "That's odd, why would Chief Giffen want to see me?"

"I wonder if it has anything to do with why he wants to see me. My call was from him as well." Liam took a sip of his coffee. "I didn't set a time. Should we go together?"

"I don't know, it may be different things he wants to talk about."

"I wouldn't bet on that. It's a nice Sunday morning at the beginning of tourist season. There can't be two things important enough to drag him into the office when he'd probably rather be with his family."

She stood, put her mug in the sink. "In any case I need to take a shower, get ready, eat something. I told the By the Sea folks I'd come down again today and do some demonstrations."

"I'll go get cleaned up and treat you to breakfast before we go. Fisherman's Friend OK?"

Roz smiled. "Yep, I don't think I want to face the crowd at Jules this morning. Before we'd even get out of there, the whole town would know we're on our way to talk to the cops."

"Why, Ms. Duke, do you have something to hide?" Liam's grin reached his eyes.

"No more so than you, Mr. Karshner,"

In less than 30 minutes, they were in Liam's truck, headed south. Gravel crunched under the tires as they pulled into the lot between the restaurant and the feed store and the familiar smell of hot, fishy grease wafted out as they went in the diner.

Jurgen loomed out of the kitchen and he and Liam went through a bro hug. "This is a treat. I don't usually see you this often." The blond grinned.

"I took a chance you wouldn't be out on the boat on a Sunday. Roz wouldn't let me rest until we came back again."

Roz wrinkled her brow and gave Liam a questioning look. In return, he smiled and mouthed "not now."

"We're a bit pressed for time this morning. Could you just whip us up a couple of omelets?" He turned to Roz. "You want salmon?"

"I'd rather have ham and cheese," she said. "If that won't offend Jurgen's sensibilities."

"No problem." Jurgen headed for the kitchen.

"What's all the hush-hush 'not now' stuff," she hissed at Liam. "And why are you blaming me for wanting to come here?"

"Nothing bad. I just want to keep people guessing. This doesn't have the local crowd that Jules does, but you can make book on someone seeing us and it getting back. Even to Patsy. The whole town saw you lunching with the Catholic contingent the other day."

Their omelets and coffee came, they ate and headed for the police department by quarter to 10. On their way, Roz told him Patsy's quick gasp and cover-up when she realized that the knife she'd seen at the murder scene, the bloody knife in the evidence bag, matched another one Roz had brought down to By the Sea for the demonstrations.

"That cat's out of the bag. Probably Giffen wants to ask one of us why we didn't mention it to him." Liam turned right, off the highway and onto the street running in front of the police department.

"I wonder, too. That's why I just told you. I think we need to go down for this together." Roz would keep Winston's murder case alive, but she wanted to figure this one out soon. On the drive, she'd watched the forest slide by and marshalled her thoughts for the story she'd tell Giffen.

CHAPTER TWENTY-FOUR

"C'mon back."

The police chief met them in the foyer, deserted on a Sunday morning. If he was surprised that they'd arrived together, he didn't say anything. "I'm pretty much by myself this morning, except one patrolman who's split between traffic and jail duty, if we need it."

Once in his office, he offered water. "I don't make coffee and the vending machine isn't what I'd call drinkable."

"Thanks." Liam took the bottle. "Although I'm not sure this is a social call."

Chief Giffen grunted something that could have been "yes." "It's not. I have questions for both of you although I surely didn't expect you to arrive together. Are you an item now?"

Roz choked back a snort and looked at Liam. "An item? I don't think so."

"How did I get both of you, then?"

"Liam met…"

"Roz and I were…"

Talking over each other, they tried to come up with a plausible reason for being together and Liam gestured for Roz to go ahead with her story, planning to agree and flesh it out as needed.

"Liam, well, I called Liam and left him a message that I wanted to talk. He met us, me and Tut, at the back of my house this morning. We were talking about getting breakfast when you called. First Liam, then me. We decided to go to breakfast then both come here."

Fine as far as it went. No mention of what they'd needed to talk about.

"Makes sense." Giffen swung to face Liam. "I understand you were a little upset the other day in Jules when Ms. Duke, here, had lunch with the priests."

Liam paled slightly. "Upset? I think that's strong word. I was surprised to see Archbishop Malone here, and sharing a meal with Roz. I've done research on him."

"And what did you find?" Giffen's voice was calm but his eyes looked stormy.

"As I told Roz, I've traced his career from a parish priest up the ladder to archbishop of the Eastern Diocese of Kansas."

Giffen watched silently for a few seconds, then: "I wondered how long it would be before you put that together. We've traced the ownership of the house back to the diocese." He turned to Roz. "And you? How do you figure in with the archbishop?"

A thin blade of unease scored its way down her arms. "I believe I told you the commission I'm working on is for a new cathedral in Colorado. The cathedral is part of the Eastern Diocese so the archbishop, Malone, is the person I contracted with. He, the bishop in Colorado, the architect and the head of the building committee came out to see how the window was progressing."

"You two may not be an 'item' but you have a lot of overlap. Did you," he pointed at Liam, "know she was working for the archbishop?"

"Good lord no!" Liam was incensed. "How would I know that.?"

"How, indeed," murmured Giffen. "And you," he nodded at Roz," Did you know that Liam was looking into the home's owner and Malone?"

She shook her head. "Absolutely not."

"Tell me again about when you two met." Giffen looked back and forth.

"I was walking my dog and when we came up from the beach there were emergency vehicles on the street in front of my house. I watched for a minute from my living room, then went over toward the house. There were two people standing in the street, watching as well. We had a few words of conversation then Liam, well I didn't know who he was, said he had to get to work. I stayed for a while and talked to Patsy, and…" She slowed.

Liam took up the story. "The next time I saw her was an hour or so later. I was in Jules and she came in. I'd noticed earlier she was attractive. Jules was packed, I asked if she'd like to join me, we introduced ourselves and chatted. After that, we found we enjoyed each other. I made a flip comment about her work, then saw some of it and felt like a fool. I had no idea she was as well-known and well-respected as she is." He was quiet, not wanting to tell Giffen too much. "Did you look her up as I suggested?"

"I did." Giffen slid a glance to Roz. "I didn't know we had a celebrity in our midst, and one with such a tragic past. Are you still working with the LAPD on your husband's killing?"

Unexpectedly, Roz felt the tears form. It was one thing to have Liam know the story, but another to have a different police department aware. She'd told herself that meeting and getting to know Giffen might help her with Robeson, but the grief and anger was always near the surface.

"I talk to Det. Lt. Robeson at the LAPD, yes."

"About once a week, I understand."

Roz felt a lick of outrage. Had he been checking up on her? "Usually." She nodded in agreement. If he knew how often he'd been in touch with Robeson what else did he know?

"And I also understand," here Giffen paused, "maybe you should step outside, Liam."

"Chief Giffen, I've told Liam everything I told Robeson. He and I know the same information."

"That so?"

Liam was standing, but at Giffen's tone, on the edge of belligerence, he sat again. "That's so, Chief. Roz and I have a couple of parallel mysteries and we've been talking about how they may overlap."

Giffen cleared his throat. "Alright, here we go. Lt Robeson told me you mentioned a bloody cross on the wall of the house where the man was murdered. As far as we know, the only person, besides the responders and police, who saw that and know about it is the murderer.

"And, I got a call from Patsy yesterday. She said that what she believes is the murder weapon, a bloody knife being taken out of the house, matched a set of knives you own."

CHAPTER TWENTY-FIVE

Silence weighed on the room. Roz sat with her eyes closed, her mind in a squirrel cage. Patsy. She was the one who knew about the cross and told Roz. She was the one who put Roz' knives together with the murder weapon. Could she have found out who Roz was, snuck in and stolen one of her knives, killed the neighbor then watched the scene, hoping to deflect suspicion away from her?

That didn't make any sense, she'd only met her that morning. And how did Giffen know that Patsy'd identified the knife?

"Did you talk to Patsy?" Liam's voice broke through Roz' frantic, racing mind.

"I did. She called me yesterday after she watched Roz do a demonstration at By the Sea. Patsy told me that Roz showed everyone a knife she had specially made for her glass work and it looked just like the one taken in evidence." Here the police chief closed his eyes and a low moan escaped.

"Are you alright?"

"Yeah. I've told the guys about evidence recovery, but they tend to get excited. For starters, they're not supposed to put anything with possible blood or secretion evidence in plastic. It degrades the sample. In addition, when they stuck the knife in a plastic bag, anyone standing around could see it…and someone did."

Now he looked at Roz. "Or maybe more than one someone."

Roz let out a breath she didn't know she'd been holding. "Yes, I saw it. I was afraid it was one of mine. I had no idea how it was taken from me, or when. I think I know why. But I don't know who. That's why I've been talking with Liam."

He smiled at her and said, "Chief, we think that before we can even begin to guess who the murderer is we need to know who the victim really was. Even Patsy isn't fooled with the William Smith name, although I don't know what else she'd found out."

"Patsy, Patsy, Patsy. Just like Rome, all roads lead back to her." Giffen twirled around to look out his window.

"Do you think she's involved?" Roz found her voice quavering and forced herself to strengthen it. "She knows everybody."

"She does. She's related by blood or marriage to half the town, including my bosses on the city council, so this place is like a swamped fishing boat in a storm, completely leaky. Whatever my thoughts or suspicions about her are, I keep them to myself." He turned back and glared at Roz and Liam.

"Now, Liam, I guess I'm glad that you and Roz are nosy together. Where are you in the search for William Smith?"

Liam looked over at Roz. This was part of what he wanted to tell her but hadn't had time. "I still don't know who he was, but I'm sure I know what he was."

"What he was?" Roz' brows raised.

"He was a retired priest."

"Retired priest? Do priests retire?" Giffen was curious.

"Sure they do. And depending on what they did, what order they belonged to, they have retirement homes, spaces in monasteries. Some live in apartments or houses in their last parish."

"Does the church usually buy them a house?"

"Not as a rule." Liam took a slug of water. "I think our mystery man was a special case."

"Was kind of special case do you think he was? Maybe my neighborhood is more mixed than I thought." Roz stopped talking, remembering that she hadn't reported the last incidence of peeping toms.

"I think in our neighbor's case, the church retired him because of pedophile charges."

Dead silence.

Giffen and Roz exchanged a stunned look. "Pedophile? Why would you think that?" She was barely able to get the words out.

"Because Malone was accused of a cover-up both as a bishop and as an archbishop."

"Was he ever arrested?" Giffen swung to his computer to begin a search.

"I doubt you'll find anything there, Chief. He was never arrested, never charged."

"But how could he get away with it?' Roz was surprised and angry. How could men, men who were supposed to be leaders, teachers, take advantage of young boys in their charge like that?

"This happens all the time, and not just here. There was a cardinal accused of pedophilia, and remember the church hierarchy in Ireland? And just recently, the archbishop in Australia? There are some very good people in the church who are working to rid the priesthood of these men, but still some get in. And some of those are protected by their friends, fellow-priests, higher-ups. There's like a code of silence, so that they don't bring shame and criminal proceedings to the church."

Roz shook herself and suddenly felt the need to take a shower. This despicable cover-up of unholy and unlawful acts made her skin crawl.

"That's an interesting theory, Liam." Giffen steepled his fingers. "If it's true, why would that make William Smith, or whomever he might be, a murder victim?"

Liam frowned. "That part I haven't completely worked out," he admitted. "I heard rumors that there might be one of the worst pedophilic priests living on the coast of Oregon. I checked through years of parish records, deaths, moves, relocations, retirements and couldn't find a specific one. What I did find, though was a pattern of priests under Bishop, now Archbishop, Malone, who were accused of pedophilia. Only one was arrested and the diocese paid through the nose, so I think Malone covered-up the rest and moved them out. In our guy's case, about a $1 million was a small amount to set him up with a house in a remote area and enough money to live quietly on."

Roz snapped her fingers. "Is this the book you're working on?"

Liam grimaced. "Working on is the right description. I haven't finished the outline to send to my agent. There are still too many holes—a major one is who this guy is, was. I'd intended to confirm he was the pedophile, interview him, write this and include some biographical information. Now that he's dead, or at least the identity of who I think he was, is gone, I'm having to shift my focus. But the hunt goes on."

Giffen stood. "We haven't answered any questions, but at least we all have the same information. Please keep in touch and be careful. We don't know who or why this guy was a victim, we don't have a suspect, even a person of interest." He stopped and looked at Roz. "Well, after Patsy telling me she thought one of your knives was a murder weapon, it raised your status, Ms. Duke. And after a conversation with Lt. Robeson I knew I wanted to talk with you. I'm urging you to be careful. Someone knows about you, your husband who was killed, your connection to the church and cathedral, your knives. Clarence reported one peeping tom at your house to Smiley, there may be more."

"Thank you, Chief." Liam rose and shook Giffen's hand. "I'm watching out for Roz. Someone is trying to pin one murder on her. I don't want there to be another."

He held the door for Roz and they walked out into the warm sunlight. A slight breeze came off the ocean, sea birds squealed and hung on air currents, two gulls fought over a dropped French fry, tourists leaned on their cars and shook sand out of their shoes.

How could such a normal day be tainted with pedophilia and murder?

CHAPTER TWENTY-SIX

"I have to go to By the Sea." Roz was quiet.

"Are you sure? Even Giffen thinks you should take care and in my book that means no more sleuthing, no more watching for knives."

Roz looked down the beach. "Liam, I'm a big girl. I'm a professional. I survived my husband's killing. I have to find out who stole my knife and why they killed the man across the street. I appreciate your concern, but I'm fine."

He grabbed her arm and turned her to face him. "And were you fine this morning when I walked into your house through an unlocked door? And have you told Giffen about the second peeping tom incident?"

Roz lifted a hand to slap him then realized what he was saying. If someone was trying to frame her for one murder, why wouldn't they do it again? Maybe this time she'd be the victim, killed with her own knife.

She sighed. "We need a peace, at least détente. I will lock my doors, I will watch for peeping toms or any strangers. I'll be careful what I talk to Patsy about." For the last one, Roz crossed her fingers, mentally. Patsy may have more information than she was letting out or she even knew. A chat with Patsy was on the agenda for tomorrow.

"OK, that's all I want, for you to be safe. And for Giffen to take you off any person of interest list. I'm headed up to not here tonight for a few days. I need to work on my book proposal, update it with the murder and tie-in to Malone coming here."

Roz gasped. "You're not going to put me in your book!"

"No, no, I'm going to add the diocese buying the house and 'retiring' the priest."

"You can do that even though you don't know his name?"

"This is a proposal. It's an outline, a beefy outline, of the book. I can add a name, change a few things around when I'm working with an editor." He knew he was telling the truth, but this made him nervous. If his agent took the proposal and pitched it to publishers, it wouldn't be to publishers of his science fiction novels. He'd be working with a different editor, a different set of people and he'd have to make them understand his vision.

"I'll be away for about a week, but please call me if anything happens. And I'll call you if I discover his name and what relationship he had to the archbishop. Remember, a man is dead, stabbed with one of your knives. I'm sure this puts you in jeopardy as well." He leaned over and kissed her cheek, jogged to his car and was off.

Roz rubbed her cheek. Was that nice or not nice? It was the first gesture of affection from a man since Win. She decided it was nice. There wasn't a total attraction to Liam Karshner but a warm feeling licked at the block of ice in her chest. She headed off to By the Sea.

Betty hadn't put the sign up outside, which Roz appreciated. She didn't want to walk into the store and face people lined up, waiting for a demonstration.

"There you are. I was hoping you'd come in today." Bob's cheerful face lit up behind the cash register. "Being Sunday, I didn't know if you went to church or what."

"No, just got busy with errands." Another small lie of omission. "Let's put the sign out and get ready for the hordes!" She laughed. "At least a few people who are interested in a 1,000-year-old craft."

Pulling out pieces of glass, straightening the lead cames, laying a few simple designs and angles on the light table, all the well-loved and known tools that she handled every day, eased her spinning mind. Routines that occupied her hands and left her free to roam into the canyons of her experiences.

Who knew her? Knew she lived here? Knew she had a collection of knives? Knew she accepted commissions from churches? Knew she was still trying to reason out Winston's killing?

No matter how many times she ran through the questions, turned the pieces around and around, tried to make them fit together the answer was the same. No one. There was no one single person who had all the answers. Patsy knew about the knife. Liam knew about the knife, churches, commission. Anybody, including Chief Giffen, knew about Winston, all they had to do was Google her. Lt. Robeson knew where she was, knew about Winston but didn't know about her missing knife. They all knew about the cross in blood on the dining room wall.

What none of them knew was the identity of the murdered man and why he lived in Hamilton.

A sound at the door. She turned. A couple with two children looked in and Roz' heart sank. She hadn't anticipated children.

"Hi. Are you interested in stained glass?" The question wasn't specific to either adult, but the woman said, "Yes, sort of. I've wondered how it stays together in a window."

"Come in and I can show you, but you'll have to leave the children in the store. My insurer gets nervous with all the sharp things around."

The mom and her husband exchanged looks. "I'll take them down the street for an ice cream," he said, then to Roz, "Would half an hour be enough?"

"Sure, we can go over the basics by then. Set your purse down here." Roz waved to a chair against the wall.

"Do I need any special clothes or aprons or gloves or anything?" The mom was hesitant after Roz' mention of sharp objects.

"Not at all. Here." She took a piece of red glass and laid it on the light table.

"What a beautiful color. What do you use that for?"

"Anywhere you want a strong accent. It's particularly effective in an east or west-facing window, when the sun is at an angle. It paints the entire room. Let me show you how to score it."

She put a straight-edged ruler against the glass and ran a cutter along it until she had a vertical score a few inches long. "Once you've scored it—and you only want to use the cutter once, otherwise you risk the possibility of chipping the glass—then you put it against the edge of the table and gently lean on it until it cracks along the score." She demonstrated and the glass fell away in two even pieces.

"After you have the glass pieces cut and laid out in the design you want, you begin measuring and cutting the cames, the leads."

She handed a length of caming to the mom, let her feel the weight and flexibility of the soft lead, then tugged the ends to straighten it. Roz eyeballed a measurement of one side of the ruby-red glass, laid the came down flat and made a quick, neat cut with one of her knives.

The mom watched carefully. "Those look like expensive tools," she said, glancing at the knife.

Ah ha, knife talk. "Those are, but it's because I had them made specially to fit my hand. Most home stained glass projects can get put together with an X-acto blade. Just as long as it's sharp so you don't squish the lead." She picked up a piece to show how easily the H-shaped came end could get mushed into a lump.

"Once you have a section of glass and leads cut to the right size and shape, you start fitting the glass into the open side of the came. You work in small sections until each piece of glass is surrounded and enclosed with a came, fit them together and begin solder the joints where the cames meet."

She picked up her hot iron, another reason to keep kids away, touched the roll of solder to the joint and watched it weld. "Do you think it's something you'd want to do?"

The mom looked dubious. "Maybe when the kids are older. For now, I think I'll buy one. Thanks for showing me, I didn't have a good idea."

"By the Sea has a selection of small pieces suitable for hanging in a window. They're made by a woman in Portland. And if or when you're ready, I have kits you can buy to make one yourself. Here's my card."

She smiled to herself, had never thought she'd be hawking retail stained glass.

CHAPTER TWENTY-SEVEN

"Patsy? It's Roz."

"I saw your number come up. What's on your mind?" Patsy's voice was cool, not frosty cold but not her usual bubbly self.

Take it slow, Roz thought, here comes some honey. "Since you know the town so well, I was hoping I could talk to you about the visitors I had the other day."

"Visitors?" A hint of interest.

"The men I had lunch with in Jules the other day."

"Oh. I don't know them."

Slow, slow. "No, I don't think anyone in town knows them…well except Liam seemed to know the archbishop."

"Archbishop?" Patsy's voice rose. "You were having lunch with an archbishop?"

"That's funny, he and the bishop said the same thing. People forget that they're just men and do all the normal human things, eat, sleep, travel."

"I suppose so." Patsy slipped into a dubious tone. "I just didn't think you hung around with a church crowd. You seem too…"

Roz waited for Patsy to take her foot out of her mouth. When she didn't, Roz said, "I'm not sure I'd call it hanging around. It's business. Don't you remember, I'm doing a stained glass piece for a new cathedral."

"I remember, I guess I thought you were working with the architect or construction guys."

"Them too, but the guy who's going to OK the costs and sign the check is the archbishop."

A pause, then: "That's not why I called. I saw Chief Giffen yesterday. He told me you called him with some information."

Wariness edged into Patsy's voice. "Information? What information?"

"That you'd seen the evidence tech take a blood-stained knife out of the house. And you saw my knife during a demonstration at By the Sea. And you realized that they were the same design."

Silence. Roz imagined Patsy making fish faces while she tried to come up with an excuse.

"Well, I did mention it to him. I want to keep on his good side, we need him here in Hamilton."

"I wish you'd talked to me, first. He looked at me as though I was hiding something. I'm wondering if he thinks I'm involved."

"Oh, he doesn't think that. He told my…"

"Your, what?"

"Well, my sister's niece, the one on her husband's side, is married to one of the police volunteers. He wants to join the force so he thinks this will help him. Of course, when he dropped out of the community college…"

"Patsy, who told what to whom? Sometimes I need a score card to talk to you!"

Patsy laughed. "I told you people call me PS. My mind just runs around and everything reminds me of something else. Chief Giffen said that he was going to talk to you, but he didn't think you were involved."

"That's good news." Roz absently petted Tut's soft ear. "Do you have time for lunch? There are a couple more things I want to run by you, and since we're both sort of sleuthing, maybe we can sleuth together."

"Sure. Today?"

"Yep, that's fine, I can meet you at Jules at, say, 12:30?"

*****

Jules' lunch crowd had thinned when Roz came in. BethAnn waved at her and pointed to Pasty sitting in a corner booth.

"I don't know why I bother to read this." Patsy put the large plastic-coated menu down. "I know it so well I could recite it in my sleep."

Roz laughed. "That's one of the reasons I wanted to see you."

"So I could recite Jules menu?" Patsy grinned back.

"Right!" She paused. "No, because you know almost everybody in town. I've decided I, we, have to figure out who the murdered guy really was."

"Do you believe his name really wasn't William Smith? I told you that."

"You did. And Chief Giffen has done a search as well. Nobody by that name lives here."

"Finally, somebody believes me! People think I'm just a busybody who makes stuff up." Patsy pushed the menu so hard it slid off onto Roz' lap.

"I know Liam believes you. He's in not here looking for the man's real name."

Patsy stared. "'Not here'? What the hell is that?"

"Oh, I asked Liam what he did here and then he said he lives somewhere else—he said 'not here'—part of the time. I asked him where 'not here' was and he said Portland. It's a silly thing, calling here 'here' and Portland 'not here'." Roz paused. Told like this, it sounded a lot like cute names and jokes between lovers.

"Portland? That makes sense. He usually leaves his truck here and drives another car down. I thought it had to be close." She looked closely at Roz. "You and Liam getting cozy?"

"I wouldn't say that." Roz slapped herself mentally at the smile she couldn't stop. "We've had breakfast together a few times, he went with me to the police department yesterday." She was careful to tell Patsy only those times she and Liam could have been seen in public then felt a frisson of guilt because there wasn't much else. Was there?

"Speaking of the police, how well do you know Clarence?"

"Clarence?" Patsy sounded surprised. "He doesn't have anything to do with the police."

"I know that, but he reported that I had a peeping tom. I wonder if he's as observant as that for all the neighborhood."

"He's a member of our Neighborhood Watch. Doesn't come to all the meetings. Some of us think he spent a little too much time tied to the rail." At Roz' look, she added. "When some of those fishermen used to go out for a few days, they'd tie themselves to the railing if a storm came up. It means they don't stop what they're doing and head home. In his case, he spends a lot of time at the Snug, drinking, when he should head home."

"Liam mentioned that, them tying themselves to the rail. Do they still do that?"

"Not so much. With GPS and cells and all the modern communication equipment, it's hard to get too lost at sea any more. Before, you went out and you came back. Or not. If you were lucky enough to be in a group of boats and someone saw you get swamped, they'd get to you and pull you out, but a lot of guys went out by themselves."

"So, Clarence drinks?"

"Used to. I think he's slowed down some. Smiley used to arrest him once a month or so, let him sober up then sent him home. He probably drinks at home now. He's pretty reliable about calling Smiley if he hears or sees something, though it's mostly kids. I'd say he's observant."

"When I heard that he came roaring out of his house with a shotgun I got a little nervous."

Patsy shook her head. "We don't even know if that shotgun is loaded. I heard that a nephew from maybe Cottage Grove came to visit and took away all the shells and bullets. It's all for show now."

"Thanks, I feel better. Did you ever tell him about the boys who came to visit?"

"The boys?" Patsy's eyebrows drew together. "What boys?"

CHAPTER TWENTY-EIGHT

"The boys you said you saw at the victim's house? This is awkward, I hope we find out his name. I hate having to call him 'the murdered man' or 'victim'."

"Oh, those boys. I haven't thought about them. Did I mention them to you?"

"You did. I asked you how you saw them because you can't see the front of the guy's house and you said they came to the back door. I've thought that was odd. I haven't said anything about them."

Patsy waved BethAnn over, ordered a club sandwich and iced tea and looked at Roz who said she'd have a bowl of clam chowder. When BethAnn swung around to take the orders to the kitchen, Patsy leaned over and all but whispered. "Don't tell anyone I saw that."

Roz almost choked on her water. "I haven't. I won't. Why?"

"Because none of those boys were from here. I thought maybe they were run-aways and I didn't want to get them into trouble with their families. If I'd told Chief Giffen, he'd probably have to take them to juvie or call in Child Protective Services. Once you get involved with CPS, it's hard to get out."

When BethAnn set her chowder down, Roz was afraid she'd vomit in it. Whatever CPS was, it was bound to be better and more humane than allowing those boys to get involved with a pedophile. To be fair, a suspected pedophile, she supposed.

"With the guy dead, have you seen any of the boys since?"

Patsy added sugar to her tea and picked up a piece of the sandwich. "No, come to think if it. If they were running away from home, the grapevine could have passed along the information that he was dead. It wasn't a safe place to stop any more."

Convoluted logic, Roz thought. How was she going to get this information to Liam? And was there a way to link occasional boys knocking on "William Smith's" door to tie him to a pedophile priest?

Carefully, she said, "You know Patsy, I wonder if any of those boys could have murdered him?"

Patsy's eyes grew huge, she inhaled and a piece of her sandwich got sucked down. Coughing, choking, she shook her head as BethAnn started over. She was bright red, but managed to rasp out, "I'm OK."

While this was going on, Roz skimmed over everything she knew about the Heimlich maneuver and breathed a rush of relief when she heard Patsy's voice. "Slow down, take a sip of tea."

Patsy sat back in the booth. "I really am OK, a crumb of bread went down the wrong way. I can't believe you said that."

"What? That one of them could be the killer? Why not? Somebody stole one of my knives, which means they had to come in my house. I've had some 'visitors' and…" she stopped. Liam and Clarence were the only ones who knew about the second peeping tom episode. "And I know that I didn't kill him. I didn't even know him. You watched kids go in his back door, Liam said they used to exchange pleasantries, 'how're your tomatoes,' kind of stuff. I'd never seen him."

"When you put it like that, I guess." Patsy sounded doubtful. "It would help if we knew who he was. Why he moved here."

"Did you ever see him have other visitors?"

"No. I even invited him to Neighborhood Watch meetings. He never came."

Roz thought, then; "How'd you invite him if you didn't know his name?"

"There are other ways of getting in touch with people, you know." Patsy was a little waspish. "Not everyone runs on email or Google or whatever. Or even telephones. I had a few flyers made up for each meeting and put them on light poles. I slipped one in his mailbox."

The simplest thing is usually right. Roz kicked herself.

"Had anyone in the group ever met him?"

"Hmmm, I don't know, I never asked."

"Are there any neighbors in the back, on your street, who might have seen the boys, or any other visitors?"

"There might be." Patsy's voice slowed while she did a mental inventory of her neighbors.

"Do you know them?"

"Of course, I know them!" Oops, thought Roz, I poked the hornet's nest.

"That didn't come out right. I mean, do you know them well enough to ask?"

"Ask what?"

This was painful and getting her nowhere. "Ask them if anyone saw the boys, or any other visitors going into the guy's house."

"Sure. But I don't want to be the only one who does that. Maybe we could ask Chief…"

Before she could get his name out, Roz said, "No, I don't think this should be a big deal. If we get the Chief involved, or even Smiley, it'll be formal. They'll have to interview people, take notes. People get nervous when the cops get formal. I think it's better if we just keep it on a neighborly basis. We're all concerned, want to catch the murderer, want to feel we're safe. That sort of thing."

"You're probably right." Patsy brightened. "Maybe you'd come with me?"

Oh. Roz winced. This was too easy, shooting fish in a barrel. "Sure, I could do that. When can we start?"

"We can talk to a few people later this afternoon, early evening. After they get home from work."

"Sounds good. Should I come over to your house? Which one is yours?"

"Do you know where Liam lives? I'm across the street and one house up from him. My backyard overlaps the murdered guy's back yard."

"Good. I'll be by about 4?"

"There are six or seven houses we can get to before it's too dark. Do you have a list of questions?"

Six or seven? Roz hadn't planned to spend more than ten minutes with each neighbor. She'd have to let Patsy take the lead on this. "A list of questions? No, not really. I thought I'd, we'd, just talk to them about the morning the man was found. See what they remembered, what they heard about it. Then ask if they knew the guy, saw any visitors he had."

"Don't you think Chief Giffen has already done this?"

"I hope he has, but he's won't tell us anything he found out." Roz looked at the other woman. "You haven't told Gifffen about the visitors?"

"No! I said I haven't told anyone. I don't want those boys to get in trouble."

"Good." Roz picked up the check BethAnn dropped on their table. "Let me get lunch. If you can help me track down who was in his house, then maybe I can figure out who stole my knife." And whether they're framing me, she thought.

With a few hours to work, Roz pulled out the design for the next section of the cathedral window, taped it down and began selecting glass. She was engrossed when her cell began to samba off the edge of the table.

Patsy. What now? "Hi Patsy, what's up?"

"I finished all my chores and can go talk to neighbors now, if you're available."

Roz looked at her phone, 3:45. Close enough and she was at a point she could stop.

"Sure. I'll be right over."

Tut was laying on the floor by the light table. "Be a good boy," she said as she went out the side door of the studio.

CHAPTER TWENTY-NINE

Northwest Coffee Roasters hit a lull in mid-afternoon and Liam used that quieter time to do some internet searching. Fewer people to interrupt, no one asking "Mind if I sit here," the barristas yelling names and orders. He could do this work in his condo, but sometimes the silence was oppressive. Probably too many years of working in a crowded, noisy newsroom, he thought, with its ringing phones, conversations, clacking keyboards.

His search for Archbishop Malone was interesting. Every site had a few paragraphs about the prelate's early years. Born in New Jersey, went to Catholic schools, was an altar boy, joined the church and went to seminary at 18. He was the oldest of six children and had one sister who became a nun, living in a teaching order.

A steady rise from parish priest to Monseigneur with a short gap in postings when he must have been about 30. Had a year's sabbatical before being assigned to a large urban parish, then the elevation. There were two different assignments as a bishop, a title he held for almost 20 years, then five years ago, the elevation to archbishop. There was speculation he might be a candidate for Cardinal, although an assignment to a Vatican post would help his odds.

No hint of scandal.

Liam sat back, turning options over and over, then logged onto Lexus-Nexus, a perk he'd kept as a busy freelancer. Put in search terms of the parishes where Malone was a priest. No hint of anything amiss, except that a member of his parish, an altar boy, committed suicide. Liam noted the place and date.

During his stay as a bishop in the first See, there was an article that said several parishioners had lodged complaints against a priest, not Malone, accusing him of molesting the boys who came for after-school activities, swimming, basketball, baseball. The church denied the charges, gave the families some compensation, two of the accusers received full four-year scholarships at Catholic universities.

Just before Malone's elevation to archbishop, another priest in another parish was accused of molesting boys from the elementary school the parish ran. This time, the parents sued. Again, the church handled it internally, there was a non-disclosed settlement, the priest was put on sabbatical and eventually retired.

Liam did the math, but this priest was long retired before the man called William Smith appeared in Hamilton. He kept looking.

Bingo. Just as Malone was taking on his role as archbishop, a group of parents accused a priest who supervised a Boy Scout troop of molesting their sons during a week-long camping trip. The priest's name was Henley Jackson. He'd served in the parish twelve years with an unblemished record to date. At the time, he was 54 years old. No criminal charges, the church put him through their own courts and he disappeared from the public rolls.

Now with a possible name, Liam backtracked, looking at Jackson's life. Nondescript. Raised in an evangelical family, Jackson had an attraction to Catholicism and converted in college. He was active in the parish where he ended up teaching sixth grade Social Studies in the public school system. After three years, he quit his job and went to seminary, joining a teaching order. As a priest and a teacher, Jackson easily fit into a parish that ran a school and he served there then was transferred to the parish where he was accused of pedophilia.

Liam knew transferring a "problem" priest was a way that the church dealt with accused pedophiles. The priest would be sent for counseling, or a rehab facility, and when he was deemed "cured", sent back to minister to a parish. And none of this happened without the hierarchy's knowledge and approval.

Had Malone been a "problem" priest when he was sent for a sabbatical? Only he, his confessor and his archbishop knew for sure. As he rose through the church, Malone kept his vow of silence, using it to cover priests who reported to him. He may not be, or have been, an active sexual predator, but he was culpable of aiding and abetting it.

Liam checked his watch, shut down his laptop and headed to his condo. On the way, he called Sam in Boston, needing to get advice on the next steps.

"I'll help however I can," Sam said, against the noise of a newsroom on deadline, "but it'll take a while. Let me get back to you in an hour or so."

"Thanks, that's fine." Liam took the stairs to his third-floor unit. If he was hauling something, groceries, bulky things like reams of printer paper he took the elevator.

Restless, he puttered, made a grocery list, washed the few dishes from this morning, pulled the duvet up on his bed, sent a text to Roz. *Have a lead on the man's name and background. Will let you know if it pans out.* Got no answer but he wasn't surprised. She was probably working in her studio and she'd told him she turned her phone off.

Sam called about an hour later and Liam realized it was after the evening news from the decrease in background noise. "What's up?"

"That LLC I asked you the check on a couple of weeks ago? I think I've tracked down the tenant. Or maybe the person who was deeded the property."

"Good work. How'd you find it?"

"The archbishop of the Eastern Diocese of Kansas is Malone, a guy who made his way up the ranks of the church over the past 30 or so years. I remembered I heard his name at one point with a possible cover-up of pedophile priests. Then he showed up here the other day."

"In Portland?"

"No, weirder yet, in Hamilton"

"Isn't that the place you go to write? Population 100 and several thousand seagulls?"

Liam laughed. "Close. It's really a small tourist town on the ocean. Think towns on the Cape."

"Still, what's a big cheese in the church doing there?"

"As Alice said, 'curiousier and curiousier'…a neighbor there, a stained glass artist, has a commission from him, from the diocese, for a huge window in a new Colorado cathedral."

"Is this some kind of strange six-degrees stuff?"

"No, it's just coincidence but it gets even odder. The guy who was murdered was stabbed, with one of the artist's knives."

"Are you writing one of your fantasy books?"

Now Liam whooped. "Stop it. Let me tell you where I am and what I need."

"OK, just email me."

"No. On top of all this, I've got some creeping paranoia. This stuff is big, big in the church. Remember the *Globe* and the Spotlight series?"

"Ah, bad boys in the priesthood. That's old stuff now."

"If the guy is who I think he is, he got himself murdered. Fairly spectacularly. I don't want anything in writing until I can pin it down, so I'll tell you."

Sam was quiet on the end of the phone. "Humor me, Sam, just take some notes the old-fashioned way, pen and paper."

"I think you've been smoking some of that cash crop stuff, but OK. What do you have?"

Liam gave up a brief rundown of the way he'd tracked Malone then did a cross-check of his assignments. Found Jackson, at the right place, at the right time. Told Sam that Jackson had disappeared from the records after the accusation.

"It's circumstantial but possible," Sam admitted. "What do you want me to do?"

"I'm using a Lexus-Nexis account that has limited search abilities, can't get into the dark web. I'm hoping you can. Look for the name Henley Jackson on any of the gay porn, pedophile sites. I know it's a fishing expedition."

"It is. I'll see what I can do. Everything leaves a trail, you know. "

"I know. I'm trusting you can explain it away with a revisit of the Spotlight series, or where does the church stand now story idea. It'll hold up with you, but I don't have that cover any more."

"OK, give me a couple of days. I'll call with whatever I find."

CHAPTER THIRTY

Roz texted back later that night. *Sorry, was out with Patsy, interviewing neighbors.* This was odd enough that Liam called.

"Interviewing neighbors? What's that mean."

"Hi Liam, and how are you? Or is this a new way of communication, don't bother with the introduction?"

"Sorry, I was on the phone with a friend on the East Coast and we talk in shorthand. 'Hello Roz, this is Liam, how are you this evening?' Is that better?"

She snorted, "Is there something in between? "

"Probably, but I'm going back to 'Interviewing neighbors?'"

"Remember when I told you Patsy saw boys come to his back door?"

"WHAT? You never told me that."

Hmmm, maybe she hadn't. Here came the deep dive. "I was sure I had, but anyway, she used to see boys occasionally come up to the back door. The guy would let them in. With the pedophilia connection, it makes sense. She didn't tell anyone because she thought boys were run-aways and the guy had a kind-of half-way house, underground way station."

"And?" Liam's voice was frosty. Was he pissed? Oh, well.

"We went to several neighbors, talked to them about the morning he was found. Asked if they'd seen anything. Asked if they'd ever seen anyone coming or going from his back door. And I found out that my bladder can hold a lot more coffee and iced tea than I ever knew possible."

A slight intake of breath and Roz could feel Liam smiling. "That's it?"

"We only got to three houses. Each one, we had to go over what Giffen has found, how the Neighborhood Meeting ended up, why I'm doing demonstrations at By the Sea, how I like Hamilton, you know the drill."

"I do. I haven't been idle," and he went through his internet search and his call with Sam.

"Liam, that's terrific!" Then silence. "At least I think it is. What does that tell us?"

"If the murdered guy was Henley Jackson, he had a checkered past in the church. The church hasn't been turning over pedophile priests to the civil authorities for prosecution, they handle it internally. Which mostly means they just sweep it under the rug. Hiding a secret like that could easily make you vulnerable to blackmail…or worse."

"If it was Jackson, do you think he was being blackmailed?"

"Don't think so." Liam stood up to get some wine and Roz heard the glass clink against the counter. "What could anyone get from blackmailing a retired priest? Maybe blackmailing the archbishop or something. Or a rich parish…" His voice trailed off. Then; "No, that doesn't wash. If it were a blackmailer, why would he, or she I guess, kill a sleazy pedophile priest. And the wounds…"

"What about the wounds?"

Uh oh Liam thought. Did I tell her the details? "Stabbing someone repeatedly with a knife is more often a crime of passion, not a calculated thing a blackmailer would do. Let alone the bloody cross on the wall."

"That makes sense. I asked Patsy if she thought one of the visiting boys could have done it. Stolen my knife and…oh my god!"

"What, what? Are you alright?"

"You're going to be mad, oh, hell, I'm mad."

"What is it!" Liam was yelling. "What's wrong?"

"You're going to hate me. I was working in the studio when Patsy called and said she was ready to go interview the neighbors. I said good-bye to Tut and went out the side door. I didn't lock it."

"How do you know that?"

"Because two of the pieces I'd cut for the window are smashed on the floor!"

"Don't touch anything! Call Giffen. Get a detective over there. Chances are there won't be any fingerprints, but it has to be reported. You had a break-in."

"Does it count as a break-in if I left the door unlocked?"

"Semantics. I'm not sure what it's called, but someone came in your house uninvited. Is anything else disturbed?"

"I don't think so. Hang on."

Liam could hear her carefully walking around the studio, moving tools, leads, glass. Then a gasp. And a moan. "Oh, Liam, they wrote on my window."

"What window?"

"The back one that looks over the beach. Oh, Liam."

"What does it say?"

"It's awful. It says, 'Roman whore, in bed with the church'." Her voice was thick. Liam knew she was about to cry.

"That's terrible, but for sure you need to call 911. Hang up with me, dial it, say you have a break-in with vandalism. Stay on the line then call me back as soon as you can. Where's Tut?"

"Tut?" Roz' voice sounded lost. "Oh good, where is Tut?"

"Go find him. I won't hang up."

He could hear her running through her house calling. Then; "Tut, oh Tut, there you are. Are you alright? Oh, my boy!" A pause. "He's here, he was asleep in my bedroom and the door blew shut."

"OK, now hang up and call 911. And please call me back when you can."

Liam stomped around his living space, itching to throw something. Why had she left the door unlocked? Did she still think this was a small matter, an accident that her knife was used to kill someone? One would think she'd been warned off a hunt enough after Winston was killed.

Winston. Liam's mind spun. Roz took the commission for the cathedral when she was living in L.A. with Winston. Was the commission, the work with the church, a key to all of this? Don't think like that, he told himself. Use your rational mind and work this out.

There was the attraction to her he felt as well. He'd never planned to get involved in a relationship. Was he on the verge of one now? No, she was interesting, attractive, fun, smart, independent, self-contained. And now, she'd dropped into his lap as part of his research for what he hoped would be a best-seller.

He poured another glass of wine, booted up his laptop and idly searched for her. Did she really do a lot of business with the church? He found four commissions for cathedrals and another ten for Protestant churches, but those couldn't count, right? Most of her work was for commercial properties, resorts, malls, or for wealthy people with huge homes.

He grabbed his phone when she called, didn't say hello, just "Are you OK?"

A slight sigh. "I am. The police came. Even an evidence technician. My studio is covered in fine, black powder, I have to leave the glass on the floor, they took pictures of everything. That horrible message is still on my window, they wrote it with a Sharpie. I don't know what will take it off. Or even when I can clean it."

"I'm so sorry this happened. If you need me, I can come back tomorrow."

"No, I think the worst is over. I'm gluing my house keys to my hand so I'll never forget to lock my doors again. At least Chief Giffen didn't say anything about that."

"He came?"

"He did. I was surprised."

"I'm glad to hear that. He's taking us seriously and knows there's still danger."

CHAPTER THIRTY-ONE

"Hello Ms. Duke. What can I do for you?" Lt. Robeson was always polite. "Wait, you missed calling a couple of days ago. Is everything alright?"

Roz thought back. He was right, in the commotion of starting classes and demonstrations, searching for the murdered man's identity, she'd skipped right by her weekly call to the LAPD.

"I ran across something up here with the neighbor I told you was murdered."

"Yes, and I told you to stay out of it."

Roz wished his attitude didn't immediately raise her defenses. "I'm glad I didn't. Some things have happened. The man was a retired priest, was accused of molesting boys and was killed with one of my knives."

She could hear Robeson suck in a breath and push his chair back.

"I'd say you've been busy. Are you sure of your facts?"

"Yes. I'm working with a friend, a retired journalist."

"How much of this have you shared with Giffen?"

She thought carefully. Robeson was asking this like a prosecutor, never ask a question you don't already know the answer to. A way to get trapped in lies if your story differed from what was already known.

"My friend and I met with Giffen a couple of days ago and went over what we found out. And, I saw Chief Giffen last night. He came to my house after I had an uninvited guest."

"A burglary?"

"No, more like vandalism. I had some broken glass but the most disturbing was what they wrote on my window."

"And that was?"

Steady, Roz thought. She closed her eyes, knowing Robeson didn't see that, but the action pulled the words up sharply. "Roman whore, in bed with the church'."

Robeson was quiet for a beat. "Provocative. Do you know what it means?"

"Whoever wrote it knows that I'm working on a commission for a cathedral window."

"Is that unusual?"

"Not really, I've done them before. This commission, though, I took while I was in L.A., before…" She took a breath. "Before Winston was killed."

"Hmmm. I don't see how a nasty slur against you in Oregon ties in with a drive-by shooting in L.A"

"What if it's wasn't random? What if it was targeted, but Winston wasn't the target, I was? What if the shooters just saw a figure get out of our car and didn't realize it was him, not me?"

"That's a lot of 'what-ifs', Ms. Duke."

"Life is made up of what-ifs, Detective."

She heard him sigh. "I'll tell you what, Ms. Duke. I'll talk to Chief Giffen again and ask him to keep in touch with any information on you or the murder up there. That's about all I can do."

"Thank you, Detective. And please let me know if you find anything new."

"I will, Ms. Duke." And there was silence.

She'd done what she could do. Her next call was to Chief Giffen. "Have the evidence techs found anything? Do they have fingerprints?"

"No. I'm sorry. The intruders wore gloves. And since you left the door unlocked, they didn't exactly break in, just walked in. The Sharpie isn't traceable, it may have even been one you had laying around."

"This hasn't been my day for working with the police." Roz told him that Lt. Robeson of the LAPD may be calling him and gave a brief synopsis of the theory she'd floated, including that Robeson wasn't buying it. From Giffen's tone, he wasn't either.

"Tell you what, Ms. Duke, since we haven't been able to recover any evidence at your house, you can go ahead and clean up. If we come across anything, I'll be sure and get in touch."

Small mercies, she could at least clean those awful words off her window, went into her bathroom and got a bottle of alcohol. Armed with that and paper towels, she rubbed the hate away, knowing that every time she looked through that window at the beach, she'd see the words.

The residue left a smear on the window. She got the glass cleaner, did the whole window and carried over her cleaning to the inside of all the studio windows. Then noticed that the outsides were coated with a thin film of wind-driven salt spray, so went to the storage area, filled a bucket with sudsy water and grabbed a squeegee.

She did the west-facing window wall first. As she moved along the glass toward the side door, she kept an eye out so she wouldn't step on the fuchsias hugging the foundation. Watching her foot for the next step, a piece of paper fluttered and she leaned over to pick it up. A receipt from a Fred Meyer in Salem. Three weeks ago, someone bought gloves, duct tape, a plastic hazmat coverall, a roll of trash bags, a package of t-shirts and a People magazine.

Roz crumpled it up and stuffed it in her jeans pocket, finished up the windows. Housekeeping wasn't her long suit, but she'd started down the road with the window washing. She gathered up clothes, changed her bed, grabbed towels. Washing the outside of the windows, she'd shaken off wind-blown sand and felt sticky so she stripped and took a quick shower. Adding her jeans and shirt to the laundry pile, she felt in the pockets, pulled out the receipt and dropped it on the kitchen island on the way to the washer.

With the load started, she thought about lunch. Plain yogurt, blueberries, topped up with a handful of almond granola. Sat at the island and read the receipt again. It could have come from anywhere. Everybody shopped at Fred Meyer, it was a popular big box store and this receipt might have blown out of someone's trash. Or blown up from the beach. Or been dropped in her yard by someone coming into her house.

Liam answered on the first ring. "Are you alright?"

"We're back to the shorthand greeting, I see." She made her voice smile.

"We are. You're now officially a friend. What's up?"

Roz went through her conversation with Robeson and her short call with Giffen "He told me I could clean up, so I washed the window, then decided to wash all of them while I was at it. Sort of a delayed spring cleaning. I was finishing up when I spotted a receipt dropped in one of the fuchsias by my side door."

"What kind of receipt?"

"Just a Fred Meyer one, but it was for gloves and a plastic coverall."

Liam whistled. "Giffen needs to see this. And pretty much right away. He can get the state cops to look at video surveillance for the date, time and store and see who bought those. This is beyond our own asking questions and doing internet searches."

"I felt the same way. I think this was dropped by my latest 'visitor'. I've touched it. Will that hurt anything?"

"Maybe, maybe not. Just to be safe, use tweezers to pick it up, seal it in a baggie, then take it to Giffen right away."

"I don't know why the cops didn't see it last night. They looked outside."

"They could have missed it. They probably didn't scour things after finding you'd left the door unlocked." She heard a keyboard clatter.

"Are you writing?"

"I am. I'm writing the book proposal for my agent. It can get put on hold though. I'm coming down this afternoon. Can we have dinner tonight?"

Was that a quick tangent from business to personal or was he just being friendly? "Sure, I'd like that. Do you want to come here?"

"Do you cook? I don't want you to go to a lot of trouble."

"Don't be a jerk! Of course, I cook. In fact, I'm a dang good cook." Roz' irritation echoed in her voice.

"Sorry, sorry. These days a lot of people don't cook. Order something in or go out." He almost added, particularly those who lived alone, as he did. *Her* singleness had only been a short time though.

"I'll cook and I'll see you at 7?"

CHAPTER THIRTY-TWO

List, lists. Roz had been miffed at Liam's question about cooking. She considered herself at the edge of a gourmet cook and collected recipes and food pairings from the times she and Winston spent in Europe. Living in L.A., there was a world of food to choose from, so she had some Latin American and Asian favorites as well. For tonight she'd do a simple fresh meal. Grilled salmon, cheese soufflé, blanched fresh green beans with tarragon and a dash of vinegar.

The ingredients went on a list. On another list, she made notes for the police. She'd picked up the receipt with tweezers, got it into a baggie and sealed it. Her list noted where, when and how she found it.

She loaded Tut in the car, planning to give him a long-leash walk on the municipal beach which had a section reserved for dogs. He might meet some new friends, she reasoned. In truth, after last night when he'd been trapped in her bedroom, she felt guilty. And he was the best reason to lock her doors. If she was going to have vandals, and they left the door open, he might take off. Finding him in the dark was iffy.

After his play on the beach, her first stop was the police department. Chief Giffen was just coming back from a Rotary lunch and he waved her in. "Were you able to get your studio cleaned? I'm sorry an investigation is so messy."

"I did, and in the process I found something." She pulled the baggie out. "I washed the windows and found this under a fuchsia near the side door to my studio."

Giffen looked at the receipt. The purchases were visible through the baggie and he whistled, sounding much like Liam. "Interesting choice of items. Did you pick it up?"

Roz made a moue. "I did. When I saw it, I thought it was garbage. I get stuff blown in my yard from idiots who leave their trash on the beach. After I picked it up and read it, I thought it was strange, but just crumpled it up and was going to throw it away. I had a goose-bumpy chill, smoothed it out and guessed I needed to show it to you. Can you get Fred Meyer to show you their surveillance video?"

"Probably. They cooperate with law enforcement. I'll have somebody drive this up to the state police in Salem this afternoon. You realize your fingerprints will be all over it?"

Roz nodded. "After I handled it a few times my brain kicked in. I put it in the baggie with tweezers, too late by then."

"Thanks for bringing it in. My guys are still learning search techniques, as you know. I'm glad you found it before the wind blew it away."

"I hope it's going to be worthwhile. Whoever wrote those hateful words on my window needs to get punished."

"What do you think would be a good punishment?" Giffen was smiling as he ushered Roz to the foyer.

She grinned. "Maybe sentenced to ten years of washing church windows, inside and out?"

He laughed. "I like your ideas. I'll be in touch as soon as we find anything out."

Tut was asleep in the back seat. He woke as she got in, leaned over her seat, rested his head on her shoulder as she drove to the grocery store.

"Sorry sweetie, you'll have to wait again. I'm leaving the window cracked for you. I won't be long."

She picked up the few items on her list, added eggs and cream and looked for fresh tarragon. It was hard to find even in larger supermarkets and she gave up. Dried would have to do. On a whim, she grabbed a couple of cartons of ice cream. Marionberry in honor of her new home and salted caramel.

By 6 she'd set the table, gotten the grill ready, put a rub on the salmon and was grating cheese for the soufflé when her phone jiggled. It was Liam.

"Are you stuck along-side the road? Do I have to send help?"

"No. Don't leave your house again!"

"Is something wrong?" Liam's voice sounded light and kidding but she wasn't sure about anything anymore.

"I didn't mean to make you nervous. I got here an hour ago and wanted to know if you wanted company before 7."

"Uh, sure? I'm going to grill some salmon and I'm doing sous chef prep."

"I can watch that. And I'll bring some wine."

Roz' voice softened. "Then c'mon over. I'll get out the glasses."

She had time to run to her bathroom, do a quick look in the mirror, swipe some gloss on and was back to answer Liam's knock. It had only been two days since she'd seen him, but he looked good, familiar, safe, easy. His black hair was wind-tousled and his smile lit up his blue, blue eyes, making the incipient lines curve up. He wore an untucked dress shirt, collar open and sleeves rolled up toward his elbows, faded jeans and a sweater tied over his shoulders. In his hands were two bottle of Willamette Valley white wine.

"Is that a little overkill? I don't drink that much."

He smiled. "Neither do I. I thought it would be a good idea to have a spare here, just in case."

"In case of what?" The quick banter was back.

"Tsunami? Hurricane? Fire?"

"R-i-g-h-t. Those disasters happen often here?"

"Maybe not often, but they could. Did you keep earthquake supplies in L.A.? And did you ever have to use them?"

"Yes and no. You win. We'll start a shelf in the fridge for 'emergency rations'."

He came around the island and handed one bottle to her. "This is for an emergency. I know you have a corkscrew here somewhere."

She handed him one and pulled two glasses down from the rack. "I'm snapping the green beans, the soufflé gets put together at the last minute, we probably have at least a half hour before we need to start the grill. Want to sit out on the deck?"

"Sure. And you can tell me how the rest of your day went."

Out the back, she put Tut on his long leash, set her glass down on the table and went to the railing, looking at the beach and the ocean behind it. "I guess it went fine. It bothers me that here, this place I came for healing and solace, has been breached. I know it was my fault, leaving the door unlocked, but I wonder if they'd have broken in anyway?"

"They may have, and in that case you've saved yourself some heartache not having to replace doors or windows."

She turned to face him. "It's such a creepy feeling, knowing that somebody was in your house, your space. May have touched your things." She shivered. "Then left that hateful, hateful message."

"I can imagine." He went over to her, put his hands on her shoulders, drew her into his chest. "What did Giffen say?"

"He took the receipt—I didn't tell him I told you, by the way—was going to have someone drive it up to the state lab in Salem this afternoon. He says that Fred Meyer cooperates with law enforcement all the time. I don't think I'll hear anything for days."

"Probably not. I have some feelers out as well," and he told her about his conversation with Sam.

"The dark net? Oh my god, Liam, isn't that where arms dealers and anarchists and conspiracy nuts and hackers and…"

"And pedophiles, and child pornographers and sex traffickers hang out. Yes. Sam knows some hackers who can trace a person down, even his physical address, through his IP. I don't know how, I don't want to know." He paused. "I gave him what I've found on Jackson, but I don't expect to hear for a few days. In the meantime, I'm staying here."

Roz moved back, picked up her glass. "You're not doing a strong and manly act for me, are you? I've been through worse."

"As attractive a proposition as that sounds, no. Don't forget, you're now part of my best-selling book. More of the answers are here, not in Portland. And I'm planning that being in the physical neighborhood of where Jackson was murdered will give me some insight about what happened."

"Good." Roz said it, but did she mean it?

CHAPTER THIRTY-THREE

The salmon was tasty, the soufflé crusty and cheesy, the beans tart and crunchy. They did finish off one bottle of wine and Roz was relaxed as she picked dishes up from the table.

"Let me do that," he said. "You cooked. And you were right, you can cook, it was wonderful."

"Leave them in the sink, then. I splurged a little on dessert."

"Do you want it now?"

"No, let's go out and look for a green streak. I have a bottle of port that I put away for a special occasion and after last night, tonight is special."

Liam laughed and took her hand, leading her out through the French doors. "It's a deal. This place owes you a green streak after having had your peace disrupted."

They leaned on the rail companionably, watching the sun sink into the rim of the ocean, the sky turn salmon, vermillion, tangerine, then easing into a vivid magenta. But no green streak.

As the sun made its descent into the Pacific, a slight breeze came up and Roz shivered.

"I know the plants and flowers think it's spring but it's still chilly. How about a small fire?" She went in, piled two logs onto the grate, hit the igniter and flames licked up. "This is easier. In L.A. we only had gas fireplaces, probably more ecologically conscious, but I missed the smell of wood smoke."

"There may come a time when that's true here, too." Liam settled on a loveseat, stretching his legs out. "We don't have to worry about air pollution here, yet."

"I have ice cream—Marionberry or salted caramel. Want some with your port?"

Roz brought glasses, bowls of ice cream and the port to a table before the fire. "This is nice. It makes me feel more comfortable in my own space."

"Being invaded, even if it wasn't violent, has to set your world on edge. I've never had it happen, but I talked to plenty of people who did."

"Why?'

He picked up his glass, swirled the dark red port around. "Mostly when I was being a reporter. I always felt invasive when interviewing people after a violent event." He smiled. "I never asked the TV question, though."

"What's that?"

"The one where they stick a microphone in someone's face and ask, 'How do you feel?' The only answer I can ever think of is 'crappy'."

She nodded and smiled back at him. "I agree. How are you supposed to feel? I feel violated, angry, humiliated, like my world is no longer mine or safe."

"I keep wondering if the intruders are local people, teens, or are connected with the visitors that Jackson used to have."

"Jackson?"

Liam looked at her absently. Then; "Ah, Jackson. The guy across the street."

"Do you know for sure it was Jackson?"

"No. It's gonna take some probably DNA or dental records to pin it down. I'm calling him Jackson because it begins to put a picture of him together. A face with the body. And I don't have to call him 'the victim' or the 'murdered man'."

Roz looked at Liam. "Isn't that grisly? What if it wasn't Jackson, or the guy wasn't a pedophile. Are you ruining his reputation?"

"For starters, it's only in my mind—and now with you. I trust that you'll stay quiet about it. Besides, everybody, including the local police and, I suspect, the state crime guys, have tried to identify him. At least all the normal ways. They haven't gone to the press yet. It's harder to get lost and stay lost today. But you can if you try."

"You're talking like Witness Protection."

"If the church hierarchy is in on it, yeah, it's kind of like that. Priests are taught to keep secrets. If they didn't, confession wouldn't work"

The fire popped and an ember jumped to the hearth and died. Roz watched the red die out to gray. There was death in everything, even in the midst of life. Was this what happened to Winston? Just living one second then a pop, a fading to gray and he was dead.

She jerked her mind back. There was a scientific reason the fire popped. A drop of moisture or sap caught in the wood that expanded with heat and burst, pushing the ember out like popcorn. And there was a reason Winston was killed. She just didn't see it yet.

"I want to know more about the boys." Liam licked his ice cream spoon. "Would Patsy talk to me about them?"

"Hmmm, probably. In fact, you're one of the neighbors who might have seen something. We're going to talk to more people tomorrow evening. Want to come?"

"I'd like to. Should I talk to Patsy first?"

Roz thought for a tick. Patsy did seem to soften, to be a little coy when she was around Liam. "That may be a good idea. Tell her that one of the other neighbors told you she and I were doing the rounds and you wondered why we left you off. You don't have to mentioned you weren't home, we didn't even get to your house."

The evening was winding down. "That was a wonderful dinner," Liam said. "Where'd you learn to cook like that?"

"I don't know. I've always loved to eat. Early on, as Winston was working on his Ph.D. we didn't have much money. I was doing free-lance graphic design. One day I drove by a yard sale. We were always looking for stuff we could fix up and use, tables, chairs, bookcases. These people had a bunch of books. I flipped through them and here was a cookbook with a picture of a beautifully roasted chicken, green beans, succulent roasted potatoes sprinkled with parsley, you know the way they stage food? The table was set. Gorgeous dishes, silver, crystal, fancy napkins and holders."

She was lost in her memories. Liam watched the fire play on her face as her eyes gazed at a faraway place. "We had mismatched dishes we'd picked up at garage sales, plain drinking glasses, cheap stainless cutlery, but I could afford to buy a chicken, beans and potatoes. So I bought the cookbook and we ate some great meals off chipped plates." She smiled.

"You must miss him terribly."

"I do." She came back from her memory and glanced at Liam. "There was this time when…"

For the next hour, she went through selected memories of dinners, lunches, travels with Winston, laughing at times they got lost or ended up in small farm villages. Always, always she came back to the food.

"It probably seems silly to spend all that time remembering the food when I was surrounded by glorious architecture and art. There was one very chi-chi restaurant we stumbled into in Orleans. It was raining and we ducked behind a heavy drapery in an archway and found ourselves in the restaurant's foyer. We looked like drowned rats and all the others had on dresses, suits, ties. The French upper middle classes are very traditional. We were shown to a table, given an appetizer and served a prix fixe meal. The mushroom soup was beyond anything I'd ever tasted." She sighed. "The meal cost us about $200 and this was ten years ago. We promised ourselves we'd always read the menu in the window first after that."

"That sounds special."

"It was. But we ate bread and cheese for two days after, we'd broken our food budget."

CHAPTER THIRTY-FOUR

In the half-dreaming state, Roz was walking up a narrow alley on Mont St. Michael. The building sides were so close she couldn't swing her arms and someone was pushing behind her. Unease overcame her before she woke enough to realize that Tut snuggled his large body against her, trapping her in the duvet. She rolled away from him and he roused.

"Time to get up, big boy? Some coffee and a run?"

He stood, shook himself and jumped down, rocking the bed. Roz closed her eyes and remembered how much she'd told Liam last night. She'd not spoken to anyone about those memories, not even Win's sister. After his killing, she'd pulled away from his family, his mother still living and one sister. They could live with their memories of him, she kept her own locked inside.

Did she trust Liam or was this a part, the next step, in the grieving process, being able to remember and talk about the good times? Or maybe half a bottle of wine and a glass of port did it? She poked around in her mind to look for regrets, was calmed when she didn't find any. Whatever allowed her to talk to Liam last night, it was healing and comforting.

Jeans, sweater, shoes, coffee in hand she opened the French doors and Tut, on his leash, pulled her so hard she had to jog to get down the steps. It was overcast, the usual morning fog, but a nip in the air. She tugged Tut back inside, stuck her pencil behind her ear, grabbed a sketchpad, picked up a hoodie and locked the door behind her. "Take that," she mumbled. Across the dunes and onto the wet sand of the tide mark, the wind hit in earnest. She pulled the sweatshirt on, even tucking her hair into the hood.

Regardless of her uninvited guests, she felt more at peace here than in L.A. There, everything reminded her of her past with Winston. Here, she could go for hours without the need to turn to him and share something. These were *her* memories she was building.

At the edge of the water, the wind was stronger and cooler. Maybe a storm rolling in from Asia? She cut her tide-line walk short, went back to the tree roots. Sipped coffee while she watched the sandpipers and gulls. She took her pencil and sketched studies of the shore birds. Some wheeling against the clouds, some darting back and forth, just out of reach of the waves lapping in.

This was a calming way to start the day, but chilly. She shivered, noticed the morning was lighter now and the fog was thinning. Time to get Tut back, fix them breakfast and start to work. She had to put more hours in if she was to make the deadline for the cathedral, plus, she needed to translate the wild berry forest to a good drawing so she could turn it into glass. For every design she added to her online catalogue, she made about half-a-dozen of them first, working out the cuts and joins the amateur glass makers needed to do. Too complicated and she'd never sell them.

After kibble for Tut and French toast for herself, she went into the studio. She couldn't look at the sea view, the horrible words were still too embedded on her retinas, but the window washing yesterday brightened the room. The salt film had grown so gradually she didn't notice it, now the studio almost glowed.

Roz tacked the sketch and studies of the birds on a corkboard, next to two sketches of berry bushes tangled in the trees. She'd work on these this afternoon, but now she had to finish the next section for the church. She was in the process of putting together a stylized comet shooting across a cluster of nebulea, but the proportions were giving her trouble. She booted up her computer, opened the Hubble page of NASA and skimmed through the pictures again. She'd used a shot of M 16, called "Pillars of Creation" as her background guide because it looked like organic growths against aqua-blue space and the comet had to be a burst of white light streaking upward. This wasn't an exact replica. She was going for the feeling of exultation and limitless space, a searching for the beyond. She sketched several renditions before finding one she liked, blew it up on her printer to the final correct size and taped it to her light table.

One of Winston's jobs when she was working like this had been to keep her focused on drinking and eating, and now she noticed she was thirsty. It had been almost three hours since breakfast. She stretched, went into the kitchen for a bottle of water. Her eco-guilt always kicked in when she bought bottled water, but she drank more of it and it didn't tip over as easily when she was moving around her work, waving her arms to look at various angles.

She idly watched the birds from her kitchen window and jumped when she saw a figure out of the corner of her eye. Clarence. Was her neighbor patrolling?

"What are you doing?" She crossed the studio, opened the side door and made him jump as he scuttled across her side yard toward his own house.

"Nothing, nothing." He turned and came back toward her. "I just decided that I needed to be seen around your house and yard. You've had two prowlers and one break-in and I don't want anybody thinking you're not protected."

Bless his heart, she thought, how much protection was a retired fisherman, probably a drunk, maybe carrying a shotgun without ammunition, going to be?

"Thanks for the thought Clarence, but you startled me. Any time I see movement in my yard, I get nervous. How long have you been doing this?"

"Oh, two or three days. I don't have a regular schedule, don't want any of the vandals getting the drop on me because they know when I'm coming by."

Roz closed her eyes and counted to ten, then, "Thanks, Clarence. I do appreciate it. Maybe you could call me before you poke around? I don't want to be surprised and smack you with my baseball bat."

"Lordy, no. I didn't know you had a weapon. Do I have your telephone number?"

"It's on the Neighborhood Watch list."

"Isn't that the thing that PS, that nosy Patsy, is involved in? I get calls from them sometimes to come to a meeting or something. Never have gone."

Roz smiled. Clarence didn't seem like the kind to get involved with groups. "Maybe you should come sometime. It's a good way to get to know your neighbors."

"Naw, I know plenty of people hereabouts. Just keeping up with the crowd of old fools who get together at Jules is enough for me."

He turned and started back toward his house when Roz called, "Clarence, did you know the guy who got killed. The one who was stabbed?"

"The one across the street? Not really. Saw him enough to nod at. Saw that he had visitors a few times."

"Visitors?"

"Yeah, you know, when people come to your door." Was he being funny?

"What kind of visitors?"

"Didn't get a good look at them, they always came at night. One time, when he opened the door, I saw the visitor had one of those backwards collar things."

Her breath stopped. "You mean like a priest? Those Roman collars?"

"Is that what they're called? Yep, like that, don't know whether they're coming or going."

"Did you tell Chief Giffen or Smiley about this?"

"Nope. Why would I? Don't want the police thinking I'm as nosy as that Patsy woman."

"Well, thank you Clarence for keeping an eye out, but please let me know when you're coming on patrol. With my other unannounced visitors, I'm a little on edge these days."

Roz spun around and headed back through her door, trying her best not to run. She had to call Liam.

CHAPTER THIRTY-FIVE

"I just heard something odd from Clarence."

"OK, I see you've taken on the 'just start in the middle of a conversation,' too." Liam's voice held a smile.

Roz stopped herself from sniping. "Sorry, this is weird and maybe stunning and I practically ran in here to call you. Did I interrupt something?"

"No, just running some questions through my mind for the interviews this evening."

"This sort of has a bearing on that." She didn't speak for a few seconds, marshaling her thoughts. "When I had a conversation with Clarence, he told me he'd seen Jackson having visitors at night."

"We already know that, that's what we're asking people about…"

"No. These people came to Jackson's front door. And at least one of them was a priest."

Liam snorted. "Now how, at night, did Clarence, a drunk, know it was a priest?"

"He said the guy turned and he saw the Roman collar. Or as he put it, 'those backwards things'."

"You have my attention now. Did he say how often? When did he see the priest? Did he ever talk to Jackson?"

"I didn't ask him any of that, I was so surprised." Roz picked up her pencil and scratched her head with it. "I don't want to spook him. Should we go back and talk to him?"

"We can, yes. How do we frame it?"

"Frame it?"

"A journalist term. What angle do we want to use? What information do we need to get from him? Unlike lawyers, we don't want yes or no answers. We have to ask questions that will open Clarence up, let him tell about his impressions."

"OK, well, we should figure out how often the priest came to visit. Was it always after dark? If Clarence was too far gone he may not be the most reliable witness. Did he see more than one priest? When was the last time he saw someone come to Jackson's house?"

A chuckle. "Now you're thinking like a reporter. Good. Those are all questions we should ask. When do you want to do this?"

"He's home now and sober. I just caught him patrolling my yard. He said he was randomly walking around to let the 'vandals' know I was protected."

This time Liam laughed out loud. "Good. I can be over in a few minutes."

Less than half-an-hour later they were on Clarence's front stoop waiting for him to open the door. Roz was ready to greet Clarence while Liam turned his back. "What are you doing," she hissed. "That's rude."

"Figuring out what his view of Jackson's front door is," he whispered back as Clarence's door opened.

"Hi Roz, I just talked to you. Are you alright?" Clarence looked to Liam and back to Roz.

"I'm fine. Liam and I are part of the Neighborhood Watch group and we're going to all the neighbors asking what they've seen and warning them to be careful. Do you mind if we come on and ask a couple of questions?"

Inside, the funk of older bachelor hung in the air. Seldom washed bodies and clothes, meals out of cans heated up and forgotten on the stove. Not dirty, more unkempt with two empty beer cans on a table next to his recliner. Roz assumed he didn't entertain much.

"Roz told me you saw some people coming to visit the man across the street." Liam started, knowing Roz would chime in if needed.

"I did. Yep."

"Was it always the same man?"

"Don't know. I only saw him a couple of times. It wasn't as though he was a regular. Come to think of it, it probably was the same guy."

Roz chimed. "Why do you think that? Did you recognize him?"

"Naw, I saw him twice in the last few months. It was the same car."

Car. Roz slid a sideways look at Liam. They hadn't thought about a car.

"Could you recognize him?" Liam this time.

"I don't think so. I only saw his collar because the porch light came on before the murdered guy opened the door. He was kinda tall."

"Tall? Over six feet?"

"I don't know about that, he was taller than the guy who lived there. I didn't see that guy open the door, the visitor was bigger and blocked him out. That's how I know he was tall. And I saw the collar as he turned to go in." Clarence stopped talking and his eyes gleamed. "Do you think that visitor was the murderer? Is there a reward for information? I didn't see him that well, but I know he had white hair…or maybe light blond but I think he was older, so white."

"I don't think there's any reward." Liam eased toward the door. "You've been helpful, Clarence."

The old man puffed himself up, seemingly happy to hear that. "I try. I told Roz I was walking around her house and yard every so often, making sure that everybody knows she's got protection. This used to be a dead quiet neighborhood, now a guy gets killed, Roz has some break-ins and peeping toms. Things are surely changing."

"They are. The whole world is. Thank you, Clarence, and I appreciate you keeping an eye out for me." Roz reached for the door handle and jumped slightly when Clarence's hand came up behind her and pulled the door open.

Waving good-by, they walked across the lawn to Roz' side door. "What do you think?" she asked, going into her studio.

"Depending on which window he looks through, Clarence has a good vantage point for Jackson's front door. He could clearly see the size of the visitor and the color of his hair with the porch light on. Not sure how much help the car will be, other than the visitor used it at least twice that Clarence saw."

"And the Roman collar. Does that help? Do bishops or archbishops wear different collars than a parish priest?" Roz took commissions from churches but didn't pay much attention to the clothes the clergy wore—unless they were wearing surpluses or stoles or cassocks.

"Not necessarily. They all can wear a Roman collar." Liam snapped his fingers. "Come to think of it, anybody can go into a store selling religious goods and buy those. Probably even online. Which means we may be leaping to assumptions."

"We have to start eliminating things, people. If any stranger can dress up and come to visit Jackson, what would be the reason? It only makes sense, if it really was Jackson, that it was someone from his past. Or knew about his past, but blackmail doesn't work." She closed her eyes. "This may have been a wild goose chase. Let's see where the interviews with neighbors, your neighbors, goes this evening. You did call Patsy?"

"I did. I couldn't tell if she was miffed. I promised her that I'd stay in the background and let her take the lead on questions."

Roz walked into the kitchen, got a glass of water. "I've forgotten my manners, would you like something to drink?"

"Ah, no thanks. I need to get back to my proposal and framing questions for tonight." He smiled sheepishly. "Even though I may not get a chance to ask anything."

CHAPTER THIRTY-SIX

They met at Patsy's house shortly after 4 that afternoon. Chatted for a couple of minutes, then Patsy laid out her plan and which neighbors would be first on the list to visit.

"I thought we'd start on the other side, your side, Liam. Roz and I talked to the two families next to me. I think your side may have had a better chance to see any of the boys, or anybody else who came to his back door."

"That's fine with me," Liam said. Roz nodded in agreement.

"We're just being friendly. I introduce myself as the chairman of the Neighborhood Watch group—most of them know that already—and ask them if they were home the morning of the murder. Probably if they went to work, they left before the cops showed up, so wouldn't have seen anything."

"We'll just follow your lead." Liam turned to Roz. "If that's OK?"

"Good. I'm too much of a newcomer. They all know you and Patsy."

"I'm not here all the time. I think most of them have at least seen me." He gestured to Patsy to lead the way.

The first house, no one answered. Not daunted, Patsy slid a Neighborhood Watch flyer giving information about the murder in their mailbox. "That should get them to call," she said with a slightly wicked grin and Roz made a mental note not to cross Patsy.

Next house held a retired couple and Patsy went into her spiel. The woman called, "Wes, it's that Neighborhood Watch lady, wants to talk to us." From somewhere back in the house, Wes said, "Well, invite her in," and they heard heavy footsteps coming down the hall.

Wes took a look at Liam and said, "Hell, I didn't know you were involved with this."

"Not a lot, but we have a few questions we'd like to ask."

"You're not selling anything, are you?" Wes' voice was suspicious.

"No, no." Now Roz introduced herself. "Patsy, Liam and I met in the street the morning our neighbor was found murdered. We'd like to talk about that morning."

Patsy found her command voice. "Were you home? Did you see anything?"

Wes said no, the woman said yes, then, "Would you like something to drink? Coffee? Iced tea?"

Once the drink orders were sorted out, Liam said, "Wes, you said no and your wife said yes. Which was it?"

"That's easy. I was down at Jules. Had an early breakfast meeting." Wes seemed self-important.

"Breakfast meeting my left foot. You old fools go down there to drink coffee and lie to each other." The woman turned to Patsy and Roz. "I was home, I don't get invited to their 'meetings' and wouldn't go even if I were. I didn't see much of anything, though."

"It was pretty loud and lots of emergency lights. I even saw it coming up from the beach," Roz said.

The woman looked at her for a long second. "You must be that artist lady. The one who bought the old Jamesson place." She smiled, having put all the pegs into the proper places.

"That's me." Roz put a cheery note in her voice followed up with a smile. No matter what happened with the murder, she was getting to know a lot of the locals.

"I was doing my morning exercise." She looked at Patsy. "I have a tape that runs on the TV for an hour so I don't hear much else." Back to Roz. "How do you like the house? Does the noise bother you?"

By now, Roz understood the "noise" people referred to was the ocean. "No, I like it. It's just background. I moved here from Los Angeles and down there, there's noise all the time."

The woman gave her a look as though she heard that noise all the time as well. "Is there anything else I can tell you."

Patsy cleared her throat. "There is, yes. Did you ever see any visitors to that house? Particularly at the back door?"

Wes and his wife looked at one another. "One night I was coming home from the Snug and there was a boy, a young man, in the backyard of that house. He was pacing. I thought maybe he was casing the joint, then I saw him go up the steps, knock on the door. The guy, the owner opened it and the boy went in."

His wife nodded. "And one time I was coming back from the grocery store and saw the owner standing on the back stoop talking to a boy, couldn't have been more than 14. Wes and I mentioned it to each other. It seemed odd that a man who lived alone as best we could tell had young visitors who came to the back. But we figured it wasn't our business."

"Do you remember when that was? What day?" Liam asked it casually, didn't want to spook her.

She thought, then, "I do. It was three weeks ago on a Thursday."

Wes looked at her. "You're making that up. How could you remember?"

"That was the day I bought a huge roast and was going to cut it up and freeze part of it. I was going through how to cut it when I saw the boy and thought it was a shame that it's just us now." She turned to Patsy. "You know, you get used to cooking for a crowd when the kids are here, then, boom, it's you and him." She thumbed at Wes.

Roz tamped down a smile. She'd never cooked for a crowd—except parties—but she appreciated the way the woman's memory worked, tying together seemingly unrelated things.

"That helps. Thanks." Liam closed his notebook, signaling the end of the visit. Roz wondered how he managed to take things over, but Patsy didn't seem to mind.

The family in the next house announced themselves before Roz, Patsy and Liam got to the door.

"Put that down. Stop it!" Children's wails overrode the woman's voice.

"Maybe we've come at a bad time," Roz said and slowed her walk.

Patsy shook her head. "No, it's just the kids, fighting as usual." She raised her hand to knock when the door flew open and a child, a boy, Roz thought, barreled out, followed by his brother yelling, "You're gonna get it!"

A woman, probably the mom Roz judged, from the baby on her hip, came to the door and halted mid-yell. "Oh," she said. "Hi, Patsy."

"Hey, Jessamine. How are you?"

"Ready to tear my hair out. What's up?"

"You know I'm the head of Neighborhood Watch…"

"I know, but I just can't make the meetings. Maybe in another 15 years." She gestured at the baby on her hip.

"You have your hands full," Liam leaned over and stuck out his hand, realizing too late it was awkward for her. "I'm Liam Karshner and I live down the street. We just have a couple of questions to ask you. Did you know the man who was murdered? Did you see or hear anything strange that morning?"

"I guess I heard that some guy was killed. On the corner? Mornings are hard for me, getting the kids off to school. I wouldn't have noticed a bomb going off."

"How about any boys hanging around his backyard or visiting him?" Patsy regained the lead.

"Nope. Sorry. I don't get out much beyond what I have to do for the boys' activities. And when we're in the car, I'm refereeing the constant uproar and arguments." She grimaced.

"I can't believe I fell for that 'have another kid, they'll have built-in playmates'."

There were times Roz regretted not having a child with Winston. This wasn't one of them.

CHAPTER THIRTY-SEVEN

Three more houses, one neighbor not at home, two others who lived farther down the street and didn't have a good view of Jacksons' back yard.

"That's about it, I think." Roz was tired of meeting people, making chit-chat, coming up with nothing. "We went to a total of seven homes and got nowhere, except for Wes and his wife."

Patsy crossed her arms. "We didn't get much about the dead guy but I think I managed to get more information out about Neighborhood Watch. We may get more members and that's good. I need to get home and make dinner." She headed off, leaving Liam and Roz to look at each other.

"Well, guess we're not invited." Liam shrugged his shoulders. "Don't think it's a big loss. Want to grab a burger or something? There's that touristy place up towards Newport."

"That sounds good. I'm kind of peopled out. I spend most of my days alone. Dinner isn't when I want to talk with lots of folks I just met. I need to let Tut out first."

"I'm a loner, too, I guess. Now. Spent work time around people but I'm getting used to living with my friends in my head. I can control them a little better."

Roz patted his hand. "I know. I can make up any designs that interest me. At least until they don't sell, then I go back to the tried and true. But I don't have someone looking over my shoulder and critiquing everything I do."

She walked up the street towards her house, calling back, "Come over whenever you want to go. I'll be ready."

She took the house key out of her pocket, stuck her tongue out in Liam's direction and unlocked the door, holding a hand out to catch pounds of dog leaping for her chest. "Tut! Tut, come on out the back and go pee." On his leash, he lunged off the deck and was brought up when it hit the end, just as he began to sniff. Roz watched him, her mind chugging along, turning over what they'd heard this afternoon. Was any of it helpful? Clarence had seen a man at Jackson's front door twice, both times at night. Wes and his wife saw a couple of boys at Jackson's back door. The only sure conclusion they could draw was whoever the man was, he knew a few people, just no one in Hamilton.

As she started to reel Tut back in, Liam appeared around the corner of the yard. "C'mon boys, she said," waving them in through the French doors. She grabbed a sweater and her purse off the peg, said "Let's go," and locked the front door behind them.

"Thanks for taking my advice," Liam said as he opened the passenger door of his truck.

"Thanks for watching out for me. It makes me a little crazy, you and Clarence appointing yourselves as watchdogs, but I'm glad. Just the thought of someone coming in and letting Tut tear off in the dark scares me. Using a key to get in is a small price to pay."

The burger place was a local restaurant right on the highway that drew customers from the traffic headed somewhere else, so Roz and Liam were anonymous. Roz wasn't big on fried food but the smell of hamburgers, onions and fries was too much. She ordered a special and fries with a soft drink, Liam went for a bleu cheese burger with mushrooms, as well as the fries.

While waiting, he said, "We did pretty well today."

"We did? I was going over things. I don't think we got much. Clarence saw 'some guy' show up. He drove. Wes and his wife saw 'a boy' twice. They don't even know if it was the same boy."

"OK, lets' see what we learned. Jackson had a grown-up, maybe even elderly, visitor. It was a priest, or dressed like a priest, and he drove the same car both times. And that happened over the last few months. The vague description could fit Malone, but he'd have to rent a car…" Silence.

"What? So he'd have to rent a car. Why is that a problem."

"If it was Malone and if he rented a car, the chances of him renting the same car weeks apart is too slim. But, if it was Malone, if he flew into Portland and stayed at one of the parishes, he could borrow the same car."

"And?"

"And I might be able to find Malone's travel records. I still have come contacts in Portland. Having the archbishop come for a visit is a big deal in parishes. It could have been announced in church newsletters or the church PR office could have sent out a press release. If he came here, we could get the dates."

"Then what?"

"We know one of the dates that a boy came to visit, although we don't know if it was the same boy they saw both times. If the boy was there at the same time Malone was there—this is making pretty big assumptions—it could tie Malone either to an active pedophile case or at least a cover up for ex-priest, Jackson, as a pedophile."

Roz was quiet as the server set down huge plates of burgers and fries, then spun around and got ketchup and mustard from a neighboring table. "Anything else?" she said absently.

"Drinks?' Liam smiled up at her, she said, "Yep," and took off again, coming back with two glasses and the check.

They were both silent as they began to eat. Roz rolled her eyes. "I'm not a big red meat eater, but this is really good. Thanks."

"You just never know about these places." Liam salted his fries as Roz frowned. "What? My blood pressure is fine." He grinned like a naughty boy, caught flinging dirt clods. "Anyway, we were comparing dates."

"Even if we can put Malone and a boy together at the same time. This may help you with your book, but how does it solve my problem? You know, the stolen knife and the 'stabbing multiple times' of the neighbor. Whether it's Jackson or not Jackson."

"It doesn't solve anything, yet. But it gives us the victim's name and a motive for the crime."

"What motive? We've ruled out blackmail."

Liam sat back. This wasn't going to be easy. "There are a few things I haven't told you. You remember I told you that one boy who was a victim of a pedophile priest committed suicide? He had a brother who swore he'd track the priest down. And you know those multiple stab wounds? A knife attack like that is pretty personal, certainly with where many of the wounds were."

Roz looked at him. "And the wounds were?"

"More than half of them were to his genitals. Giffen said his penis was all but severed."

"Wow." Roz whispered it. "Wow, that's a pretty strong case for anger at a pedophile. Are you thinking it may have been the brother? Do you know his name?"

"Not yet. That information came up in an interview a year or so afterwards. Suicide of a juvenile isn't covered with names, as a rule, particularly if there was a tie-in to an accused pedophile priest. Protection of the family and protection for the priest."

"How are you ever going to sew this all together?"

Liam chewed the bite he'd taken. "I don't know yet. That's why I've asked Sam to spend some time in the dark web. It's like fishing. Everybody told you this was a good spot to catch your limit, but you're not sure there are any fish there, what kind they are, how big they are. You hope when you do get a bite it's a 10-pound trout."

"Good writerly analogy." Roz grinned at him. "How long before you know anything?"

"First, I have to do some date research. That'll entail phone calls, maybe a trip to Portland. Bless Wes' wife's heart for remembering when she bought a roast. By the way, do you know her name?"

"No, Patsy declined to introduce us, didn't she? I can go back again tomorrow, introduce myself again and chat a bit. I hate to keep thinking of her as 'Wes' wife'."

"Somehow I thought that would bother you." Liam stood, picked up the check and waited while Roz gathered up her things.

CHAPTER THIRTY-EIGHT

"I must be slipping." Liam shook his head and the truck veered a little. Roz sucked in a breath as he brought it back to the center of the lane and said, "I can't believe I didn't ask that."

"Ask what, besides 'Is your license up to date?'"

"Ha. At least I didn't slap myself in the head, we'd probably be in the sand now. That I didn't ask any of the neighbors if they'd spoken to the police. Were we the only ones who talked to them?"

Mentally, Roz went over the conversations. "No one said anything about the police. I'd think someone would say, 'I told the cops, why are you asking again?' if they'd talked to anyone else."

"Yeah, I don't know if this is a bad or good sign. Either Giffen's crew interviewed them and ruled everything out, or we have information they don't. I hope we're not spinning our wheels."

Roz watched the sun begin its slide into the Pacific. "It feels like a time bomb. It's ticking but will it really explode or is it all a big dud and I'm wasting my time?" What had she done in her life that put her in situations she couldn't control? First Winston, now this. Possibly involved in a murder without her knowledge and facing break-ins and vandalism. It didn't feel random, but she couldn't see the connection; the closest was the church, not enough to hold together.

"How are you coming on your prospectus?"

The question startled Liam. "What prospectus?"

"For your book. Is that what you call it?"

"Ah, proposal. I have about 50 pages done, detailing the background and the research. The facts haven't changed, these events happened. The difference is that some of it has never been made public before, so I have to be very careful in any conclusions I draw."

"Does it make you crazy?"

"A little. I'm convinced I know what happened years ago that led to this guy, Jackson, getting murdered." He was silent. "That's what made me move to Hamilton."

She whipped around to look at him, the sunset forgotten. "You knew he was going to be murdered? How?"

"No. God no. I had no idea he was in danger. I'd done enough research to suspect a retired priest, a pedophile, was living quietly in Hamilton. I was planning a book about the ways the church dealt with these priests, and that so many of them were never punished for their crimes. I was just as stunned as anyone when he ended up being stabbed to death."

"This all seems slippery. How can you prove anything?"

Liam pulled the truck into his driveway. "I don't have to prove anything, exactly. I have to do first-class research in tracking down names, dates, accusations, police reports. Until either the church or the individual priests confess, these are allegations, backed up by as many facts as I can dig up. And having the central person of the book be a murder victim—this is causing a big shift in my narrative. I'd planned to knock in his door when I'd gathered enough information that I was confident I knew who he was and what he did. Have the thrust of the book be an interview with him, asking why? Although I'm not sure even he would have known."

"Have you interviewed any of the survivors?"

"'Survivors?' That's an interesting choice of words." He walked through the garden and held the door, silently inviting her in.

"I had some friends in L.A. who were active in groups against domestic abuse and sexual assault. They hated the word 'victim' as though the person brought it on themselves. They started using 'survivor' as a term for someone who got through a horrific situation and was stronger for it. I like it. It gives those people who've been taken advantage of by someone more powerful recognition for their ability to survive despite the abuse." She walked around the living room of Liam's cottage, trailing her fingers across books, pictures. "Where do you write?"

He flipped on a lamp by a window and Roz saw a work area, a library table, couldn't accurately be called a desk, laden with papers, files, a laptop, a printer. "Here, when I'm here. In Portland, I have a space as well. My condo there is a converted loft. I like working in places that hold some human history. Sometimes I imagine I can hear the ghosts whispering secrets to me."

Roz shivered.

"Are you cold? Let me make us some tea. Do you drink tea?"

"I do. I'm not cold so much as goose-fleshy. Do you believe in ghosts?"

"Ah, that's what has you shivery." Liam's voice came from the kitchen and Roz heard him fill a kettle with water, then put it on a burner.

"What kind of tea would you like? I have chamomile, Darjeeling, mango. No. I don't believe in ghosts. I do think something from the past can still be around. Our bodies run on an energy like electricity, so it could be that's what gets left behind."

He came out with a tray holding cups, sugar, sliced lemons, cream, spoons and a tea cozy.

"I haven't had service like this since I visited England." She smiled. "I had no idea you were an Anglophile."

The kettle whistled, Liam went to get it, came back with a pot that he covered with the cozy. "Not sure I'd say an Anglophile, there are customs and rites that other cultures do that I think are civil, and civilizing. I haven't traveled as much as you have, but I plan to. Now that I have the time, well, can take the time, I don't have the money. It's always one or the other."

Roz grinned. "That's right. I need to drum up commissions in other places. Colorado's fine, and lots of places where I've done windows in the U.S. are wonderful. People who can afford my windows tend to live in spectacular homes in astounding places. If I got a call from someone in Europe, or Australia or South America, I'd go in a flash. I keep my passport up to date and my fingers crossed."

Liam poured and handed her a cup. "Do you have a favorite place?"

"No, there are so many astounding places and cultures, I don't think I could just choose one. Do you do research anywhere else?"

"I have. I've written a few pieces on the way some of the European countries are working with climate change, for instance. Several of them are far ahead of us in renewable energy—wind, solar, water. And Europe has always been better at us for moving people. They have autobahns, M roads, autoroutes, but they have railroads and people still travel by train. Much smaller carbon footprint than freeways jammed by cars."

"Have you ever driven in Paris?" Roz was laughing. "The traffic circle around the Arc de Triomphe looks like a seven-lane parking lot most of the time."

"Well, I can't imagine asking any European to give up his or her car." The corner of Liam's mouth quirked up. "I'm not bashing our car culture, lord knows I have two. I would like to see people work together to solve problems, though."

Roz sipped her tea. Liam was an interesting man, she enjoyed his company, he was easy on the eyes, had a quick wit, seemingly like to flirt. This was the first time since Winston she'd felt any interest in getting to know a man better. Was she betraying Win?

She thought not. He'd always admired her interests and zest for living, all her appetites. He hadn't been a dried up old stick, himself. Every year there were girls in his classes who made no bones about finding him attractive. They'd send emails and write comments on their papers—nothing so out of line that they'd open themselves up for a harassment complaint. Invitations to parties or coffees or a drink, Comments about one-on-one tutoring. Usually, at the end of each semester, he'd do a class on Medieval art and include stained glass. Guest lecturer for part of that class was Roz, who came with a small power-point portfolio of her own work.

The invitations dropped off after that, every time.

CHAPTER THIRTY-EIGHT

The church's reactions to allegations of pedophilia in its ranks of parish priests must stop. Even after complaints in the U.S., and the volume of allegations in the Boston diocese, the patterns of abuse continue. Ireland, Poland, Australia. No place in the world is free of priests preying on children or worshippers.

Liam reread his words. Was this too strong? He stood up, paced around his living room. Decided it could stand as an introduction and went back to his laptop.

This book will examine one priest, his crimes, the church cover-up and his ultimate murder.

A proposal, something he was proposing to write. He would include his research, how Archbishop Malone and Henley Jackson were interrelated, interview some of the victims—wait a minute, he liked Roz' use of "survivors"—went back and changed it.

This book wouldn't be a psychological profile of who pedophiles were and why they existed. He wasn't able to do that depth of work, but he could interview some experts as an addendum to the story he wanted to tell.

He couldn't remember when this idea hit him. He'd always loathed people, he had to admit it was almost always men, who took advantage of their power and position. Whether it was police officers who used excessive force, men who sexually blackmailed women, soldiers who raped or men working with children. The older and stronger who assaulted the weaker, forcing them into a sort of sexual slavery, with the implied threat of violence if the weaker told anyone. And those who took advantage of their hold over children were the worst. Assault and molestation could and did happen in the family. But when parents turned their children over to organizations that were supposed to be a safe haven and they weren't, Liam's blood boiled.

It was particularly galling to him that the institution would put the secrecy of the assaulter ahead of the rights and health of the survivor. The church may have paid out millions to the children. Did this erase the lifetime of psychological problems that child felt? Not only did it happen, but the assaulter was never punished for his crime.

There was an incipient unfairness in this. Liam knew life wasn't fair. Maybe that's why he went into journalism, writing. To tell some stories to balance the bad that people faced every day.

Stop it, he told himself. If he started down this slippery slope again, he'd never get this written. Was it better to stew about the weak in the world, the starving children in India, the orphans who were made every day in the countries at constant war or to write a book that told the story of one abuse? He'd learned that telling one story to illuminate the whole made more impact. People could gloss over hundreds killed in a flood, an earthquake, genocide. When that large-scale death took on a human face, though, people reacted in a humane way.

Back at his laptop, he began adding to and fleshing out his outline. When he wrote fantasy he didn't plot out the book, he focused on the characters and the reasons for their behaviors. Way easier than this non-fiction. In his fantasy world, Liam could write anything he could imagine, and that was pure fiction.

This though, was fact. He was writing about events that happened, people who'd been damaged through no fault of their own. It had to be written in an interesting enough way that people, the readers, could empathize and relate to the survivors and their families. Creative non-fiction, and it was fashioned after Truman Capote's *In Cold Blood* and Dominick Dunne's books and articles about celebrities

He gave himself another five minutes to get a glass of water and wander, then sat down again. He was a professional and he'd taken this on for reasons he didn't completely understand. First was a deep-seated anger. He wasn't Catholic, but one of his friends growing up was and had been molested, once, after a communion lesson. The friend told his mother, his mother marched down to the church, told the priest off, got in touch with the bishop, filed charges with the church and the police and dragged the family off to the nearby Episcopal Church.

Second was the need to distinguish himself as a serious writer. His journalism pieces were good, his fiction had a following in the realm of fantasy, but he wanted to be known, wanted to be invited to one of the talk shows. He never told anyone about this, he was too embarrassed to be blatantly needy but the desire stayed there like an ember.

He typed the heading for Chapter VI and his cell rang. The screen said "Unknown." It was from the Boston area code.

"Hello?"

"Is this Liam Karshner?" A voice he didn't recognize. "You don't know me, and you don't need to know my name. Sam told me to call you."

"Is Sam OK?"

"He will be."

"What happened? Is he hurt?"

"He was run down by a hit-and-run driver. He has some broken ribs and a broken leg but they're letting him out of the hospital tomorrow."

Liam slumped back against his chair. "Oh my god, does anyone know why? Or who?"

"No, and Sam's not talking about it, except he told me."

"Why you? Who are you?"

"I told you, you don't know me. I'm Sam's lover. We've been together for four years. I know he was working the dark web for you. We think someone tracked him through those searches and went after him."

"Do they know what he was searching for?" If his friend had been run down because of what Liam asked him to find, he'd never live down that guilt.

"Not really. Neither do I. They followed him to some gay porn sires, some sex trafficking sites but people go to those places every day. He thinks they found out somehow that he works in TV and he might be working on an expose."

Holy crap, was this the search Liam asked him to do? "Why are you calling me?"

"When I went to the hospital today, he told me to call you and mail something off to you. I asked if he could wait until he got home and he could email you and he said no, that you didn't want an email record of it. I'm calling you on my phone so there's no record on his. What's your mailing address?"

Liam thought a split second then gave the caller his Hamilton address. Few people knew it and written correspondence went to his Portland home.

"Thank you for calling and please give him my best wishes. I'm so sorry this happened. I'll call him in a few days." Then there was dead air.

He was gobsmacked. Was this because of him? It must have been or why else did Sam's lover call? What had he found out? What was he sending? He figured he was probably being overly cautious telling Sam not to leave an email or phone call trail. Now Liam was in the clear and Sam, who was only doing a favor for a friend, was in the hospital.

How would he make this up to him?

CHAPTER FORTY

"Roz?"

"Hi Liam. What's up"

"Are you free? I'd like to come over and dive into the emergency rations."

Roz pulled the phone in front of her. Yep, it was Liam's number alright. What was all the secrecy?

"Sure, come on over." This time she didn't even bother to look in a mirror. He was curt, in a hurry, and he'd get what there was.

Minutes later Tut's ears perked up. Roz looked up and Liam was at her side door, frowning.

"Why are you lurking around my side yard?"

He sidled in the studio and closed the door after him. "I could use a glass of wine, how about you?"

"Uh…I guess. Come on in the kitchen." She kept glancing at him as she got two glasses down. Why was he skirting the question?

"Something's got you spooked. Are you going to tell me or do I play 20 questions?"

"I just got off the phone with some guy is Boston."

"There are probably a lot of guys in Boston…wait, is this your friend, Sam?"

"No, it was Sam's lover calling to tell me Sam's in the hospital, after a hit-and-run accident."

"Oh lord, is he OK?"

"He will be. They're releasing him tomorrow. He has some broken ribs and a broken leg. As bad as this is, it isn't all."

"What's the rest?"

"Sam asked his lover—no, he wouldn't tell me his name—to mail me a package today that was on his desk. The lover doesn't know what's in it and didn't even have my address,"

"That's pretty cloak-and-daggerish."

"I know." Liam took a swig of wine. "The lover told me that Sam was afraid someone had tracked him to the gay porn and pedophilia sites and was afraid that he, Sam, was going to do an expose on them."

"Is that what Sam does? Investigate?"

Liam shook his head, frowned again. "No, that's what makes me nervous."

"You? Why you."

"Because I was the one who asked Sam to go into the dark web. Asked him to specifically look at porn, gay porn and pedophilia, sites. I feel responsible for what happened."

"Wait a minute. Does anyone know for sure that the hit-and-run is connected to what Sam was doing?"

"No, not really." He stood up, paced to the French doors, gazed at the dunes. Turned back to her. "It could just be a pure accident. I doubt it. Sam had something ready to send me and this happened before he could. I'm the one who said I was worried that I might be traced. Wanted him to use old-fashioned communications that couldn't be tracked."

"Why don't you wait to see what's in the package? It may just be some innocuous information."

"Ha! If he found nothing, he'd just call me. I need to call his lover back. Tell him to tell Sam to buy a burner phone and send me the number on a postcard. Then I'll buy one, too."

Liam shoved the pieces like dominos, searching for the matches. If Sam found something, it shook someone's tree. Their reaction was fast and could have been deadly. Just a warning? A warning from who?

"I can't do a lot until I hear from Sam, either get the package or a burner phone number."

"Use my cell phone to call his lover. I still have my L.A. number. Only my landline is traceable to here. He can get a burner then call back with the number."

"Arrrugh. That's a head-desk."

"What?"

"I'm mentally hitting my head to get my brain working. Not a very good spy, I was making convoluted plans that would take weeks. Thanks for the voice of reason. Want to go with me?"

"Go where?" Roz looked at him, then down at her faded jeans and sweatshirt.

"To buy a phone. They have them at the hardware store." He noticed her assessing her clothes. "You don't have to even get out of the car. Since we're using your phone, I thought it might be better to have it with us, me."

"You can just borrow it." She went to get it from the counter, bemused. Liam always seemed together. This news must have gotten to him.

He pulled his car keys out, fiddling with them. "No. In case you get a call, I don't want to answer it."

"Liam, you're making this way more complicated. Take my phone. If someone calls and it's not the guy's number, let it go to voice mail. Come back, have a glass of wine while you wait for Sam to call on the burner."

"Gaaahhh. You're right. Be back soon." He took her phone, ran out the side door.

Roz stared after him. She didn't know him well, but this seemed to be out of character for him. He'd struck her as the kind of person who was capable, calm in emergencies, thought things out. When this was taken care of, when he found out what Sam had for him, maybe she'd get an answer to his odd behavior.

"Come on, Tut." It was turning out to be an unexpected day, she'd take advantage of it and surprise him with an afternoon run.

There were others out in the spring warmth, a couple holding hands as they walked, a male jogger running along the damp sand, Tut's usual track. She headed the opposite direction from the others, walked him for a while, then leaned over to unleash him. "Not too far," she said then wondered why she bothered. He wouldn't understand and wouldn't care. It made her feel better, though, a competent pet owner.

She let him go until he was a dot down the beach then whistled. It took three tries before he turned around and headed back. Why had she chosen to get a greyhound? She could have found a cute, fluffy lap dog, one who came when called and didn't rove far from home. But she didn't. She'd wanted a complete change, a challenge, wanted to have a companion who had some independence, and she'd gotten one in Tut.

Telling Liam she'd come to Hamilton for solitude, solace, anonymity was true, to a point. The routine she'd developed over the past few months was soothing. No one to have to care for, or about, no jarring incidents in her schedule, no surprises.

Then, boom. Jackson got killed. With one of her knives. The Cascadia Fault might as well have opened up, her world was so shaken. She was proud and pleased with herself that she was coping, asking questions, meeting people, getting a place in this small community. And making friends, maybe even with a man who could be more than a friend.

Coming over the dune, she saw Liam, pacing outside her studio, talking on a phone.

The errand hadn't taken long. Was it successful? From a distance it looked like he was using a much smaller phone than hers. She waved, he glanced up and waved back, still talking. She came up to him and he hit the end button. It was a different phone, he handed hers back.

"Well?" She took her phone.

"Well, Sam has a burner, I have his number, he'll be home from the hospital tomorrow morning. His lover overnighted the package a few minutes ago."

They started back into the house. "I know I don't know you well. This seems to have jolted you. I'm curious why."

In the kitchen, he rinsed out his glass and poured some wine. "It has, it did. Going along prying into people's lives to bring light on horrible crimes, horrific actions, is fine. Even good. These are people I don't know and don't care to know. Sam, though. And you. Are my questions, my probing, putting people I care about in danger? That possibility hit me like a sledgehammer."

CHAPTER FORTY-ONE

They sat at the kitchen island. Roz was absorbing Liam's confession, his fear. He cared for her?

"I don't want you to worry about me." She leaned her head on his arm. "You didn't involve me in this, someone else did. You're just helping me figure out who. And I care about you, too."

He blew out a breath. "I'm glad to hear that. The minute it was out of my mouth, I wanted to cram it back in. 'Stupid' I told myself. She's getting over that her husband was killed. She doesn't need to have some guy putting moves on her."

"I wouldn't call what you've been doing, 'putting moves' on me. You've been helpful, interesting, funny, nice and good company."

"As have you. You've even put up with the fish stuff."

"Fish stuff?"

"The stories from the guys at Jules, and Jurgen. Most women don't care about men beating their chests telling tales of machismo. You may not care about them, but you're polite enough to listen."

She laughed softly. "Thanks. It comes from always working with men. Most artists who work in large pieces like I do are men. And most of my commissions come from men. Not the first contact. If it's for a home, a woman usually calls first. But the architect, the builder, the installation crew, are men. I just listen, wait for them to get over themselves and sort out the information I need. Are you hungry?"

"I could eat something. I managed to miss lunch."

"I could make a sandwich, or I have some cheese. Just snacks?"

"Or, I could feed you at Jules."

She looked down at her clothes again. "I'm pretty disreputable."

"I'll wait for you to change, then. I want to run home and pick up my phone." At her questioning look, he said "My real one. I was rattled and ran over without it. Need to check my email."

She stood. "OK, I'll come over in a few."

In 15 minutes, she was at Liam's door. He'd left it open and waved her in while he finished writing an email. "Glad I checked. I just got an assignment to do a piece on wine. An airline magazine is putting together a package on the 'New Northwest, a survey of food and drink in Oregon and Washington'. Guess California is too trite."

"Do you know who's doing the food piece? You could tell them about the Fisherman's Friend."

"I'll mention it. Jugen has a good crowd now, I'm not sure he'd want more publicity. Drive or walk?"

They drove, found a parking spot behind Jules.

"Hmmm…not too busy. A quiet lunch?" Liam pocketed his keys and phone.

Inside, less than half the tables were full. The café was getting ready for dinner, but BethAnn pointed out a table by the window. As they ordered, Patsy came over. "Saw you guys through the widow. Wanted to tell you I talked to Chief Giffen about our questioning. He thanked me for the Neighborhood Watch aspect and said he'd have one of his guys go back and talk to Wes. No one ever mentioned the boys who visited the victim."

Of course not, Roz thought. You were the one who saw them most and kept it to yourself.

"Good, Giffen needs to follow up on that." Liam raised his coffee cup at BethAnn. "They may have been run-aways as you thought, Patsy, but if the Chief could track one of them down it would help the investigation."

Patsy glowed. "I also asked him about all the blood and he asked where I'd heard that. I told him I'd seen a lot of it when they came out with that awful, bloody knife."

Roz choked on water, spat.

"Are you OK?"

"It just went down the wrong way," Roz said, taking a slow breath. "I'm fine." She raced through her mind. Did she know that Patsy told Giffen the bloody knife was hers? She couldn't remember who'd said what to whom. That was the trouble with having a lot of information and trying to keep much of it under wraps.

"How are you going on identifying the man?" Liam chummed the water, fishing for any leads Patsy'd found.

"Nowhere, really. The chief did tell me the house was owned by a church group, an LLC? Is that the right term?"

"It is." Roz smiled at Patsy. The woman was too far away from the whole story to be able to find the truth, the connection. Her nosiness had been a catalyst to get Roz and Liam involved, now they'd gone beyond where Patsy's knowledge took her. A good thing. Patsy had no filters and spread the word better than social media.

"I need to run, I have to pick up my husband at the Boys and Girls Club. He volunteers there two days a week. Gives him exercise and get him out of my hair. See you?" She gave a jaunty salute and left.

A few others raised hands in recognition, but Liam and Roz finished their lunch without interruption.

"Now what?" Roz gathered up her phone and purse. "I have some work to do."

Liam pushed his chair back. "So do I. I let myself get pulled away this morning with the phone call from Sam's lover. It was important and may add to my research, but I'm way behind. I promised myself my agent would have the proposal by now."

"Do you have a deadline?"

"More of a self-imposed one. I've told my agent I want to write this and I'm sending a proposal, but no time set yet. It'll be a month or two before she starts bugging me for something. If not the proposal, an outline for another fantasy. If you let too long go between books, you can lose your audience."

"The price of fame?"

"Hah, you're more well-known than I am. You must have commissions lined up."

She grimaced and reached for the truck door. "Not lined up, no. I do have two people who want quotes on pieces to be done in the next year. I've told them that I swamped and will get back to them when I can."

He drove the short distance to her house in silence. In her driveway, he said. "Does it make you comfortable knowing that you have a few years work ahead of you?"

"It eases my money worries, sure. And it's nice to know my ideas and skills are in demnd. There's a bit of pressure, though."

He came around the truck, helped her out and held her hand to the door. "Being self-employed, relying on your wits and contacts to have income has ups and downs. I like the freedom, though."

She took her hand from his to unlock the door, turned to say good-bye and his lips brushed her cheek. She looked up at him startled.

"I'll see you tomorrow?" he said.

CHAPTER FORTY-TWO

There was a strange sound. Liam tried to pin it down. He fished around on the table next to the bed, hitting the alarm, his phone, then something unexpected. The burner phone was chiming.

"Hello?"

"It's Sam."

"Hey man, why are you calling so early?"

"Ah, you were asleep. It's 10 a.m. here, remember?"

"Sorry, I'm not functioning yet. How are you? Where are you?"

"I'm fine, sort of. I'm at home, Brad picked me up this morning."

"Brad, ah, that's his name. He wouldn't tell me."

"Yep." Sam's voice was quiet. "I told him not to tell you. You're digging around, well, I guess I'm digging around, in some nasty stuff. "

"You think the accident wasn't an accident?"

"Man, I don't know. Two witnesses said it was a black SUV with tinted windows and it sped up after it hit me. I just remember feeling a whoosh of air then I was on the ground, in a lot of pain. It wasn't a dead-on hit, a fender must have caught me."

"That's lucky. Brad said you had a package for me ready to go, except for my address."

"Yep, you'll get it today. When you take a look, and understand what it is, call me at this number. I don't think I can go much farther on this."

"That's cool. I don't want to endanger you anymore than I have. You've gone beyond what I asked. I'll call. Thanks."

Awake now, Liam made coffee, brought a cup to his work table and opened email. The contract for the magazine article was there as well as a note from the food writer, thanking him for Jurgen's information. The food guy said he'd try and make a quick trip down from Portland but if not, would at least mention The Fisherman's Friend, based on Liam's recommendation. "Love to find strange, out-of-the-way places, thanks," he'd ended with.

Liam was antsy. There was a lot riding on what was in the package from Sam—at least he hoped—and he couldn't settle down. He felt cooped up, it was a beautiful day, with a few puffy clouds and no morning overcast. His garden called. Grabbed a pair of leather gloves, a spade, clippers and headed out to trim and weed.

In the soft sun, he thought about the brief conversations he'd had with Jackson. Was there any clue there? Jackson's accent was so slight that Liam couldn't place it, which could have come from years of being moved around by the church. Particularly if Malone was watching out for him and assigning him to places far away from accusations.

How could anyone tell Jackson was a pedophile? They didn't look differently than anyone else, didn't act is a way that aroused suspicion. Their dangerous and aberrant desires weren't stamped on their foreheads. Initially, people trusted them, and trusted their children to them. Liam wasn't qualified or interested into delving into the why, there were professionals working on that. He wanted to tell the story on one, Jackson. He owed it to his friend.

He cut berry bushes back, trimmed rhododendrons and lopped off dead blooms. Pulled weeds from the daffodils and tulips that were breaking through, and his back was starting a low ache. One more chore, getting two planter beds ready for tomatoes, zucchini, cucumbers and green beans. Those would get planted in another couple of weeks, depending on the weather. Maybe even some strawberry sets. Fresh strawberries, in Champagne, to toast Roz' completion of the cathedral window, would be a good reward.

Enough work for one day, he put his tools away, went inside and took a shower. Clean, and with a nice ache in his muscles, he made some soft-boiled eggs and toast, sat down and began researching Washington and Oregon wineries. He was engrossed in the Willamette Valley when a knock at the door pulled him away. Before he could get there, the person left. Liam looked up and down the street then noticed an overnight envelop balanced against a pot on his porch.

It was from Boston, a return name and address Liam didn't recognize but it had to be from Sam. Cut it open and a thumb drive fell out. No note, nothing but the drive. Stuck it in his laptop and sat back to see what Sam found.

First file was a note from Sam.

"Liam, I may have hit the Mother Lode. It's more, and more frightening, than I suspected. I've copied most of this off the sites I found, but I've also listed links if you want to see it for yourself. I wouldn't advise it, though, these guys are born hackers and can follow any search you do. You don't want them digging around in your computer. I used an old IP and program that the station had from previous dives into dark web stuff, but they may be able trace me."

Liam stopped reading. Whoever "they" were they'd probably been able to trace the search to Sam. Was this the hit-and-run? Could he prove it? Went back to reading.

"In general, I found an IP that showed up a lot in the gay porn and kiddie porn sites. Got my hacker friend to track it and traced it back to a street address in Hamilton, Oregon. The screen name was 'godguy1956' and he was active in sharing pics of young boys. There was also another screen name, 'ettuirish' that showed up in the same groups. It could be 'et, tu, irish', maybe an alias for your archbishop Malone? The physical address is in Kansas City."

This was incredible, beyond what Liam thought he could get. He went into the kitchen, made another pot of coffee and prepared for a long haul at the computer. Should he call Roz? No, leave her alone for now. No matter what he assumed, or found out, about Malone, she still had a commission for the cathedral to finish. What Malone did in his private life had no bearing on that.

Yet, someone or something was dragging her in. The horrible message on her window. Being framed for Jackson's murder because of her knife. Did he owe her a front row spot for seeing whatever he discovered? If he didn't share it with her, was he trivializing her involvement, her emotions?

Knowing there wasn't a right answer, he opened the next file on the drive.

It was a listing of dates and times when "godguy1957" logged on to look at pictures and chat with others in the group. The conversations were comparing physical characteristics of the boys pictured, including their ages and locations. Some even included towns where they lived. Most of the conversations were masturbatory but some detailed actual meetings with the children.

Liam homed in on those from "godguy1957." They were fairly regular, about twice a week, then a flurry when he'd post new pictures. There wasn't any pattern for his postings. A batch of pictures, maybe six or seven, then he'd be quiet for a month or more. Then Liam hit a run of five batches of picture over a two-week period.

Sam hadn't zoomed in on the pictures but to Liam's eye, each batch looked like a single boy and they ranged in age from about ten to 14. Just on the edge of manhood. The recent batches, in the last five years, were boys in the older range. Did that match up with the date Jackson arrived in Hamilton? Could he have been preying on parishioners then, when he was "retired," he was forced to look elsewhere? Maybe Patsy's theory of run-aways wasn't so far-fetched.

In the last nine months Liam noticed "ettuirish" had joined in a discussion with "godguy1957" about two specific boys. The conversations centered around who the boys were, how old they were and where they were from.

And one chilling line. "I'll come and meet him at your place."

CHAPTER FORTY-THREE

After spending an hour pacing and dithering with ideas, Liam put together a spreadsheet with "godguy1957" postings, dates and interactions with "ettuirish" over the last five years.

He couldn't tell whether the two men had gotten together earlier or just talked online about the boys. "godguy1957" spent time in chat rooms with a lot of other users over the years, but his direct interactions with "ettuirish" were less than ten, and only two were about "coming to meet him."

He had only one firm date, when Molly, who turned out to be Wes' wife, saw a boy at Jackson's back door. Liam plugged that into his spreadsheet, but no conversations popped up. For the three weeks before that, though, there was a posting of photos of one specific boy and a discussion about meeting him.

If "ettuirish" was Malone, he wouldn't be able to just drop everything and get to Hamilton, his movements were scheduled in advance and he didn't travel alone. With a date range of about a month, Liam needed to go to Portland and look for church records of an archbishopric visit.

He stuffed a few things into a travel bag, called a friend who used to cover religion and headed out. Just north of Salem, he kicked himself. He hadn't called Roz. He pulled into the Fred Meyer gas station in Salem to call her then realized where he was. Had the receipt been traced?

She answered on the fifth ring, just as he was getting to leave a voicemail.

"Ah, is this you?"

"Who did you think it was?" Roz' voice was terse.

"I meant I thought I was getting voicemail. It's Liam."

"I know. What's up? I hear traffic."

"I'm in Salem, on my way to Portland. I found some interesting stuff on the thumb drive Sam sent me. That's what was in the package." He gave her a brief run-down of what he'd discovered and that he'd put all the dates and conversations into a spreadsheet. "We'll go over it when I get back. I'm tracking down Malone's travel. And right now, I'm getting gas at the Fred Meyer in Salem. Have you heard anything about the receipt you gave Giffen?"

"No. I'll call him today. When are you coming back?"

"If I can get with my guy today, tomorrow. And, if you can stomach it, I want you to look at some pictures."

"Ugh, porn?"

"I'll blow them up and crop out the explicit stuff. Maybe even show one to Molly."

"You think it's the murderer?"

"No, if this is one of Jackson's victims, I think he's too young I'll call you and see you tomorrow."

Roz stared at the phone. She had no strings on Liam, but there was a disquiet that he'd opened the drive, had time to make a spreadsheet and headed to Portland, all without telling her. She was the one in danger, she was probably being framed for Jackson's murder, although Giffen had been careful not to make her feel watched and suspected. It was time to take better control of the investigation, or whatever it was. She called the police department and made an appointment to meet with Chief Giffen.

She had to wait a few minutes in the lobby of the police department while the Chief finished up a phone call, then he motioned her into the interrogation room. Roz was surprised, then thought it was better. She knew this room would have cameras and she wanted everything she said recorded.

"What can I do for you, Ms. Duke?"

Ah, Ms. Duke, this was going to be formal.

"I was wondering if you'd been able to track down the receipt, who bought the things at Fred Meyer? I'm not usually nervous, but I've had some unwelcome visitors lately."

"I realize, but we don't have a lot to go on. Whoever is doing the stalking or break-ins has been careful. No, we don't have an answer back from the crime lab yet on the surveillance camera at Fred Meyer. I'm hoping tomorrow. Oh, I do have a small piece of news. The peeping toms you had after the Neighborhood Watch meeting? The ones who Clarence warned off with the shotgun? It was two high school boys. They'd watched everyone leave and were looking for something small to steal."

"High school boys? Did you catch them?"

"Catch isn't quite the right word. Their parents brought them in after word of Clarence's escapade got around town. The parents wanted to scare the kids, told them they could have been shot."

"Did you arrest them?"

"No, we let them go with a strong warning and 20 hours of community service. They're on clean-up patrol at the town beach. Did you have anything else?"

Roz took a deep breath, squinched her eyes shut. "I wanted to talk about the murder weapon."

"Ah, yes, the bloody knife."

"Yes, well, first I want to thank you for not assuming I had anything to do with the murder. Second, I wanted to ask you if the break-in or the peeping tom incidents have anything to do with who stole the knife from me."

"Things are related, Ms. Duke. I understand you talked to Det. Robeson about you being somehow responsible for your husband's death."

Whoa, wait a minute, she thought. That was a strong statement. And had Giffen and Robeson become buddies? "I don't think 'responsible' is an accurate description, chief. There are some coincidences that make me wonder. He was shot in front of a mall that we didn't shop at. But the mall commissioned me to do a window for them."

"Was he there to look at the window?"

Roz was quiet. "I have no idea, why would he?"

"Let's go down a different street. You use dangerous things in your work, right?"

"Not dangerous. The glass could cut you. And the knives are sharp, but the blades are short. Except for the one that was stolen, I deliberately had a longer blade on that one because I needed a longer reach for some of the leads. I even use an X-acto knife for some work, not a good murder weapon unless you managed to hit a major artery."

"Whoever this was, he managed to hit quite a few major arteries judging from the blood. And a lot of the wounds were…" He paused, and Roz said, "In his genitals. Liam said his penis was almost severed."

"It's such a pleasure having lay people run around with confidential information. This is why law enforcement doesn't share everything. I thought Karshner would keep quiet."

"He only told me recently, when we talked about pedophile priests. That seems like such a motive."

"It does to us, too, Ms. Duke. Most things point to a dislike, hatred, of the Catholic church. Here you sit, working for the church, handling the murder weapon. Someone steals it from you, Clarence sees someone watching you, someone breaks in and trashes your work, leaving a nasty anti-church slur on your window. And you've managed to learn things about the murder that aren't common knowledge—the cross on the wall in blood."

"Even I would wonder if I was involved." She paused. She was involved, who was she kidding? "I guess I mean actively." She grimaced. "Good thing we both know that's not the case."

"Yes, if that's the case."

Now was the time for the theory. "It is the case. I think I'm being framed. Someone has put the pieces together of what I do, figured out that if they stole my knife I'd be implicated."

CHAPTER FORTY-FOUR

***On** my way back. Do you want me to stop and pick anything up? Wine? Fingerprint powder?*

Oh, ha ha Roz thought, reading Liam's text. It was better that he'd regained some of his humor. She'd worried at his letting his control slip and show his concern about her. It was nice that someone cared, but the trade-off for caring might be to lose some of her regained strength and balance. She didn't intend to be overcome by another man who'd learn her secrets, fears and intimate thoughts. She wasn't going to take a chance on losing him again.

No, I'm fine. Come on by when you get into town. Short and to the point, she thought.

She was cutting glass when he tapped on her side door, making her jump and taking a nick out of her finger.

"Damn, Liam, don't sneak up on me like that."

"It's a little hard to understand you with your finger in your mouth. Did I make you do that?"

"Yep, and now I'm going to the bathroom to get a bandage." Then she noticed he had a paper bag, a bottle of wine and a sheaf of papers in his arms. "Set that stuff down on the island, I'll be right back."

"Since it's my fault, I'll help you." He trailed after her, putting the bag, wine and papers down and following her into the bathroom.

She poured peroxide into the small nick and handed him a bandage. "Open this and wrap it around, tight. It should stop bleeding soon. In the meantime, what's in the bag?"

"I stopped and got Thai." He stared at her. "Do you like Thai?"

"I do. A lot. Is there a Thai place here?"

"No, this is imported. The wine's pretty local though."

Roz narrowed her eyes. Whatever spooked him had been resolved. The teasing, light, flirty Liam was back and she was glad.

"Let's start with the news first. I spent some time with Chief Giffen yesterday. They have no leads on the vandals, haven't gotten anything back on the Fred Meyer receipt and he finally told me about the wounds, genital wounds, on Jackson. When he laid out all the information they found out about me—everything from my theory of involvement in Winston's murders to my links with the church to my knife being the murder weapon—I had to admit I'd make a good person of interest. Then we chatted a bit about me being framed. I think he believes that, but it doesn't get us any closer to the murderer."

She could smell the food as they came back to the kitchen and her mouth watered. Liam reached over the counter and pulled two wine glasses out of the cupboard.

"Dang, you're finding your way around." Roz leaned her head on her uninjured hand.

"I have to, you're the walking wounded."

"Right. Have you ever looked at my hands?" She colored. "I mean my fingers? I have enough small scars that they probably couldn't get decent prints off me. If I don't cut myself several times for each commission, I haven't done it right."

He poured wine, moved the bag of food to the countertop under the cupboard and started shuffling through the stack of papers.

"Is that all the spread sheet stuff you did?"

"And some. I managed to get the Portland diocese's newsletter and press releases for the past year, but I haven't sorted through them yet. And if you can, I'd like you to look at a few of the photos I found."

"I never saw any of Jackson's visitors!"

"I know, but these boys could have been around the neighborhood for a day or so before they went to visit. We're shooting in the dark. I think we're getting a better picture, but we don't know what we don't know." He separated stacks of paper. "These are the diocese's records. It should go fast, we're only looking for mention of the archbishop's visits. This stack is the spread sheets I did on connections between Jackson and Malone."

He paused. "I need to be careful. This is assumption still. Don't want to miss something because I'm so focused on those two."

Roz eyed the stacks. "That's an awful lot of paper to go through. We could be here for days."

"Hah, welcome to the glamorous world of investigative journalism. Or for that matter, law enforcement. It's not all spying and guns and arresting and phone calls from Deep Throat."

"Point taken." She started flipping the stack of newsletters and releases from the diocese. Half an hour in, she stopped and stood, stretching her back. "They have a lot of activities; Scout groups, catechism classes, confirmations, group counseling for young marrieds, potlucks, alter society meetings, plus listings for all the masses at all the churches in the area. No mention of any archbishop visits, though."

"Here, let's look through the communications. It's at least in order." He spread the printouts across the island in rows, sorted by date. "I didn't include all the times 'godguy1957' went on line. There were places when he was chatting for an hour or more several times a week. I pulled out the dates he uploaded pictures, particularly in the last five years. Each upload was maybe ten or more photos of the same boy. Do you want to see the pictures?

Oh my god, did she? Intellectually, she thought she knew what the photos would look like but emotionally could she handle looking into the eyes of a young boy being forced to do things no child should know about? She steeled herself.

"Yes, I'll look at the photos. How many are there?"

"I'll just show you the ones from the last year. I think I counted 15 different boys." He thumbed through the stack. "Here they are."

Roz peeked through her fingers, not quite sure what she'd see. In fact, they were somewhat normal photos of a boy, pre-pubescent, standing or sitting. The difference was that he was naked and the photographer had moved him into provocative poses. His back to the camera, coyly turning his head and smiling. Him leaning down and looking back at the camera from between his legs. Him on a couch with one leg up, slung over the arm. And half-a-dozen of just his genitals, still child-like.

She moaned. "Why did I look? I don't like any kind of porn." She looked again, studying his face in the ones he was seated. "He's so young, a child. So innocent. How could anyone deliberately take that away from him?" She turned to Liam. "If this is Jackson, maybe I don't want to find his murderer."

"Strong words. I do know what you mean, though. Even if it's Jackson, he's only the symptom of the problem. One man out of the thousands who prey on children. Pedophiles, abusers, sex traffickers have been around since we lived in caves and no one noticed or cared. It's probably good that the age of technology has brought much of this into the open. Well, not open but findable if you know where to look. The bad part is that there's volumes of it and of users, the good part is that law enforcement is able to track them now."

"Which are the most recent ones? Are there any where we could just crop it to head and shoulders and show it to Molly and Wes? And maybe even Clarence? If he was here for a day or so, they may have seen him but not realized he was 'visiting' Jackson."

"My thoughts, too. Here, these were uploaded over the last six months." He pulled out pictures of three boys, two dark-haired and one with long blond hair. "Jackson didn't seem to be too interested in coloring, but he never went for any who were African-American or Asian or looked Hispanic or Latino. That would have made them more memorable locally."

CHAPTER FORTY-FIVE

Liam went home to crop and print the pictures, leaving Roz to continue through the diocese newsletters.

When he came back, she handed him some sheets. "I think this is what we're looking for." It was a newsletter from two months ago with a story that a Sunday Mass would be led by Archbishop Malone. "We are honored to have the Archbishop here with us for this event" the story gushed.

"Good work. That's it exactly. What are the dates." He cross-referenced them to the spread sheets, found a match with the upload of pictures. "Here we go. Malone was in the area, at least in Portland, when this boy was here. It probably wasn't the boy Molly saw, a little too early. But we have dates. I wonder if we could pin Clarence down?"

They looked at each and frowned. "You know him and the town better than I do." Roz tapped her lips, wincing as she remembered the bandage.

"It's worth a try. Want to go over now? Catch him before he's too many beers down the road?" Liam picked up the cropped photos and Roz grabbed the newsletter which had a picture of Malone.

The smell of pad thai hit her again. "Can we eat when we get back?"

Liam laughed. "That'll give us incentive to cut to the questions. Fast and done."

Clarence was home and didn't slur his speech or lose his balance. Roz thought they'd hit at a good time. "Hi. Do you have a minute for a few more questions?"

"Sure. Come on in. Can I get you a beer or something?" The older man must be sober to be able to put his visitor's manners on.

"No thanks, we have some dinner waiting." Liam was matter-of-fact, not wanting curtness to put Clarence off. "We have some pictures of a young man and an older man, as well as a date when he could have been here."

"Dates run together for me. I don't track them much anymore, but I'll try." Clarence held his hand out for the pictures. "Hmmm, I don't recognize the young one. The old guy, maybe." He squinted his eyes. "What's the date?"

Liam gave him the four-date spread that Malone was in Portland. He could have driven down in the late evening any of the days. "It's a Thursday, Friday, Saturday, Sunday, if that helps."

Clarence stared at Malone's picture. "This could have been the guy who visited the dead guy. Let me think." Silent for a few seconds, then, "I had a meeting of the Fishermen's Society that weekend. Friday night we held a fish fry to make money." He turned to Roz. "We go to a couple of salmon or crab festivals every year up and down the coast. This way, we rent a bus in case anyone drinks too much to drive." He giggled.

"Yep, I think this guy showed up that Friday night. I was getting ready to go down to the hall and help the last cooking shift."

"Thanks, Clarence, this is good." Roz smiled and took a step back.

"Now that I remember, there was one odd thing. When I got home, the car was still there. I thought those guys were too old for a sleepover."

"Clarence, you've been extremely helpful." Liam shook Clarence's hand, stepped off the porch and began walking toward Roz' house. She waved good-bye to Clarence and ran. "Hey, hey, wait up!"

She caught up to him just as he reached the side door. "Don't say anything yet. I wanted to whoop for joy, but don't want Clarence asking why we're so pleased. You know if we make a big deal of it, it'll be all over town by tonight."

Roz pulled her key out. "You're right, but let's get inside and jump up and down." She saw Liam smile at the key and this time, did stick her tongue out. "OK, you were right, but don't get all puffed up about it. Let's go stick the food in the microwave and plan next moves."

Over dinner, they got Malone's visit tied to the same date that Jackson posted the pictures of one of the dark-haired boys. This visit had been set up six weeks earlier when "ettuirish" asked "godguy1957" if he had any "new friends" because "ettuirish" was planning a trip. "godguy1957" said yes and they set a date.

Liam thought Roz' eyes looked worried. "Do you think Malone is still molesting boys? Or do you think he's covering up for Jackson?" She stopped taking and stared. "Or is he covering up for more priests? How many parishes are in a diocese, anyway?"

"I have no idea. I think a lot. Regardless of now, Malone has been a rising star in the church hierarchy for a few decades. He could possibly know thousands of priests."

The scope of what they may have uncovered made Roz' head reel. Until the Boston *Globe* broke the scandal in the Boston diocese, most of the pedophile priests were individuals, accused by parents in their parishes and moved elsewhere by the church. A few had actually been arrested, tried in a civil court and were serving sentences. If Liam was right, they'd uncovered a systemic pattern involving parishes at least across the Americas that were being protected by men working their way up the ladder of church authority.

"OK, before we leap off into the sublime, let's focus on what we know. We know; 1, a man was murdered; 2, we know he had some visits from an old man who arrived by car; 3, we know that occasionally he was visited by boys who came to his back door; 4 we know that at least two of the boys were seen by reputable witnesses; 5, we know the house the murdered man lived in is owned by the Eastern Diocese of Kansas; 6, we know that Henley Jackson lives or lived at that house; 7, we know that someone in that house spent a lot of time on the deep web, looking at and interacting with porn and pedophilia sites."

"And we know he was murdered using one of my knives." Roz didn't want that overlooked.

"We do know that. Can we pull all these facts together into a whole that would stand up in court? Or can become a best-selling book?"

"The LAPD always went over the motivation as well as the means. The means in Winston's death was the gun. Neither the cops nor I could figure out the motivation, though. They thought I may have had a motive—he was having an affair with one of his students, he had control of money, one of us had a problem with abuse, drugs, alcohol, gambling—and either I found out or he found out that I knew and I had to kill him. Nonsense, and they finally realized it. They're still hung up on motive, they don't have one."

"Nice speech." Liam was up, putting left-overs back into cartons, stacking dishes in the sink. "Are you saying we don't have a motive yet?"

"Yep, that's pretty much what I'm saying." She moved to load the dishwasher. "Hating a pedophile, blind anger at a priest who's taken advantage of a son or a brother or a relative. Those all could be motives for killing someone and we know, in the abstract, that Jackson did that. Took advantage, probably right up until his killing. We may have a motive, but we don't have a suspect."

"*Au contraire*, we have too many suspects. If we assume Jackson molested, say, two boys a year, not an extraordinary number, and did it for 35 years until he was forced to retire, that's 70. And we know he continued after he retired, maybe even stepped it up a notch because he didn't have access to as many boys. We could be looking at close to a hundred survivors. How would we even begin to look for them?"

"Wait, just wait. That's negative thinking. We're not trying to find, or prove, that Jackson was a pedophile, we're only trying to find the one person who murdered him."

CHAPTER FORTY-SIX

"Oh…oh!" Roz threw the dishtowel across the room.

"What? What did I do?" Liam scanned the room for broken crockery, cracked wineglasses, missed cutlery, an escape hatch.

"You didn't do anything. It's that son-of-a-bitch!"

Liam had known a few sons-of-a-bitches in his life, but he didn't think Roz had met any of them. "Is this a particular one? Do I know him?"

"Yes, that bastard, Malone. *Archbishop* Malone. He came to my house a few days ago. I entertained him. We had lunch together. And all this time, he's laughing at me, at my simplistic chatter about the area, how serene and peaceful it is. How I'm loving the solitude. And that, that…liar has been here. Across the street from me."

She started off to her studio, murder in her eye, but Liam rushed to the door to stop her. "Don't get too upset!"

"I want to smash every piece of that window! Crumble it into a mass of lead and toss it into a bonfire. That, that…"

"Before you can come up with every cuss word you've ever heard, listen to me."

She stopped her rant because Liam had hold of her arms. He spoke directly to her. "Think about this. This is a commission for a cathedral. Sure, he's the archbishop, but the cathedral is for all the church, for all the people. You said you were working with the architect, the building committee, the bishop. Those are people who represent the congregations. Malone is just a man. He can and will be replaced with another man called Archbishop. The people are interchangeable, the cathedral will last for years. Centuries, maybe."

His words seeped in, dribs and drabs as though through a clogged drain. "Are you religious? I know you're not Catholic."

He reached out and smoothed her hair. "No, I'm not at all religious, but I can respect others who are. I have no beliefs, guess I'm an atheist. I'm astounded, though, at the beauty of things, objects, buildings that people of faith, all faiths, have made as worship for their gods. It's terrible and unfortunate that there are some who demean and deface that faith and beauty, but those are just the people. Not the buildings, not the congregations, not the faith."

She leaned against his chest. "You're amazing. I know you're at least as upset as I am. Maybe more. But you can disassociate the man from the title, the job. Even the faithful who are being duped."

"That's just it, they're being duped. A lot of people in this world get duped every day. By politicians, by conmen, by liars, by thieves, by self-titled men of god. They lose their innocence, their families, their money, their beliefs because some guy shows up and convinces them to give it away. That doesn't make the people bad or stupid, just misled.

"Look at you. You've said you're not religious, yet you make these amazing, soaring designs in glass that lift eyes and souls, searching for something beyond themselves. And what you make transcends the individual men who pay you."

Roz pushed back and stared at him. "Are those some of your writerly words? You use them well. I was on my way to smash things, to grind them into little pieces like I want to do to Malone. Maybe I'm not sorry Jackson was killed." She looked into his eyes and saw truth and caring. "Thank you."

"Come out on the deck and we'll look for a green streak." He tugged her arm.

"It's too early."

"A bit, but I think there's nothing to help you remember how small a speck you are, and how little our problems and hatreds are than watching the sea and the sunset."

She took a deep breath, put Tut on his long leash, picked up the bottle of wine and led the way. Liam followed with two glasses and sweatshirts, for any breeze that might come up.

Leaning comfortably on the rail of the deck, she scanned the sea and the sky. Far out she could see the outline of a freighter headed north and a fishing boat headed in. A couple walked the edge of the water, their arms wrapped around each other, their dog running up to the hissing waves and jumping back. Birds, starlings she thought, swirled like looping clouds of smoke, feeding before settling down for the night. As she watched, a mist of yellow came low across the dune grasses then veered off towards the forest.

"What are those?" She was entranced.

"A flock of wild canaries. There are some along the coast as far south as California."

"They can't be native?"

"They're not. It's supposed that some canaries got loose, or were let out, by owners who didn't want to take care of them anymore. They managed to find one another and breed."

"How strange." She was looking at the flight path the birds took.

"Not really. Horses, cows, sheep, goats were all brought here from Europe and got loose. The strongest were the pigs. Domesticated when they got here, they became feral and took over a lot of territory. And how about the parrots of Telegraph Hill in San Francisco?"

Roz laughed. "You win! I guess I'm learning not to make off-hand comments to a writer. Where'd you get all this from?"

"Oh, I don't know. Weird places, odd books and papers. I love to read, so just pick up different and obscure things. It's a dubious pastime. On the other hand, I used to beat everybody at Trivia and friends tell me I should try out for Jeopardy."

She looked at him, his profile. A smile teased the corner of his mouth and she had an overwhelming desire to kiss it. What? What was she thinking? What would Winston think? A wave of melancholy rolled over her like an incoming fog bank. Winston *wouldn't* think, about anything anymore. She shivered.

"Cold?" Liam handed her a sweatshirt.

"A little chilly. Maybe someone walked over my grave." She made her smile reach her eyes. "Thank you for talking sense to me. A year or so ago, I was just going along, married to a man who I adored, working in stained glass and getting an international reputation. Then one day, two men came to my house. Archbishop Malone and the head of the building committee. They were finishing a new cathedral in Colorado and wanted to talk to me about a commission for a window over the nave. It seems so innocent now."

"What you're suffering from is knowledge. You have first-hand experience about the changeability of life, the transitory nature of it, the ability of people to wear different masks."

She turned her back to the ocean. "I'm not sure I'm happy with this knowledge. It was simpler believing I knew where everything belonged and that it wouldn't change."

"Would you want to go back? Oh, lord, what a stupid question. Of course you would." Liam smacked his forehead.

"Yes, I would. But I'm finding out that I have strengths I never knew about. Can make decisions I thought were too hard. It never crossed my mind that I could live after Winston died. That I could find creativity and joy in making different pieces, stretching my craft, even teaching others. I thought I'd always live in L.A. Loved the hectic pace of life, the way ideas bubbled up, burst and were replaced. Loved watching all the people…what a variety! Different races, different cultures, different ages. At the Farmer's Market you could see Hassidic Jews mixing with guys in kuffiyeh head scarves, Chinese women trying to talk to their grandchildren who sported Mohawks dyed red and green, piercings in their cheeks, tongues."

Liam laughed. "And here you are in Hamilton. Oregon, where the broadest cultural difference you see is when the retired fishermen take off their winter flannels and expose their white arms. Or the tourists walk funny because they forgot sunscreen because it was cold on the beach, and everybody knows you can't get a sunburn when it's cold or overcast."

By now, she'd sloughed off her melancholy, laughed out loud. "More writerly words!"

"I may not be a best-seller—yet—but it's nice to know that my words affect people. You're being too hard on yourself. You've been through a major life trauma and now you're facing another. Pollyanna I ain't, but there is a lot of good in your life."

CHAPTER FORTY-SEVEN

Liam was right she thought, as she sipped her coffee and waited at the driftwood tree for Tut to finish his run. The beach was sunny, one of those clear mornings she hadn't gotten used to yet. No overcast, no mist, no high fog, just sun so bright it made the tops of the small waves sparkle, as though electrified.

She had gone through an event she wished on no one. Winston's killing had fractured her world far more than she'd let herself believe. Only here, now, in this place where the ocean whispered its ceaseless knowledge, could she take out the anger, the grief and examine it, turn it over in her mind. It frustrated her because she wasn't finding the why. There had to be a reason he was killed and she couldn't see it, couldn't find it. She had to begin to let it go. There were other things, terrible movements, happening right now.

Life was happening. Someone had invaded her space, stolen something close to her, used it to kill another person. There was also work to do. Tut to care for. Possible feelings for another man bubbling up inside her that needed to be nurtured.

As disorganized as she felt, Roz was a list-maker. Writing things down, making tasks solid, let her take them out of her head. Once they were physically put somewhere, she looked at them objectively, checked them off, accomplished them, felt satisfied.

Today's list began with packaging up and sending off two orders for Van Gogh's *Sunflowers*, a perennial favorite in her catalogue. While downtown, a quick visit to By the Sea. Were there any sign-ups for a stained glass class or was it only going to be demonstrations? The need to pry information about her knife out of people was fading, now that she knew there were specific reasons for Jackson's stabbing.

A quick lunch at Jules? A chat with Patsy? Roz didn't want to call her and make it a formal date, better just running into her. She wouldn't share any of the information she and Liam gathered. Was there a way to show her some of the boys' pictures, the head and shoulders shots? Once the car was packed with boxed-up kits, she stood for a minute. Should she?

No harm, no foul. Roz ran back to the kitchen island, snagged the prints of the last three visitors, hugged Tut, slammed out the front door, remembering to lock it.

One person had signed up as interested in lessons at By the Sea. "Don't be discouraged." Betty stopped stocking shelves with guides to the Oregon coast. "It's not even summer yet. Once school lets out, you'll have more. Moms will either sign up themselves to get away from the kids or they'll sign their kids up."

This was a possibility Roz hadn't imagined. Older kids, teens, maybe OK, but not younger ones. "Do you think I need to say there's an age limit? I can't have little ones cutting themselves on glass."

"I think I'd wait. Most people won't want their young kids messing around with glass and knives. Will you want to do demonstrations again this weekend?"

"Maybe Sunday." Roz hesitated. Betty was on a need-to-know basis and what Roz planned was way beyond her need. "Right now, I'm off to mail some stuff then drop in for a quick bite at Jules." She waved at Betty, got the packages from her car, went into the post office/gift shop.

It was almost noon as she pushed the door open at Jules and the place was packed. She looked around, saw Patsy about to sit at a small table. Waved, made her way over, only having to step over one child sobbing on the floor.

"This is crazy! I thought I was early enough. Are you alone? Mind if I join you?"

"Get used to it, it'll be this way until probably November." Patsy pointed to an empty chair. "Grab that one and sit. They won't take it from you then. What brings you downtown today?"

What to start with? "I had to send some kits off and stopped by By the Sea to check if anyone signed up for my class."

"And did anyone?" Patsy smiled at BethAnn who brought two waters then scooted off again.

"One person. I'll give it a few days before I get in touch with any of them to set a time. I imagine it'll mostly be locals."

"Don't bet on it. There are people who rent houses and cabins around here for weeks at a time during the summer. Hamilton in the summer is different from Hamilton in the winter, even though our seasons don't change that much. More fog and rain in the winter, less in the summer." Patsy slowed. "Have you had any feedback on our interviews?"

Dropped into her lap. Roz almost forgot her speech she'd worked up to get into that conversation. "Well, sort of. Maybe. I think." She took a breath, told her herself to stop being a doofus and said, "Liam got some pictures."

"Pictures? Of what? How?"

Careful now, Roz said "He worked with someone he knows in Portland, got some pictures he thinks might be young boys who were run-aways. Not high profile one like the ones that go to Amber Alerts. More like kids who were in group homes or foster care kind of thing. I've looked at them, but they don't mean anything to me. I've never seen these boys before."

"Let me see. Maybe I have."

Roz told her conscience this wasn't sinful. She hadn't lied to Patsy, the woman asked in her own right. "Hang on." She pulled the papers out of her bag. "These were ones he found."

Patsy took the prints and stared at them. "I can't be sure about all of them, but these two I've seen." She tapped the photos of the blond and one of the dark-haired boys.

"You have? Where?"

"At the neighbor's back door. Both times it was just dusk and I didn't clearly see their faces until the man opened the door. It looked like they knew each other."

"Knew each other? How?"

"Maye not knew each other, but that the man expected the boy. He reached out his hand and put it on the boy's shoulder, kind of welcoming him in." Quiet. Then, "Come to think of it, it was kinda like he pulled the boy inside. Like he didn't want anyone to see,"

BethAnn was back. Patsy said, "Club sandwich," without looking at the menu so Roz went with the flow. "Me, too. And iced tea?" BethAnn whisked off.

"Jeez, Patsy, that sounds a little, I don't know, clandestine?"

"See, that's why I told you they might be run-aways. Didn't want anyone to see them, report them to the police."

"Ah, and you probably were right. I'll tell Liam this and…"

"No, don't!" Patsy shushed Roz. "If those boys were running away, running to a safe place, I don't want them to get picked up. The man is dead now and whatever was going on with the boys is over. I want them to be safe."

Oh lady, Roz had difficulty keeping silent. If only you knew what you're saying. Out loud, she said, "Alright, I won't tell him I showed you the pictures or that you saw the boys. And I hope you're right, that they're safe now."

CHAPTER FORTY-EIGHT

If Hamilton had a speed limit, Roz broke it driving home. She waited until she was in the front door before punching Liam's number in, then bounced back and forth on her toes until he answered.

"Guess what?"

"Who's calling, please?"

"Liam, no time for games! I just had lunch with Patsy."

"OK, that's big news. What did our pal have to say?"

"She recognized two of the boys!"

"You showed her the pictures?"

"Just three of the most recent."

"Well, well. Things are tying together nicely. Good work. Are you free now?"

"Uh, sure. Why?"

"Come on over. We'll take a couple pictures and go visit Molly and Wes."

Roz had to pass Jackson's house to round the corner to Liam's. The crime scene tape was tattered, trailing in pieces across the bushes and porch. The house looked forlorn, as through it was embarrassed at what had gone on inside. "It wasn't your fault," Roz whispered as she came around to the back then stopped.

There was the back porch, three steps up from the yard. A metal pipe acted as a handrail for the unadorned cement steps. The porch was small, screened in with a screen door. A fixture as big as a shop light hung down from the porch's ceiling and would have illuminated anyone on the steps or the porch. Jackson would probably have left the door into the house open as he came out on the porch to let the boys in. He wouldn't have wanted them to stand outside for any length of time.

Roz shivered. Until now, she hadn't paid any attention to the house, it was one just like all the others, unremarkable. Not interesting, like hers. Not a cottage like Liam's. Just a middle-class two-story house, a well-kept if unimaginative yard with a space marked off for a vegetable garden. Would it ever be normal again? House a family? Have children running up the stairs, a yard with a swing set, lawn littered with bikes and toys?

Liam stood at his door and watched her walk slowly up his front path. "What's eating you? A minute ago you were effervescent with news, now you look like a funeral march."

"It's the house. Jackson's house. Walking by it and knowing what when on inside just made me sad."

"The murder? Yep, a lot of houses where someone was murdered, or even where someone died, never recover. That reputation stays with them."

"It's not just the murder. I took a good look at the backyard. I never paid attention to the cyclone fencing, but now I see exactly what Patsy watched, what Wes and Molly saw. Where are those boys now? Will they ever recover?"

"Ah, hard questions. Come on in and have a glass of wine."

"I don't think I want any alcohol. Tea, maybe?"

"Tea it is. Which pictures did Patsy recognize?"

Roz sat and pulled the pictures out again, "I showed her these three and she recognized these two." She tapped one of the dark-haired boys and the blond.

"Good. We'll take those to Molly and Wes. I think we're homing in on what happened when."

"Does this tell us who the murderer was, though?"

"Not yet, but when we get all the dates together, with all the players, we'll be close."

They drank tea, chatted about the warm day and she asked Liam if it was too crowded in Hamilton during the summer. "Too crowded? Well, it's different. All the restaurants are packed, lines at the grocery store, no place to park at the beach. The merchants love it, though. They rely on the four or so months with heavy tourist traffic to get them through the winter. The couple who own the antique store have an RV and head off to a campground in Arizona for the winter. It's peaceful then and I look forward to it."

Roz sighed. "We've put this off long enough, probably. Let's head out."

Liam nodded in agreement, then picked up a complete set of pictures and they went across the street to Wes and Molly's.

The couple was home, Molly offered coffee, Wes offered beer, drinks were turned down. They moved to the kitchen table where Liam laid out his pictures. "I talked to a friend in Portland who works with run-away youth—not the Amber Alert kind, mostly from group and foster homes." Roz marveled that independently she'd come up with the same story for Patsy. This was good.

"I asked for some pictures and they sent these. These boys have gone missing over the past year or 18 months. I wondered if you recognized any of them?"

"Hmm," and "Umhum." Both Molly and Wes were responding.

"This one," Wes picked up the picture of the blond boy, "this is the one I saw that night pacing in the yard. Then he finally went up the steps and man let him in. I guess the light reflected off his hair."

"You may have seen him, but this is the one I saw that Thursday afternoon." Molly picked up the picture of a dark-haired boy.

"Any others?" Liam spread the pieces of paper out across the table.

Both Wes and Molly shook their heads. "No, those are the only ones I recognize," Molly said. "It's a shame to have so many run-aways."

"It is. Social service organizations are constantly trying to figure out ways to keep the boys safe, in housing and counseling situations where they bond and stay, finish school, move on with their lives."

They stood and Roz said, "Thank you both so much. We're hoping this information will help the police in their search for whoever murdered out neighbor. I know we'll all sleep better at night knowing he's been caught."

Molly nodded and waved at them as they went down the walkway.

"That went well, not too many lies and no blurts of information." Liam grabbed Roz' hand as they crossed the road.

"You think someone's going to come zooming down the road? Is this part of keeping me safe?" Roz lifted their linked hands and Liam grinned.

"Absolutely. You can't be too careful in Hamilton. Oregon, the Northwestern hotbed of crime."

Was this an act of protection, of manly control, or a simple move to let her know he cared about her well-being? Whichever it was, she liked it. She'd been bereft of human contact other than shaking hands at business meetings, and the few times Liam had touched her in commiseration, since getting hugs from friends and family at Winston's remembrance celebration. Now, there was no danger, no grief, just a man taking the hand of a woman he might be interested in.

It felt so good that she squeezed back. He gave her a long look, she nodded yes. Not right now, not at some future specific time, but there may be a time when everything in their worlds aligned. Then she would say yes.

CHAPTER FORTY-NINE

Answers were tantalizingly close. They knew who the murdered man was, they knew who came to visit him, both at the front and back doors, they surmised a motive, they knew the means. There were a couple of gaping holes still. Who'd come into Roz's house and taken a knife? And why did he, probably one of the boys, choose Roz' house?

It was time to talk to Chief Giffen again.

Walking up Liam's front path, she ran a continuous loop of "who" and "why" then turned to him. "I'm going to talk to Giffen. Want to come?" Like jerking a bandage off in one quick tear, getting it over with.

"Uh, sure? What do you want to tell him?" A pause. "Or ask him?"

"I want to tell him that we've done some Neighborhood Watch stuff and talked to two people who saw boys go up to his back door. Do you want to let him in on your dark web findings?"

"No, not now, maybe not ever. What Sam went through has me spooked. I don't know who came after him, but I'm sure it had to do with his batting around in the porn site scum."

"I'll take my car?"

Liam raised his eyebrows. "Getting tired of being seen in a pickup?"

"No." Roz let out a sigh of exasperation. "Don't go leaping off the cliff of assumption. I'm being nice. We always seem to take your truck and I'm offering to use my gas."

"OK, OK." He threw hands in mock surrender. "Let's go then."

In her car, she said, "Since I'm driving, do you want to call him and make sure he's in?"

"Ha, hhat's your plan, you drive, I call." Liam looked over at her with a smile. "You didn't want him to turn you down."

"Oh, right."

Downtown, she found a parking spot behind the department's building. Liam had made an appointment for them and the civilian receptionist waved them through the foyer and into the chief's office.

"Are you two being a pair now?" Giffen stood and shook hands. "What can I do for you?"

"We have some information," Liam said as Roz, talking over him, said "We have some questions."

"You want to start with information or questions?"

They glanced at each other, then Liam started. "We spent some time with Patsy doing a Neighborhood Watch group, uh, committee, uh self-described delegation."

"Formed yourselves into a posse, huh?" The words stung but Giffen was grinning. "I know Patsy. I'd rather have her going off with you two than on her own. What did you find?"

"Patsy told Roz that she, Patsy, had seen boys coming up to the back door of the house on the corner. She hadn't mentioned anything to you, or to anyone, I guess, because she assumed the boys were run-aways and didn't want to get them in trouble."

"Just being there, they weren't breaking any laws. I doubt we'd have done much. Is that all?"

"No." Liam cleared his throat. "A couple of days ago we, Roz and I, went with Patsy to some of the neighbors on the street behind the house, asking if they'd seen any boys."

Giffen tapped his lip. "Is this great minds think alike? Smiley went canvassing, asking if anyone had seen anything the night or early morning of the murder."

"We started out asking that," Roz said, "but then asked if they'd ever seen any boys in the man's back yard."

"Interesting question. Why would you ask that?"

"Patsy said she's seen boys 'a bunch' of times. And I'd had suspicions about the man and his relationship with

Archbishop Malone. Turns out that Wes and Molly each saw a boy, two different boys, in the yard." Liam slowed.

Roz began. "My question is, did you ever hear anything back from Salem on the Fred Meyer surveillance tape?"

"Why are you two making me feel that these things are related? Yes, I did hear. Got an email with a video this afternoon. I hadn't had a chance to call you. I don't know how much it'll mean to you but you're welcome to watch it." Giffen turned his screen toward them, scrolled through emails and hit play. "This is not for public viewing right now, but since you, Roz, brought us the receipt I'm treating you more like a witness. Have you ever seen this person before?"

Roz watched the jerky video play as a boy came up to the checkout with a roll of duct tape, a plastic package that could hold a coverall. They watched as he threw a People magazine on the conveyor belt at the last minute. His head was down, but there was no mistaking that he was blond. She sucked in a breath.

"I'm taking that as a yes?" Giffen hit stop and the screen went dark. "Do you know him?"

"Not know him, no. But I have seen his picture before."

Liam said, "We have to say we haven't been fully forthcoming. I suspected there was a pedophile ring, or some pedophile interest at least, in this area. I've been working with a friend of mine on the East Coast to use some of his search abilities. He discovered Malone and an ex-priest named Henley Jackson were chat room friends on a pedophilia site. Occasionally they'd exchange pictures and the boy on the video was one of the ones whose pictures were shared."

Through the silence in the office, Roz could hear the front door open and voices. Giffen got up, went over and closed his door, after telling the receptionist, "No one comes in. Not even any of the officers. I can't be disturbed."

He turned, watched the gulls circling out of his window. Roz was quiet, afraid she'd see steam coming out of Giffen's ears. Even Liam lost his easy-going way and looked subdued.

The chief swung around, a vein in his temple throbbing. "You two have been, have been…what? Obstructing justice? Involved after the fact in a murder? Concealing evidence?"

"Chief, we didn't do anything deliberately. I'll admit to asking questions. It's research for the book I'm writing about a pedophile priest who's still in the clergy and moving up the ranks to high office. I kept hearing rumors that he was somehow involved here, at least in northern Oregon." Liam paused and looked over at Roz. "All of this just sort of got dropped in my lap when the guy was killed, I met Roz and she ended up being involved because of the weapon. Believe me, it's a string of coincidences. And now, she and I are some sort of weird material witnesses or something, even though we didn't witness anything first-hand."

Liam gave Giffen credit, he was listening quietly, the red draining slowly from his face. He stared at Roz. "And your story?"

She froze, then found her voice. "You know my story. I told you I recognized the knife as one of mine. I don't know when or who stole it. You know about my husband's murder, you've talked to Det. Robeson in L.A. You know I'm concerned that I've somehow been responsible for both the murders, you've come to my house for the meeting, I've come to see you when I had any questions or anything to add." She stopped. A prickling behind her eyes warned her she might cry and she didn't want tears in front of these two men. One might see it as a sign of weakness, the other as a sign of guilt. It wasn't either, nor was it emotional manipulation, as some liked to claim. Those tears were deep in the reservoir of age-old hurts that rose from the shock and unfairness of being ambushed by people who should have known better. They were from the frustration of not being understood.

"I have to admit you've been open about things." Giffen sat down and slid his office chair around to the side of the desk so that he was facing Liam and Roz. "When you came in the other day, I was honest with you. On the surface, there seemed to be a lot of circumstantial things that pointed to you, Roz, as involved, if not the murderer. But I just couldn't bring myself to believe it. You didn't have a motive, although you had the means. But this was an intimate murder. You hadn't lived here long enough to know him intimately." He pinned Liam with a glance. "And if your assumptions about gay porn and pedophiles is correct, she never would have known him intimately in any way."

The three sat in silence for what seemed like a quarter-hour, probably a minute or two, until Giffen said, "OK, are there any other things you're keeping back, or can we come up with some solid leads and a road to head down, together?"

"That's why we're here Chief," Liam said. Roz nodded in agreement. "I want this settled, over. I came here for peace. I'm tired of asking questions about Winston and I'll have to find a way to deal with that on my own. But Hamilton can't be an open sore as well."

CHAPTER FIFTY

Liam, Roz and Giffen spent the next two hours laying out all they knew about the murder, Jackson, Malone, the boys, the porn sites.

Giffen was surprised and appalled at the information Liam dug up with Sam's help. One piece of information that Liam held back was where Sam worked. And, maybe, another piece was Sam's hit-and-run. That may have no bearing on this investigation, although it was probable the dark web and porn activity was included.

They agreed the primary person of interest, possibly suspect, was the blond boy. They had the video of him buying an odd selection of items. The date and time were a few days before the body was found. The pictures that Liam now shared with Giffen gave the boy a probable motivation for the viciousness of the attack. They doubted that Jackson would have hidden his past as a priest, so the anger at the church—the bloody cross—would have added to the motive.

The boy had been seen in the neighborhood, so could have easily taken Roz' knife. She had to tell Giffen that she hadn't been locking her doors, at which Liam gave a big "I told you so" look and she kicked his shin under the desk. With the overwhelming anger at the church, the boy could certainly have written the horrible message on Roz' window.

"But why was he still around?" Roz bought all the connections, except why, after brutally murdering his torturer, the boy would stick around.

"Until we find him, we won't know," Giffen said.

Liam added, "Maybe Patsy was partially right. If he is a run-away, he may not have any other place to go."

Giffen put together a Be On the Look Out poster with the boy's picture, calling him a "person of interest" in a murder investigation. Liam offered to email the poster to all the social services organizations he knew in the northern Oregon area, and to blanket Portland as well as Vancouver, Washington.

There wasn't much Roz could offer, until they came up with a tethered goat.

"A what?" She looked back and forth between Giffen and Liam. When they explained that she would be the bait, she was angry and frightened.

"Once we start handing out hundreds, thousands, of these flyers we'll be swamped with calls, a few maybe good, most time-wasting. What we hope will happen is that the boy will see them and panic. Logically he'd run, get as far away as possible." Liam watched her. "But he's a teen, a boy who probably thinks differently from an adult. If he's the murderer, and wrote the message on your window, he may think shutting you up permanently will solve his problems."

"I'm not comfortable with this plan." She looked at Liam then shifted to Giffen. "Is there another way to do this?"

Giffen leaned toward her. "I wish there were. We have some assumptions, and some flimsy evidence, but all we have is a picture of a possible suspect. No name, no whereabouts, no background. We have to flush him out and I think inundating this whole area, from here to Portland, is the best idea. I doubt he's old enough to have a driver's license so he's not easily mobile. He'd have to rely on a bus or a friend or hitchhiking to get around which means someone must have seen him."

"What do I have to do?" She hadn't said yes, she'd at least hear through this cobbled-together plan.

"Nothing. That's the beauty of this." Giffen sat forward. Roz watched Liam nod and encourage her with a smile. "You go about your usual routine, we get people, officers, planted around your house and yard. Remember, this is a boy. He's probably able to move fast, outrun some of our guys, but he'll always be on foot and there aren't a lot of ways to get out of here. The minute he shows up, most likely at night, we're on him."

It still seemed a barely formed plan. Then again, Roz thought, there wasn't much else to do. She wanted to find the person who killed Jackson, not because she felt anything about the murder, just that she wanted to have any suspicions the cops might still hold about her and her knife erased. If the assumptions were right, this was the same person who trashed her studio and wrote those terrible words.

They went over times carefully. Giffen didn't have the budget to cover many days of intense surveillance and Roz said she couldn't stand too many days of feeling like prey.

"I'm not going to change my routine. I know I'll be nervous, jump at any sounds. Let's make the time frame short."

"We'll start with two days." Giffen shuffled through his staff assignments. "If we have to, we'll extend it. We'll always have at least one officer in your neighborhood." He tore his focus away from the computer and looked at her. "Because of you, we're going to make a few of my guys happy."

Roz raised her eyebrows. "Because they might catch a murderer?"

"Well, that too." Giffen hit print. "No. Overtime."

In the end, she agreed. Not enthusiastic, she just didn't see any other way to find the boy, question him.

CHAPTER FIFTY-ONE

Home again, Liam insisted on walking through her house with her.

"Looking for bad guys under the bed?" She was nervous enough she had to make light of this.

He gave her a glance that chilled her. "No, I'm checking all the ways someone could get in. We want to force him to use the side door to your studio. That side of the house is where Giffen will assign most of his people."

She shut up and let him continue his tour.

In her bedroom and bath he found two open windows. "Even covered with screens, these windows need to be closed and locked."

"No! That's too much like L.A. I'll feel smothered with the window closed. Besides, if someone wanted to get in bad enough, they'd break the window."

"The point isn't them getting in at all, it's pushing them, or him, to find the easiest way in, and that has to be the side door. That side of the house doesn't have a deck, they can get to the door without being seen and maybe that's the door you forget to lock."

"Forget to lock? You… oh. Keep my old habits."

A nod gave her the answer. "Have you ever seen pictures of those old-fashioned hunts that people went on where they used beaters to form a line and force the game right up to the 'hunters' guns? That's the theory."

"OK, I'm understanding. When is this going to begin?"

"The chief and I think night after tomorrow. That gives a day to get the flyers out and seen. If he's not in this immediate area, he'll need several hours to get here. If he doesn't show up in four days, Giffen will cut back to one officer patrolling in the neighborhood. Do you have my number on autodial?"

"I do. I'm nervous. I think I'll be OK, although I don't have a lot of physical courage."

"You shouldn't need any. Would you be more comfortable if I slept in your guest room?"

Roz shook her head. "No, I have Tut and a baseball bat."

"Armed, huh? I'll leave then. You will call, right?"

"I will. I'm fine." Closing the door after Liam, she took a deep breath, went to fix dinner and give Tut a treat. Work in her studio nagged at her. Tonight, she ignored the nag, chose to watch a comedy on TV and went to bed early with a book. Tomorrow, in the daylight, she'd tackle the commission.

Out on the beach in the morning with Tut, Roz watched the birds hustling around for breakfast, calling to one another, dodging the waves. It was another clear morning, sunny and warm. She stripped off her sweatshirt and draped it over the roots where she'd wedged her coffee holder.

This was comforting. How could anything go wrong on a day when the sun, sand, ocean, animals were going about their safe, solid routines. Being there, being a piece of this normality, eased her nervousness. Even if the "Roz as bait" plan went well, she sucked in salt air and knew she would handle it. And she did.

Over the next three days, life was calm and uneventful. She worked on cutting the glass, making the joins, for the commission. Liam's lecture about the stained glass window and the cathedral being larger and outlasting the archbishop who commissioned it helped. Some of the intense anger at Malone was tempered in piecing together a representation of the cosmos, which certainly overwhelmed any problems that petty men had.

She had lunch again at Jules, chatting with Patsy who had new gossip. It seemed that one of the retired fishermen, maybe Yonson, had been kicked out by his wife. She, the wife, lost it when he came home three nights in a row from the Snug, drunk and having lost close to $100 in the back-room poker game.

"Where's he staying?" Roz thought she'd have kicked him out before that.

"I heard at Clarence's. You haven't seen him over there, have you?"

"No, I haven't seen anyone. Not even Clarence, come to think of it. He's appointed himself my one-person watch committee and sometimes 'patrols' my property. I have a feeling he didn't used to take a walk until he ran off my peeping toms; now he's outdoors at least once a day."

Patsy snickered. "Imagining the two of them living in the same house stretches the mind. I hope they're recycling all the beer cans."

"Yep." Roz remembered the empties sitting in Clarence's living room when she and Liam were there.

"My second cousin's son-in-law's father works for the sanitation department. Wonder if he'd tell me how much is in Clarence's recycling bin now, with Yonson there."

"Patsy. You wouldn't, would you?" Roz coughed on the strawful of iced tea she'd inhaled.

Patsy signed. "No, I suppose not." Then, "But it would be fun!"

Roz thanked whatever impulse made Giffen close his door while the three of them talked over the plan for luring in the boy. All those suppositions would be dynamite in Patsy's gossip central.

Four nights later, when there was no noise, no movement, Giffen pulled two officers off the duty at Roz's house, leaving just one to patrol the neighborhood on foot. Roz relaxed a bit, still kept all the windows and doors closed and locked except for the side one of the studio. She talked to Liam by phone a couple of times a day. He said that flyers were out, the police had been swamped by possible sightings or other reports of missing boys they were following up on ones that seemed promising but hadn't found the boy yet.

"I can come over tonight if you'd like."

"No, I'm fine. Are you sure this was a good plan?"

"It's good, yeah. We may need to leave it running for longer than we thought." Silence before he said, "It wasn't just as security, I'd like to see you. It's been a few days."

"Oh…oh." Roz had been cautious, was she was reading Liam's messages wrong? This proved he had intentions of knowing her better, being with her. Now the next move was hers. "Not tonight, maybe lunch or dinner tomorrow?"

"Tomorrow it is. Take care, sleep well. Give Tut a hug from me."

Too much of Roz' heart was still healing. If anyone could help the process, it would be Liam. Funny, caring, easy-going, intelligent, interesting and interested in so many areas. He'd never replace Winston. Maybe she could care about him in a different, parallel way.

Despite the possible danger, she'd slept well the last two nights, so planned to stay in the studio tonight, catching up on the commission. Some of the glass was large pieces, requiring careful handling to work it into the cames. She was fitting one piece of rose-colored glass when she felt a chill. She looked up to check the door was closed and saw two figures coming in from outside.

CHAPTER FIFTY-TWO

"Archbishop Malone! What are you doing here?"

Malone was dressed in casual clothes, jeans, a t-shirt and a windbreaker. He had tennis shoes on and Roz finally registered he wore gloves. Behind him, a young blond boy was dressed the same.

"It became clear I needed to take care of things myself," Malone said. "Gunther has been a great help. It got too hot when his picture was circulated around Portland. I'm curious, how you managed to get a print of it. It's old, Gunther's growing up and we're not so interested now."

Gunther grimaced. "We're still friends, though. Close friends, right?"

"Right." Malone spoke over his shoulder. "Gunther is a clever boy, figured out how to get into your studio, wrecked some things, wrote on your window. I thought it might be enough to get you to lay off, you and that nosy writer." Lay off? Take care of things himself? A flash of intuition. He'd killed Jackson.

"How long have you been trying to frame me? Did it start in L.A. when you came to sign the commission?"

"Oh, heavens no. You didn't know anything about me then. I confess, I wasn't concerned when your husband was killed. I figured you'd stay in L.A., the commission would take a bit more time, all was well." He took a breath, reached into the pocket of his jacket. "Then you decided to move to Hamilton. Why? Of all the places in the world, why here?"

He pulled out another one of Roz' knives. "You haven't missed this one yet, I take it. Gunther picked it up the night he vandalized your studio. I'm returning it. We don't need it. You're going to use an X-acto knife to slit your wrists."

"What? You're crazy. I'm not going to commit suicide."

"Of course not, my dear, it's only going to look like it. I'll testify that you've been so despondent since your husband's murder, you're not the same person we hired in L.A. The commission is too big for you, you're overwhelmed. You acted out your frustration by attacking a harmless old neighbor, a person you didn't even know, because he told you to keep your mangy dog off his property."

She gasped. "That's not true! Everybody here knows that I never talked to him."

"And who told them that? You did, right?" Malone's voice was smooth, hypnotic. "The people in this town have only known you since you moved here. I, a clergyman, an archbishop, met you more than a year ago when we contracted for the cathedral stained glass commission."

He moved closer to her, against one of her light tables, picked up an X-acto knife, pushed it toward her. "Here, dear. Oh, I almost forgot." He reached back and Gunther put a small gun into his hand. "My little persuader."

A voice outside shouted, "Put that down! I have a gun!"

Was it the cop, Roz wondered? No, it was Clarence standing at the edge of the pool of light, pointing his shotgun at Malone. Who turned to look out the door, said, "You crazy old man, what do you think you're doing…" when 70 pounds of dog hit him in the middle of his back, knocked him into the corner of the sharp-edged light table. He lay still.

All hell broke loose. Clarence kept yelling, "I've got a gun," Gunther ran at him, bowling him over as he took off, Tut's genes revved up and he took off after Gunther, the roving cop came running, gun unholstered, Liam showed up around the corner of the house with a baseball bat.

And then the cops arrived in force, lights and sirens. The red and blue strobes reflected off the high fog rolling in from the ocean.

Roz vomited into the fuchsias.

*****

Malone wasn't dead, just had a nasty concussion. Tut ran Gunther down and sat on him until two cops showed up, panting after the chase. An ambulance added its lights to the swirl in the fog, EMTs loaded Malone in with a police escort and wailed off, after checking out Roz' vitals and suggesting she lie down.

Liam made tea, shooed Clarence home with a promise to tell him the whole story tomorrow. Giffen, who'd arrived with his officers, told Liam and Roz to come down to the office in the morning and get this sorted out. "And bring your dog, too, Roz. He's got carte blanche tomorrow in the police department. No waiting in the car for him after tonight."

"Are you alright?" Liam laid a hand on Roz' forehead once they were alone. "Do you vomit easily?"

"No, I hate to upchuck. I guess it was the fear, the tension, all of a sudden I knew I had to lean over. Guess it won't hurt the fuchsias."

Liam laughed, handed her a cup of herbal tea. "I wouldn't think so. You probably need to be drinking this in bed. Can you make it by yourself?"

"I'm fine, sort of. Still shaking." She held up the cup, rattling against the saucer. "Maybe you better put this in a mug."

Liam did, escorted her to her bedroom, said "I'll turn out the light and lock the doors."

"Thank you, and please give Tut some treats. He's our hero tonight."

CHAPTER FIFTY-THREE

Another warm and sunny day. Tut came back from his run after only one whistle. Roz wondered if last night's activities had bonded him to her even more. Whatever, he was Velcroed to her now. She fixed his breakfast, called Liam.

"Do you think we have time for breakfast at Jules before we go talk to Chief Giffen? My treat."

"I'll call him," Liam said. "You don't have to treat."

"Knock it off, this is the same as the gas. If we're going to be friends, we share. We'll take my car so I can leave Tut in it."

"Giffen said he was welcome at the department."

"That's the department, I'm not so sure he'd be welcome at Jules."

The diner was packed and the noise level bounced off the walls. Patsy came up. "Have you heard? There was an attempted murder last night in our neighborhood. Close to your house, Roz."

"Really?" Liam steered Roz toward an empty table. "After breakfast we're meeting with Chief Giffen. We'll let you know what we find out."

"That was kinda mean." Roz hid her grin in her napkin.

"I couldn't resist it." Liam waved BethAnn over with a "drinking coffee" movement, she swung by, filled two cups, left two menus.

"I'm going to treat myself." Roz decided against her usual omelet. "After last night, and going to bed on an empty stomach, I'm having waffles. Hmmm. With a side of ham."

BethAnn delivered her waffle, along with Liam's scrambled eggs, bacon, hash browns and toast.

"We're going to be in carb overload." Roz smiled. "Hope we can remember everything."

Liam smacked his forehead. "Remember. I forgot to tell you, I heard from Sam. The cops found the hit-and-run car. It was registered to a guy who was active on one of the pedophile porn sites. They've arrested him. Sam was targeted because he works in tv news. The guy thought he was being targeted for an expose."

Back in her car, Tut was surprised when Roz put his leash on, tugged him out of the car at Giffen's office. "It's alright, the Chief invited you," she told him. "Come on, but be a good boy." His big, liquid eyes showed trust.

Giffen came out to the foyer and tousled Tut's ears. "Here's the guy who was our ace last night." Turned to Roz and Liam. "Are you two recuperating?"

"I didn't do much, as it happened." Liam seemed rueful. "By the time I got there, Tut, Clarence and your officer had it under control. Mostly what I did was provide tea and sympathy for Roz. And treats for Tut."

"Where is everybody?" Giffen understood Roz' question to be about Malone and Gunther.

"Malone is in the hospital, under heavy guard. His fall last night not only gashed his head but gave him a concussion. They're keeping him for a day. Gunther is here, in a holding cell. He's a minor still but we don't have any juvenile facilities here. Tomorrow, both of them are getting shipped off to the county."

"Have you interviewed either of them?"

Giffen closed his eyes. "Yes, Liam, I have. Malone was formally arrested and charged with murder this morning. He waived his right for an attorney and confessed." He grinned at both of them. "You know that confession is good for the soul, right?"

"Well? I need to know for my book."

"You and Ms. Duke here are conspiring to make me crazy, you know that. You can't use any of this until he's arraigned, he pleads and it's in the public record."

Liam nodded and Roz sat quietly, waiting.

"You've discovered the dead man was Henley Jackson, a disgraced ex-priest. He and Malone had known each other for around 15 years. Spent most of that time involved in the same pedophile group. About five years ago, Jackson was accused of sexual molestation and pedophilia by four families in his parish. Malone helped cover it up, got him a retirement from the church, snuck a million dollars to him in a trust fund. Part of that is what bought the house here.

"Then something happened, Malone wouldn't say what, but Jackson started threatening him. Jackson didn't have much to lose, but Malone did. He had his eye on a red cardinal's hat."

Giffen shrugged. "I don't know church hierarchy well, but he may even have been thinking about the papacy. He had big ambitions. A charge of pedophilia, even an accusation of cover-up, would kill any chances for advancement. Whatever Jackson wanted from Malone, he swore he'd reveal their history. Malone had to shut him up."

"Where did Gunther come in?"

"As you know from the pictures, he was one of their victims. He was in care with foster parents who were abusive and Catholic. They dragged him to church, he was so well-behaved he made it to alter boy. Malone saw him on a visit here—he usually took part of his vacation in the Portland area, even renting a cabin up the coast—and was hooked. He provided Gunther with all the caring and sympathy he didn't get at home and eventually seduced him, got him to pose for the pictures. Those were taken at the cabin during one of Malone's shorter vacations. Gunther was so brainwashed, he'd do anything for the man he believed loved him, including sneaking in through an unlocked door," Liam looked at Roz, "and stealing a knife."

"But why me?" Roz was puzzled. She had nothing to do with any of this, hadn't even met Jackson.

"Malone had as many twists and turns as a Borgia pope. It added a fillip to his plan when he discovered the artist he hired to design his cathedral's centerpiece had moved across the street from Jackson in this small town no one knew. He could visit, see how the commission was coming, drop in on Jackson, spend some time with some boys and leave.

"He hatched a plan to kill Jackson and frame either you, or if things got too hot and Jackson's identity was exposed, frame Gunther. Gunther had been sexually abused, by both Malone and Jackson, was in love with Malone, he'd stolen your knife, he'd come in, smashed your work and written on your window. One of you was going to be a fall-guy and Malone was rid of an irritation growing into a danger."

Roz was stunned at a motivation that turned out to be simple greed and the deviant sexuality of pedophilia. As Liam pointed out, the archbishop was just a man, not the church.

Her cell rang, interrupting the silence. She reached into her purse to send the call to voicemail, then looked at the screen. "Oh lord, this is Robeson from L.A. He never calls me. Do you mind if I take it?"

Giffen and Liam shook their heads, she said, "Yes Det. Robeson? I'm here with Chief Giffen." Then, "Just a minute." She turned to Giffen. "He wants me to put this on speaker. Do you care?"

"Not a bit," the chief said, as Robeson's voice filled the room.

"I have some news, I think good news, and thought I'd tell you together. We have a strong suspect in Winston Duke's murder."

Roz gasped, fought wetness behind her eyes. "Who, why, how?"

"He's a gangbanger, a member of a small group who claim that mall as theirs. It was totally accidental, their target was the other guy who was hit. Your husband just stepped the wrong way at the wrong time."

"How did you find him?"

"Pure police slog and forensics. The bullet we took from your husband matched up with a bullet we took from another homicide two weeks ago. Another gang member. That one, we had a witness. I hope this helps you get some closure and some peace. You deserve it."

Roz said, "Thanks," hit end. Sat, stunned into silence. After all the anguish, the months of anger, worry, of feeling lost and hopeless, Win was just an innocent victim, killed by the gun and shooting culture that had taken over her country, her city, her life. There was no why, it was as random as lightning from a clear sky and she had had no way to focus her anger, which grew as she understood the randomness of life. It could have been a speeding car, an earthquake, anything that brought him to the nexus of his death.

But now, when she knew Winston's death was caused by a specific person, the killer would learn his actions had consequences. She wanted to testify at his murder trial.

She wouldn't cry here, now. That grieving would happen at home, surrounded by those things she'd kept from their life together.

"Are you OK?" Liam's voice came to her as from a long tunnel.

She turned to him with a quavery smile. "I am," she said.

ACKNOWLEDGEMENTS

Books don't write themselves, it takes some dedicated people. Hamilton, Oregon is fictional but I grew up on the north coast of California and love spending time on the Oregon coast.

When all the news about pedophilia in the Catholic church began breaking over the past two decades, it seemed that a tiny town on the coast would be a good place to hide and so Hamilton came into being.

One of my most consistent and stalwart readers and critiquers was my cousin, Beth White, who died in June 2019 without seeing this book into print, but she loved it and said it was my best so far. That's wonderful praise and she helped me shape this story and the one to come. I loved her very much and she is dreadfully missed.

Also, my critique partners, Linda Townsdin, June Gillam, Tarra Thomas, Cathy McGreevy, Rick Meredith, Lynda Markham, Karen Phillips, Nuvia Sandoval, Cherie O'Boyle and two new beta readers (thanks Pam Stack for sharing this with your reviewers).

Roz Duke is already well into her next adventure on the south coast of Kent, England where she runs afoul of international art thieves.

If you enjoyed Stain on the Soul, please leave a review. I can be contacted with any questions or comments at mjdrier@gmail.com or on my facebook page.

67749397R00165

Made in the USA
Middletown, DE
12 September 2019